Cast of Characters

Flikka Ashley. A gifted young woman sculptor with a past. Every man who meets her falls in love with her.

Bee Chattock. Flikka's no-nonsense aunt, who considers herself old enough to say exactly what she thinks to everybody.

Detective Sergeant Arnoldson. A loathsome, lecherous police officer who would like nothing better than to see Flik hanged for murder.

Deputy Chief Constable Mahew. He'd much rather be at home with his wife and four dogs than investigating a murder.

Inspector Lane Parry. A Scotland Yard man and great friend of Mahew's, who is terribly afraid of where the truth might lie in this murder investigation.

Dr. Abbot. The sardonic, ill-tempered village doctor who fears he will lose Flik either to Inspector Parry or to the gallows.

Sergeant Congreve. A merry, kind-hearted fellow given to telling tall tales and passing on village gossip. Both Mahew and Parry cherish his companionship.

Clive Harris. He lost his leg in Normandy and his heart to Flik.

Phil and Tim Ambrose. A married couple whose hobbies are black magic, drinking too much, and having monthly rows.

Gwen Hunter. A silly woman who dabbles in homemade cordials and herbs.

Camilla Pain-Wentworth. A reformed drug addict who's still quite attractive in middle age and would cheerfully flirt with a broomstick if it wore trousers.

Captain Belairs. Retired army and a crashing bore, with an opinion on just about everything.

Susan Merridew. A fussy, dithery spinster who spends most of her time sewing curtains for her tiny cottage.

Molly Pritchard. An old family retainer who "does" for Flik

Old Harry. Their ancient gardener, who

Plus assorted police officers, villagers, and

Books by Maureen Sarsfield

Green December Grows the Graveyard
which is now published as
Murder at Shots Hall
1945

Gloriana
1946

A Party for Lawty
which has also been published as
A Dinner for None
and is now reprinted as
Murder at Beechlands
1948

Murder at Shots Hall

by
Maureen Sarsfield

The Rue Morgue Press
Boulder / Lyons

The Mystery of Maureen Sarsfield

British writer Maureen Sarsfield had all the tools necessary to make it as a major mystery writer, but after publishing just three novels—two of which were mysteries—between 1945 and 1948, she completely disappeared from the literary landscape. Whether she died young, commenced her short career at an advanced age or simply grew tired of the writing life is unknown. The biographical copy on the dust jacket of the American edition of *Green December Fills the Graveyard* (reprinted here as *Murder at Shots Hall*) merely identifies her as a new writer, making no comment on her age. Many of the characters in her three novels are in their thirties or forties, and she writes so believably about the sensibilities and attitudes of that age group that she herself probably either belonged to it or had recently entered the early stages of middle age.

Although other mystery writers had been known to give up the form after gaining financial independence (Anthony Berkeley and Ernest Bramah in Britain and Phoebe Atwood Taylor in the United States spring immediately to mind), it seems odd that Sarsfield would have retired after only two mysteries, especially since she began publishing at a time when it was somewhat unusual for an unknown British writer to be picked up so quickly by a U.S. publisher. There is no evidence that her books, although widely reviewed, made much of a splash in the U.S. Other than an appearance in 1950 in *Two Complete Detective Novels* (a pulp magazine) by *Green December Fills the Graveyard*, her books seem not to have been reprinted. Her one mainstream book, the very British *Gloriana*, a look at the bickering inhabitants of a neighborhood in London awaiting the arrival of the young woman title character, failed to attract an American publisher.

Her choice of titles for her mystery books may have been partly to blame for what we assume were unimpressive sales. *Green December Fills the Graveyard* is not only a mouthful but perhaps a bit too literary. Her second and final mystery was published under equally nondescript titles on either side of the Atlantic: in Britain as *A Dinner for None* and in the U.S. as *A Party for Lawty*. We make no apologies for giving both

5

mysteries somewhat more genre-driven titles (we have scheduled her second mystery to be reprinted as *Murder at Beechlands*). However, while dull titles and mediocre sales would immediately condemn a mystery author to literary oblivion in today's cutthroat publishing world, in the 1940s publishers gave their writers more time to develop an audience, which makes it all the more puzzling why there were no further books from an author who achieved the critical success that Sarsfield did. This is, of course, pure speculation. All our efforts, going back several years, to discover anything at all about Sarsfield have failed. Hopefully, the republication of her two mysteries will rectify this situation.

Those two mysteries are gems of the British school. Both feature the fortyish Lane Parry, a Scotland Yard detective who twice finds evil deeds in the backwaters of Sussex. Parry is a complex and well-drawn character, yet it is Flikka Ashley, a 36-year-old sculptor, who dominates the action and the minds—at least of the male characters—in *Murder at Shots Hall*. You would be hard pressed to find another nonseries character in the crime fiction of that era who so completely steals the stage from the investigating sleuth. What is even more remarkable is that she manages to do so in a book that is filled with so many fully realized subordinate players. Adding to the virtuosity of Sarsfield's debut is her ability to move smoothly and efficiently from one point of view to another.

Eccentric characters also abound in *Murder at Beechlands*, whose plot and setting are very much in the Agatha Christie tradition. When Parry's car fails him during a raging snowstorm, he seeks shelter at a private country hotel, where the murdered body of one of the guests has been ejected from the premises via an upstairs window. Cut off from his usual police assistants by the blizzard, Parry functions almost more like an amateur sleuth than a Scotland Yard detective. In addition to the Christie-like setting, the characters trapped in the hotel may remind you of the inhabitants of *Gosford Park*, the recent Oscar-nominated period mystery film from Robert Altman.

One can only speculate where Sarsfield career would have gone had she continued in the vein of these two books. Even so, she made her mark on the field. If the brevity of her career prevented her from becoming one of the masters of the field, she stands, as W. Somerset Maugham so honestly described himself, in the front rank of the second raters.

Tom & Enid Schantz
Lyons, Colorado
June 2003

CHAPTER 1

"NO," Flik's aunt had said. "No, Flik. This is really too much. I'm deaf enough not to be driven mad by your chipping at blocks of wood, but I'm not nearly deaf enough to stand your infernal attacks on that rock. For ten years we've lived amicably together, but I refuse to be amicable if you make that noise. Take it away. You got it here from Wales, so you can get it out again. Take it away and dump it somewhere. Down in the woods. You like woods, so can't you work in them? God knows, it's too big for anyone to steal except some lunatic Gargantua."

So Flik had sent for Tom Barker and his farm cart, the breakdown gang from the garage outside the village, six farm laborers, old Harry the gardener, several large bottles of beer, and the rock had been removed from the study at Shots Hall down to the stone shanty along the road which had once, during the days of war from the air, been a temporary wardens' post.

Flikka earned a precarious and not very profitable livelihood carving from oak, from chestnut, from any wood that took her fancy, busts, heads and masks of people she met and a lot of people she had never met. Sometimes someone bought one of the effigies. Sometimes even a definite order turned up from someone who wished to be perpetuated in wood. Occasionally she made quite a lot of money; more often than not, none at all.

Three of her efforts had once been squeezed into an exhibition at Bratton's Galleries in Bond Street. Of them, Andrew Innis had written in the *Morning News:*

"...Flikka Ashley's head of a sleeping child, carved from cherry wood, is a subtle masterpiece of repose. Her head of a young man shows a wild but restrained charm, while her small bust of a girl shows a dynamic talent... This young sculptor should go far..."

The young sculptor, then rising thirty-four, had turned down her mouth in a rather grim smile, and been glad only that Innis' complimentary remarks had brought her in six orders, one after the other. The profits thereof

7

had gone in mending the roof over the kitchen at Shots Hall, the ancestral home of Aunt Bee Chattock. When she died, Flik would have the dubious pleasure of becoming its sole and rightful owner.

It was, as the two women constantly told each other, one hell of a place; a white elephant, a blot, a disgrace, an expense and a beast. But it was a place to live. No one would buy it, and, unless it was sold, there was no money forthcoming to move elsewhere. Except to a nasty little bungalow in a row with a lot of other nasty little bungalows. And used to the large open spaces of Shots Hall, the confines of a bandbox were terrifying to contemplate. Both Flik and Bee Chattock suffered from a claustrophobic dislike of being shut up in small places for very long.

Mercifully, more than two-thirds of Shots Hall had been burned down by a glut of incendiaries during an air raid. The gutted walls, aided by gales of wind and rain sweeping in from the sea, had fallen in, and the ancient Harry had turned the tumulus-like mound of rubble into a monstrous rock garden, from which burst forth, in due course, not only flowers but a mass of strange and alien weeds. Harry called them fireflowers. They were very odd. No one attempted to weed the rock garden, so, in time, it crawled with pallid convolvulus, which strangled everything in turn, except the hardiest of the fireflowers, in a kind of gloating satisfaction that was almost cannibalistic.

With two-thirds of Shots Hall gone, there remained only the gray stone tower, the echoing cavern of a hall, the study where Flik carved, the kitchen quarters and a small drawing room. In the tower were Bee Chattock's and Flik's bedrooms. Bee's on the ground floor, Flik's on the first floor. The winding staircase that passed Flik's door led to an emptiness of moldering flooring and plasterless ceilings. One of the sculleries near the kitchen had been turned into a bathroom and lavatory. This home-from-home, or what remained of it, was built on the foundations of the original Shots Hall by a great uncle Chattock in 1860.

Down below, deep in the bowels of the earth, the original cellars still survived, and in them, untidily stacked in bins, a lot of bottles. Some empty, some still full and worth a small fortune. The Chattocks had liked their liquor. From time to time, Bee or Flik sold a bottle of brandy or Chateau Yquem to keep the pot boiling. Toward the end of 1944, they had got as much as £60 for six bottles of port. It was a pity, but still—

From the outside, the 19th century monstrosity looked fairly grand. It was only a pity that, fifteen years before, the local rural district council of Pelsey had gone into a huddle with the borough council of St. Arthurs, and between them had run a road right through the grounds of Shots Hall, almost touching the house, cutting it off from the rest of the estate. Bee Chattock had been very inadequately compensated and nobody cared for the road, which was supposed to be a short cut from Pelsey to the St. Arthurs sea front, so it was seldom used except by a trickle of local motorists. Bee had sold the land on the opposite side of the road at a knockdown price to Tom Barker, the farmer, on the condition, which he had so far kept, that he did not resell it as building land.

Down the hill was the village—Shotshall, called after the old house of three hundred years ago. It consisted of the pub, a row of cottages on each side of it, some more cottages down a lane, and the Ambroses' beautifully and richly converted farmhouse. Opposite Flik's stone shanty Miss Merridew's prim and pretty sham olde worlde cottage somehow reflected, in its appearance, something of Miss Merridew's fussy but birdlike charm.

An ancient dame by the name of Molly Pritchard did for Bee and Flik. She had been in the Chattock family for heaven only knew how many years. As there was no room for her in the house, she lived in what had once been a gamekeeper's cottage almost next to Flik's shanty. There, after she had got the dinner all ready to serve, she retired for the night at precisely quarter past eight. At half past eight, Flik, on her way to attack the Welsh rock with all the feverish strength and energy of someone without any real physical strength at all, knocked on the door, was told by Molly to come in, and went in. This procedure was almost exactly the same every evening. The same dialog must have taken place a thousand times and more, with scarcely a variation.

"Well, Miss Flikka, dinner all right?"

"Yes, thank you, Molly. You all right?"

"I'm all right, except for my rheumatism, Miss Flikka. Just going to wash up my teacup."

"Had a nice cuppa?"

"Lovely, thank you, Miss Flikka. I never can get into the way of calling you 'Madam,' or 'Mrs. Ashley.' It's from knowing you when you was little."

"I'd rather be Miss Flikka. Good night, Molly, sleep well."

"Good night, Miss Flikka, and same to you."

Then Flikka would walk on to the shanty, let herself in, look round, peering into the darkness, turn the lights up, select her implements, and attack the rock. She had found it by the side of a lane in Wales. It was an odd, pale-greenish color. It was as hard as iron, and it must have weighed quite a ton. The rock had appealed to her because of its strange color. From its sea-tinted implacability would spring a life-size sleeping mermaid.

After two years hard labor, the mermaid lay there with closed eyes, a half smile on her carved lips. Flik preferred to work on the mermaid at night. Somehow, she was a thing of the night, not of the prosaic happenings of the day. The noises of Flik's nightly occupation were, from the road, only a dim thudding. The old blast walls of the erstwhile wardens' post had never been taken down, and they effectually dulled the sounds within.

The doddering Harry, on the way home from the pub to his lonely cottage hidden in a muddy lane, used to wobble his head as he passed by and heard Flik at work, and mutter, "At it again, at it again, that's what comes of 'aving no man to look after." He was a confirmed bachelor, but his rather muddled ideas on the subject of sex were, he was sure, quite right. Women should have a man to serve. Stay at home, so they ought to, look after their man, go to bed with him, bear him children, and then they wouldn't be so restless.

Thus Harry thought to himself every evening as he groped his way home. He was regular in his habits all right. Nothing restless about him. At seven o'clock every evening, after he had knocked off work at Shots Hall and had his supper of bread and cheese, followed by a cup of tea, he went down to the pub. There he slowly drank two pints of beer. At nine o'clock he was home again, five minutes later he was in bed. There was, indeed, an almost awful regularity in the habits of the village. Willard, the boss of the garage, got drunk and stayed drunk for four days every six weeks. Not every month, not every seven weeks, but exactly six weeks to the dot. And he was never drunk for more or for less than four days. Once a month by the calendar, the Ambroses had a family row. Once every five weeks they threw a party. Every night at six o'clock Mr. Fewsey from the butcher's shop banged on the closed door of the pub and shouted the same remark, "Tom, yer clock's slow, open up, can't yer?" Mr. Fewsey never went to the pub at five minutes past six so that he wouldn't have to wait on the doorstep. Every night unless she was out to dine, Flikka Ashley knocked on Molly's door at half past eight. And so on.

Until, on the dying day of December 1st, out of the fog that wreathed in from the channel, out of the sloughing mud, the wet, tangled hedges, the leafless, dripping trees, the murk and the darkness, as if it was born of these things, secret as them, murder sneaked out and invaded the village, upsetting its routine and disarranging the regularity of its program.

The first to die was old Molly Pritchard.

CHAPTER 2

AT half past eleven on the night of December 1st, Detective Sergeant Arnoldson lounged at the main door of the Central Police Station in St. Arthurs. Behind him, entrenched on the other side of the long desk that cut the room in half, the duty officer for the night, P.C. Brewin, picked his teeth. Behind Brewin, an open door disclosed a small office where a fire burned and a kettle hissed on a gas ring.

"Filthy night," Arnoldson complained. "The seaside's all right in the summer with all the bits in their bathing suits, but it's bloody awful in the winter. This is a bloody place, anyhow—no real life. Give me Brighton or Hastings every time."

"You can have 'em," Brewin said. "Give me London. Have some tea before you go home?"

"Anything to put in it?"

"Not a damn thing."

Conversation temporarily flagged, while Arnoldson silently contemplated, in his mind's eye, bits in bathing suits, and Brewin silently indulged in a bout of dislike for Arnoldson. Not that he wasn't matey. Tell you a dirty story any time; but he was sly. Say one thing to your face, and another behind your back. The kettle started to boil over, and then the phone bell rang.

Brewin picked up the receiver.

"Centralp'licestation St. Arthurs," he said without interest. "Who? What's that? Mrs. Ashley of Shots Hall? Oh? Oh? Oh?"

Maddened by the string of oh's, and his imagination titillated by the sound of the name Ashley, Arnoldson took the receiver away from Brewin, and rang his tongue over his rather red lips. "That Mrs. Flik Ashley? Oh, I beg pardon, Mrs. FlikkAH Ashley, quite. How're you, Mrs. Ashley? Know who this is? Clever of you to recognize my voice. What? Who? Who's Molly Pritchard? Dead, is she? Sorry, I'm sure, cooks are hard to come by." He laughed at his own crack, and then paused. He tried to picture the face at the other end of the line, to drag it toward him so that it was close to his; so that he could look right into the secret, smoldering eyes, the pale, pointed face, the dark rings, but no lines under the eyes, the arched eyebrows; so that he could see the light on the heavy, soft hair that was such a deep chestnut it was almost purple. "What? Beg pardon? Yes, I'm still here. I was just thinking over what you said. Haven't you sent for a doctor, then? Oh, of course, old Bannard's dead a long time, isn't he?

He was your doctor, of course. Oh, come now, how can you say someone's murdered her? Of course she looks queer, people do when they die. Oh, very well then, Fl—Mrs. Ashley, I'll bring our chap along, and come up myself. Where is she? The cottage south of Shots Hall gates— If you'll hang on— Blast, she's gone."

Brewin perked up. "Something wrong? She started in on talking about murder."

"She says," Arnoldson grunted, "that someone's murdered her old cook that works at Shots Hall. Now why'd she jump at the idea of murder?"

"Hysterical, probably," Brewin suggested. "Rattled."

"She's not the sort that gets rattled. If she says someone's murdered the old woman it's either her imagination, or it isn't, and she knows something about it."

"Oh, go on," Brewin said, trying not very successfully to hide his impatience with Arnoldson. "Why should she know anything about it? That is supposing the old woman was murdered, which she probably ain't. Just dropped off the hook from old age, or something like that. Where'd Mrs. Ashley find the body?"

Arnoldson ran his tongue over his lips again. "She said she noticed a light under the old woman's door, thought it was funny she hadn't gone to bed, and went in to look. Now why should she be wandering about in the night outside the old woman's cottage anyhow?"

"How should I know?" Brewin shrugged. "You'd better ask her."

"Get me Dr. Abbot on the phone. Then go and tell Norton I want him to come with me, and to get Roberts to bring a car round. She might've chosen a less bloody awful night."

Arnoldson slowly put on his overcoat, and wound a muffler round his neck while he waited for Brewin to do his bidding. Flik Ashley—her waist was so small and her legs so long. He'd never seen her in a bathing suit, worse luck. Now he'd have an excuse to find out how old she really was. She looked such a kid. But knowing, and she wasn't any kid, either. Bedworthy.

"Dr. Abbot?" Brewin hallooed. Evidently Dr. Abbot had already gone to bed and was half asleep. "Dr. Abbot? Oh, Centralp'licestation St. Arthurs here. Detective Sergeant Arnoldson of our C.I.D. department wants to speak to you. Yes, sir—"

"Hullo?" Arnoldson said ungraciously to the far-off Dr. Abbot. "I'm sending a car for you—no, wait a minute, I'll call for you on the way. Some old woman's gone and died up at Shotshall, and I want you to have a look at her. The Ashley woman's just rung up and's in a flap saying the old woman's been murdered. Poppycock, of course, but there it is. I'll be round in ten minutes."

"A pox on you," Abbot said to the telephone. "A thousand maledictions on policemen who ring me up at night when I'm trying to get some sleep." He lived alone, but for a housekeeper, and so was in the habit of sometimes talking out loud to himself.

As he dressed, he talked. The words that flowed from his mouth called on devils and saints to witness to the revolting life of doctors in general and himself in particular. Why, in the name of sin and shame, couldn't people die and be born at decent times of the day? Why always at night, or in the middle of breakfast, lunch or dinner? "A thousand revolting diseases on them," he told his shoes, jerking at the laces. "The Ten Commandments go sour in their stomachs, and may Abraham, Isaac and Jacob spit in their eyes." Then, ruefully, he began to laugh. His private blasphemies, both biblical and medical, gave him a sort of bitter satisfaction and amusement. For to his patients, his female ones at any rate, he was a model of decorum. Inwardly, however, he was not in the least mild.

Tonight, he was not even decorous in his exterior. He stuffed his long length into his clothes, gnashed his teeth at the looking glass and was glad they were still all his to gnash, neglected either to brush or comb his hair or tie his tie properly. A lock of his graying hair fell down over his forehead, and flicked the top rims of his spectacles when he moved his head.

"You ugly old bastard," he said to his reflection. "And damn Arnoldson, the greasy-haired, fat-mouthed, slick-brained moron."

Who was this woman Ashley? Where was Shotshall? Of course, it was that dreary village stuck up on a hill four or five miles outside the town. Shots Hall—some old girl by the name of Buttocks—no, Chattock, lived there. If anyone had been murdered, then Arnoldson would pick on some innocent person as the murderer. He'd probably picked on someone already. Anything to get a nice case and have his name in the papers. Only it wouldn't be murder. It would be a clear case of senile decay or an embolism.

"All right!" He flung up his bedroom window as a car hooted in the road outside. "All right, all right!" The fog slid into the room, a gray, uninvited guest.

Dr. Abbot took his time going downstairs and letting himself out of his front door. No one was dying for want of his attentions. They were already dead. He sniffed the fog. It smelled of the sea, and, somehow, decay. The long black shape of the police car bulked outside the gate, its lights dimmed by the fog. Norton patiently held one of the doors open. The lumpy shoulders of P.C. Roberts hunched over the wheel. Arnoldson sat in the back, and invited Abbot to join him there.

"What's all this about?" Abbot asked petulantly. Arnoldson had plastered his hair, by the smell, with some sort of scented hair oil. "Can't the unfortunate cadaver wait till the morning?"

"The Ashley woman insists someone murdered this Molly Pritchard, who's the cook and what not at Shots Hall. Seems fishy to me. If she was murdered, how'd Ashley know? She said this Pritchard looked queer. Course she does. Who doesn't look queer when they're dead?"

"Some people look better dead than alive. Who's this Ashley woman?"

Abbot could hear Arnoldson draw his breath in, and didn't like the sound of it.

"Flik Ashley. Mrs. FlikkAH Ashley. Accent on the AH, Please. F-L-I-K-K A. Lives with her old aunt, Miss Chattock, at Shots Hall, and she's no good, pretty Flik isn't. She's a divorcée, amongst other things."

"A what?"

"Her husband divorced her ten years ago. Well, we all know what that means."

"What does it mean?" Abbot asked, disliking Arnoldson more than ever, and beginning to side most violently with Flik.

"Why, only one thing, of course," Arnoldson sniggered. "Another man. And more than one. When part of the Hall was burned down in the blitz, of course all the Fire Services were up there, and I went up to the incident as well. Hauled Mrs. FlikkAH out of bed myself. The man was downstairs in the hall, flapping, but I know he'd been in her room because I saw his notecase lying around on her table. He was a Yank. Yer. She was had up in Court before she sold her car, too, for using abusive language to a constable on point duty down in the town."

Norton looked over his shoulder. "The chap asked for it. He held up the traffic just as she was right on top of him, and she locked her brakes trying not to run over him. If I'd been her, I'd have felt like clouting him as well. Anyway, she swore in French, so's he wouldn't understand, only he did, him being able to talk French."

For a few moments, the atmosphere inside the dark car was strained. Then Arnoldson went on, "All the men fall for her. There's something damn fishy about her. Something she's done and won't tell about. But the men think she's a wow."

"May I inquire," Abbot asked, "what your sex is?"

"What d'you think it is? What a damn silly question."

"Then you think she's a wow too?"

"Not me," Arnoldson boasted; and Abbot thought: you blasted liar.

"She and the old Chattock woman," Arnoldson said, "keep themselves very close. Hardly ever see them about. Just stick around the village. They're concealing something they've no business to conceal, to my way of thinking."

"You're a policeman," Abbot said, his dislike seething inside him. "So why don't you find out what it is?"

"You wait. I will— Left, Roberts, not right. Don't drive us into the ditch. Take it easy. The fog's always worse up here than in the town, it's so high. You get fog and clouds mixed. Stick your head out, Norton, and see if we're on the right road."

Norton stuck his head out. They were on the right road, though it was almost impossible to see more than two yards ahead. Abbot shut his eyes, and wished he were back in his bed. Why had he ever got himself mixed up with the police? Giving the once-over to drunks—harmless wretches who'd been on a night out. And his evidence got them into trouble. Once he had tried to make out a rather charming drunk was sober, but it hadn't worked. Postmortems—bits of insides in bottles—coroners' inquests— Here and there a suicide, some poor devil's life was a bit too much for—

Flik heard the car in the distance, and her feelings, already overwrought, were mixed. She had stood outside Molly's cottage, now, for three-quarters of an hour. She couldn't bear to wait inside with that dead body. She hadn't waked up Aunt Bee. Why ruin her night for her? There was nothing Bee could do at the moment. So she had sneaked back to Shots Hall from Molly, when she had found her dead, telephoned the police, and sneaked back to the mud and fog, and that thin line of light under Molly's door, and waited. Somewhere there was a murderer. Somewhere in the fog was someone who had killed Molly. She'd tell Arnoldson so—— "There's a murderer near here." Only why had it to be Arnoldson? But after three-quarters of an hour she would have almost welcomed the devil. The dripping of the trees was like the ticking of a deathwatch beetle. There were queer noises. She kept looking over her shoulder. Her whole body was cold and clammy as ice, though it wasn't really cold. If only it would freeze, or snow, instead of the eternal fog and damp that turned the fields an unnatural green. Old Harry had been wagging his head and saying a green December filled the graveyards. Mr. Fewsey wagged his head and said the same thing. So did old Mrs. Vale, as if it was a matter for rejoicing. There wasn't much more room in the Shotshall churchyard to fill. She mustn't let Arnoldson see she was all shot to bits with nerves.

Poor Molly. Now there'd be no one to get breakfast in the morning. But that wasn't it. It was Molly lying in there dead. She had seen dead bodies before, when she was in the Ambulance Service, but they weren't like that body hunched inside there in the chair by the cold fire. It was horribly dark. If only the fog would clear.

The lights of the car, pale glowworms, were upon her. The brakes squeaked a little as it pulled up. They ought to be oiled, Flik thought. Three figures, black lumps, got out of the car. A fourth figure remained inside, leaning on the wheel. The fog trailed round them as if they wore long, gray widows' weepers.

"Well, well, Mrs. Ashley?" Arnoldson greeted her. "Nasty night you've chosen, haven't you?"

"What for? It's none of my choosing," Flik answered coolly.

"This is Dr. Abbot, Dr. Abbot, Mrs. Ashley. Norton, don't leave that door hanging open."

"Good evening," Abbot said to the tall bit of blackness which was Flik. Her face was a white blot in the darkness. "In my nonexistent spare time, I'm the police surgeon. Where's the body?"

He did not feel in the mood to be tactful. It was no near relative that had died. There was a body; well, let him see it.

"There'll be an ambulance come along later," Arnoldson told Flik. He moved closer to her, so that his arm brushed her side. "Now, Mrs. Ashley, let's have a look at your body."

Was that, Abbot wondered, a deliberate insult by any chance? Wrath boiled inside the doctor's long, thin frame, and words, unrepeatable, shook on his lips. "Come along, for God's sake," he fretted. "Must we freeze in this damp?"

Without saying anything, Flik pushed open the small wicket gate that was separated from the door by a yard of brick paving.

"Half a moment." Arnoldson pushed her on one side, and flashed his torch on the wet bricks. A pair of footprints showed muddily and plainly leading to the door and away from it again. Just one pair of footprints, going and coming.

"They're mine," Flik said briefly. "I'm wearing a new pair of gum boots."

Arnoldson opened Molly's door. The room was cold, dank. The old lamp on the table smoked a little. The grate was filled with dead, fine wood ashes. There was a clean cloth on the table, a bowl of red berries on the small, well-polished dresser. On the mantelpiece china ornaments and a photograph of Flik when she was a child gave an air of decoration. On the edge of the table nearest the fire were a cup and saucer, the cup empty, and a half bottle of port, the cork drawn, but the wine untouched.

Huddled in the chair by the cold fire was Molly Pritchard, or all that remained of her.

CHAPTER 3

"NOW then, Mrs. Ashley, what made you think this old woman didn't die naturally?" Arnoldson was enjoying himself. To enjoy himself at other people's expense was, to him, the height of enjoyment in more ways than one.

Flik stood up against the table, her back to Molly, her knuckles pressed down on the table's edge, rucking the cloth. "I've seen dead people before." Her voice was even, too damned even, thought Abbot. "I've seen people that've been mangled up in air raids, and people who've died in bed. Molly didn't die naturally."

"Well, of course, Mrs. Ashley, if you know all about it?"

"If I were you," Abbot said to Flik, "I wouldn't answer this man's questions till you've had legal advice. You're not bound to."

"Dr. Abbot?" Arnoldson was suddenly red with temper. "Are you conducting this case, or am I?" Without waiting for an answer, he returned to the attack on Flik. "Very well, you say she's been murdered. How?"

"I'm not a policeman or a doctor," Flik said. "As there's no knife, no blood, no struggle, then by poison, I presume. It's obvious when you look at her it must have been some sort of poison."

"Well then," Arnoldson said in a sugary voice, "take another look at her, and make sure."

"Don't do anything of the sort." Abbot's dislike of Arnoldson was nearly choking him. "Go to hell, Arnoldson. This isn't a scene from the Spanish Inquisition. Tomorrow there'll be a postmortem examination of the remains, or, if you prefer to call it by another name, an autopsy. Until you know the result, then your job's to make routine inquiries, and not badger Mrs. Ashley by forcing her to poke about with the corpse."

A slow smile spread over Norton's face, which he concealed by wiping his nose with a large handkerchief. Flik pulled her overcoat more tightly round her. She did not look at Abbot, but her stiff shoulders relaxed a little. Her face was as white as a newly laundered dress shirt. But it was perfectly calm. Arnoldson had turned down the lamp a little, so that it smoked no longer. The room, even with the presence of three living people in it, had that unmistakable smell of death, and it was very cold; the fog seemed to seep in under the door.

"Now then, Mrs. Ashley." Arnoldson ignored Abbot. "Just tell me what happened in your own way. Begin at the beginning."

"Beginning of what?"

"Beginning of this evening. What Molly did, what you did." He was being very nice now.

"Molly got the dinner ready to serve," Flik began, her voice running evenly along, as if she were repeating a lesson. "Then she did a bit of tidying in mine and my aunt's bedrooms. While she was doing that— turning down the beds, pulling the curtains, and so on—I put the dinner in the oven."

"What time d'you dine?"

"About eight. I put the dinner in the oven about quarter to. At eight my aunt and I fed. Molly went back to the kitchen, got the breakfast trays ready, and went home at quarter past eight, as she always does."

"Did she seem all right?" Abbot asked. "In her usual health and spirits?"

"Yes." Flik gave him a nod which was more of a little, discourteous bow. "She was all right. Half past eight aunt and I finished dinner, I put the remains back in the kitchen, and went out. It was all just the same as it's been for years. I knocked on Molly's door as I passed, went and asked her if she was all right, said good night and went off to my—to my work." She paused, as if she expected Arnoldson to ask some question, make some comment. He said nothing, so she went on. Abbot noticed she was breathing quicker.

"I worked till about half past eleven. I'm not sure of the time as my watch doesn't keep good time. But it must've been round about then. On my way home, I noticed there was a light still shining under Molly's door. So I knocked—"

"Wait a minute." Arnoldson licked his lips. "Why did you knock?"

Flik looked at him for the first time, a look of surprise. "Why, it was so odd. She goes—she went to bed at the same time every night. Quarter to nine. So I knocked. There wasn't any answer, so I tried the door. It wasn't locked. So I went in, and there she was. I shook her by the shoulder, then I saw she was dead. I ran back to the house, phoned you up, and came back and waited out in the road. That's all."

"Is it?" Arnoldson's voice was banteringly familiar. "That was just all? I don't think so, surely, Mrs. Ashley?"

Flik pressed her lips together. Abbot got up off the hard chair he'd been perching on. "If that's all she knows, it's all she knows. D'you propose keeping Mrs. Ashley in here with her dead cook till morning asking fool questions? Blast you," he added under his breath.

"Pardon?"

"Granted," Abbot sneered.

"Now, Mrs. Ashley——"

"Can't I go home?" Flik said unexpectedly.

"Just a few more minutes. For instance, this bottle of port, with the cork drawn, and nothing taken out of it?"

"Oh, that? We give—we gave Molly a half bottle of port every month. She liked it, so why shouldn't she have it? She was one of the family."

"Oh, she was, was she? Then she knew all about you?"

Flik took a packet of cigarettes out of her pocket, then put it back again. "Nothing to stop you having a smoke, is there?" Arnoldson said.

For the first time Flik showed emotion. "If you've no respect for the dead, then I have. Yes, I suppose Molly knew all about my aunt and me."

"You suppose? However. Did you notice, when you came in to say good night to the old woman that she hadn't drunk any of the port?"

"No."

"Did you notice anything unusual about the old woman when you came in?"

"I—I didn't notice anything. She was sitting in the chair by the fire with her back half turned. I think her teacup was empty. I go in every night, so I wouldn't notice. It's just a habit, like cleaning one's teeth. I'd have noticed if she'd been standing on her head, or singing at the top of her voice."

"You'd have noticed if she was dead or alive?"

"Naturally. She was alive. I said, 'You all right, Molly?' and she said the usual thing, 'Yes, thank you,' and so on."

"Can you swear to that?"

"She isn't bound to swear to anything," Abbot said. "This isn't the Old Bailey or the Lewes Assizes."

"I can't swear to anything," Flik said. "We say the same sentences every night, and I had the impression that the same thing happened tonight. But it mayn't. I told you, it's a habit of years. I thought she said to come in, as usual, when I knocked, but I may have only imagined it because I was so used to her saying come in. I can't have been in here more than a matter of seconds, and I didn't go right up to her."

"We'll leave that, then, for the moment." There was a nasty gleam in

Arnoldson's eye which Abbot didn't like. He didn't like anything about Arnoldson for that matter. "Now then, Mrs. Ashley. Did Molly have many visitors?"

"None at all. Unless you count my aunt or me. She didn't have anything to do with the villagers, except when she went down to the butcher, or something. She thought they were a bit—well, she didn't want any visitors, anyway. She kept herself to herself, as they say. She was at the house all day, or most of the day, so when she was at home she didn't want to be bothered by outsiders."

"No little tea parties, or ports and lemons in front of the fire with her pals?"

A slight twinge of disgust twisted Flik's mouth. "No. And she knew enough about good wines not to spoil them by putting lemonade in them. She hadn't any 'pals,' as you put it. She was a cut above the villagers."

"Snobby? I see. Then her only visitors were you and Miss Chattock?"

"Yes."

"What'd she have done if someone else had come to the door and tried to pay her a visit?"

"Told them to go away and banged the door in their face."

Flik's calmness was doing her no good with Arnoldson, the doctor thought fretfully. She ought to cry, to be frightened of the corpse. Upset. It was as if she had steeled herself to be calm under these circumstances for days beforehand. Stupid girl, why didn't she show some emotion? Arnoldson, in his mind, saw her in the dock already.

Arnoldson sucked his teeth genteelly. "Then you can say that the only two people who had legitimate permission to enter the cottage were you and your aunt? And that the only person who came in tonight was yourself?"

"Yes."

"No," Abbot contradicted. "The murderer came in as well. Don't try and push Mrs. Ashley into admitting what she doesn't mean. You aren't counsel for the prosecution, and anyway there's no one to prosecute." The doctor's fury rose and tore inside him like a gale of wind. "Your job's to find the murderer. Well, go on then, and find him or her. And while I'm about it, as Mrs. Ashley's medical adviser, I insist that she goes home immediately."

"Oh, you do, do you?" Arnoldson made no attempt to conceal his angry resentment of Abbot. "Since when've you been Mrs. Ashley's medical adviser?"

"Since old Bannard died, and I took over most of his patients who wanted me to take them over. I bought his practice—"

"And Mrs. Ashley along with it, I suppose? Funny you knew nothing about her when I mentioned her this evening—or rather, tonight."

"Last night. I didn't know her as I'd never met her. I've never been sent for by anyone at Shots Hall."

Flik moved her shoulders. "Dr. Abbot sent a card to say he'd taken over Dr. Bannard's practice, and we wrote back and said he could attend to us if necessary."

Good, thought Abbot. Lies like a trooper, and showed his teeth at Arnoldson.

Arnoldson leaned back against the mantelpiece. There was a gleam of triumph in his eyes. "Well now, how odd. When I was talking to Mrs. Ashley on the phone she said she hadn't sent for a doctor for Molly. She said as old Bannard was dead she didn't know who to send for."

For the first time Norton spoke up. "If you was a young lady that'd just found her cook what she'd known all her life dead, you wouldn't know much either. You wouldn't know if you were going or coming. You'd be all arsey-tarsey, as one might say. Beg pardon, Mrs. Ashley," he apologized to Flik.

"Why?" she said. She hadn't really been listening. And anyway, Norton was right. Arsey-tarsey was the word.

"I insist on Mrs. Ashley going home," Abbot repeated. "Apart from anything else, this place'd give anyone pneumonia."

"Just another minute or two. Mrs. Ashley, we've got to check up on any fingerprints there may be around. Mind my taking yours?"

"No," Flik said. "Not in the least. Why should I?" She spoke with sudden insolence, which, Abbot thought, suited her pale face and her secret eyes. She was tall; not as tall as he was, but tall for a woman.

Arnoldson hauled a small box out of his pocket and took Flik's fingerprints on a piece of white paper, then on a piece of black. He did the job neatly and swiftly, and managed to touch Flik's cold hands several times, which roused Abbot to a quite unreasonable anger.

"Just two questions, Mrs. Ashley, and then you can go. Does, or rather did, Molly have a cup of tea every evening when she came home?"

"Yes. Every evening. Every evening at exactly the same time. When I called in at half past eight, she'd just have finished it. She used to come back here about seven, make the fire up, and put a kettle on the hob, so that it'd be simmering till she came home at quarter past eight and all ready to make the tea."

I see." Arnoldson dug his hands in his trouser pockets and jingled his money with an irritating satisfaction. "That means she'd have made her tea directly she came in, and would have drunk it just before you came in?"

"Yes."

"Take sugar?"

"Yes. She liked her tea very sweet."

Abbot began to fidget. The room was getting more and more dank; the smell of death more and more apparent. He wanted to go over the body, but he couldn't do that with the girl here.

"Ah." Arnoldson returned to the attack. "Then as you and Miss Chattock were Molly's only visitors, you were the only people to know about her tea-drinking habits?"

"No, we weren't." Flik's contradiction was flat. "Everyone knew. Everyone in this village knows everything everyone does, says, eats and drinks, and a lot more besides. You don't appear to be used to village life."

"How could anyone else know about Molly's tea if they'd never been in here?" Arnoldson demanded truculently.

"A chance word dropped, and everyone'd know. I know that Mrs. Fewsey, the butcher's wife, cooked haddock for dinner tonight. It's a kind of secret service. Like the African jungle where the news travels invisibly, no one knows how, over hundreds of miles."

Flik pulled her coat more tightly than ever round her, so tightly that she looked like a slender pole. Then she turned and made for the door.

"I've not done yet, Mrs. Ashley. When you were out tonight, after you left Shots Hall at half past eight and before I arrived up here, did you see anyone but Molly?"

"No. At least—" Flik hesitated and was lost.

"At least who?"

"I saw Miss Merridew. I stopped outside the place I work and leaned with my back against the door and watched her. She was making curtains. Her windows were all gold through the fog, and she was all blurred. She's making new curtains for her house. She put one pair up while I was watching."

"At half past eight, or a minute past? And you stood and snooped?"

"I was not snooping. I simply watched."

"Why?"

Flik didn't answer. She stared over Arnoldson's shoulder, keeping her eyes away from Molly.

"How long did you stand there?"

"I don't know," Flik shrugged. "I didn't time myself. I just stood there. Maybe ten minutes, maybe quarter of an hour, maybe half an hour.

I don't know. I'm not interested in how long I stood there." She opened the door, and without looking behind her, without saying anything more, walked out into the fog.

"Sssh—" Arnoldson held his head on one side, listening Abbot listened too, not knowing what for. Half a minute passed, another half minute, another half. Then a dull boom sounded from the distance.

"My God," Abbot exclaimed, suddenly shaken. "What was that?"

"The Shots Hall main door," Arnoldson grinned. "It makes a row like the crack of doom when it's shut. She's gone home then. Wake up, Norton, fingerprints. Now doctor, what did old Molly-O die of? And when did she die?"

Abbot frowned. "D'you expect me to give an opinion before I can hold an autopsy? Just because her pupils are pinpricks and she appears to have died of asphyxia doesn't mean she took an overdose of morphia. There are plenty of other poisons. As for the time of death, I won't commit myself now. I'm not omnipotent, even if you think you are. Keep that teacup intact, just as it is. I can tell you this, she hasn't been dead long, but I can't tell you yet at approximately what time she took the poison. You can't lay down rules, except for things like cyanide, which kill almost immediately."

He peered into the dead face. The pinprick eyes must have seen the poisoner. Unless she poisoned herself. It was all, he thought, bloody nasty. Moving quietly, Norton was blowing white powder on the old, polished furniture. Arnoldson, wearing gloves, was poking about, avidly curious, in drawers and cupboards, prying into Molly's small and intimate privacies. I shall, thought Abbot, make a point of going home after this and destroying everything private I possess, because if I don't the same thing may happen to me. And suddenly he felt a violent revulsion against death, though he had seen so much of it.

He straightened himself, and Arnoldson, pushing him aside, proceeded to take Molly's fingerprints.

"Wonder how she got those scars on her fingertips?" he said. "Makes them easy to identify, anyhow. I wonder how old this old geyser is? I forgot to ask FlikkAH."

"Even the gods have their failings." Abbot buttoned up his overcoat and pulled on his thick woolen gloves. "I'd say she was nearer seventy than sixty."

"Where're you going?" Arnoldson asked suspiciously.

"To see if my patient's all right. You can sound your hooter when you're ready to go."

Arnoldson stuck his lips out in what was meant to be a smile. "So you've fallen for pretty Flik, have you?" he jeered. "Going to put your five bob on the mantelpiece and try your luck?"

Abbot stared at the fat, moist mouth. "I'll put five bob each way on for you, and your horse won't run."

The door banged behind him.

"One day I'll skin the pants off that old bastard," Arnoldson grunted.

"Don't forget to take his shoes off first," said Norton amiably.

"Why?"

"I'd hate to tell you. There's only one pair of fingerprints I can find round here, and they seem to be the old woman's."

"I suppose FlikkAH wore gloves."

CHAPTER 4

THE doctor had actually no intention of going to see Flik. It would, however, have been a pity to disabuse Arnoldson and tell the truth, which was that he wanted some fresh air, even mixed with fog. He also wanted to let off steam before he violently assaulted the man.

"To hell with him," he muttered, stumbling up the muddy road, leaving the police car behind him, Roberts asleep behind the wheel. "May his skin itch with scabies and every nameable and unnameable disease."

The fog gathered on the lenses of his spectacles, so that he was nearly blind. Unseen trees dripped and the silence was solid; a cloak that had wrapped itself around the hilltop hiding everything, hiding the secrets of Shotshall. Very likely hiding a murderer. Or had the old woman committed suicide? Abbot found he had walked up against a stone gatepost, and looking over the top of his spectacles saw the faint glimmer of a light. It seemed to come from between the chinks of curtains. Behind one of the windows of Shots Hall, Flikka Ashley was awake. The doctor groped his way up the short drive. He couldn't make out the shape or size of the house at all; whether it was large or small, beautiful or ugly, built of stone or built of brick.

Shuffling his feet along, so as not to fall over any unseen obstacle, he made for the light, tripped over a step, and found himself pawing a heavy door studded with nails. The light came from a window next to it. What now? he wondered. Should he knock, or should he go back to the car? He knocked, hurting his knuckles on the hard wood. Nothing happened. He knocked again, impatient and getting cross. The door began to open, and a slit of light shone out straight onto his eyes.

"Oh," said Flik's voice. "Dr. Abbot?"

"It's me. I'm alone, I left the arm of the law poking about, and the nose of the law nosing. My God, how I detest that man."

Flik pulled the door open wide, and he went in, looked round him and stared. He had no idea what he had expected, but it certainly wasn't this vast, pseudo-baronial hall, like a stage setting. The ceiling disappeared high up into a mass of carving, which he could not see properly as the only light came from two standard lamps and the logs burning in the enormous open fireplace. The walls were of stone, or what appeared to be stone. In the worst possible taste they were ornamented with carved shields and emblems. There were four high windows opposite the door he had come in by, and two high windows on each side of the door. And yet, the general effect was, somehow, pleasing, for the furniture,even though the covers of the chairs, and the curtains, were worn, was very old and very good. Probably very valuable. There was not much of it, but it was well arranged. The room must have been heaven knew how many feet long— quite fifty, and its corners were dark.

"The ancestral hall of the Chattocks," Flik said, amused. "Vintage 1860. I'm sorry the drawing-room fire's out, otherwise I'd take you in there. I can't take you into the study, either, as that's all cluttered up with my carvings. Do sit down."

Abbot sat himself in a huge wing chair by the fire. "I'm sorry to burst in on you like this, but I saw the light."

"What did she die of?" Flik's question shot out of her mouth with sudden violence.

"Postmortem tomorrow. I'll tell you then. Morphine, maybe. Maybe not." Abbot sighed, tired and dispirited, angry at the same time.

"She was murdered," Flik said. "To begin with, she hadn't any morphia, and she wouldn't take it if she had. She didn't approve of suicide."

"People don't," Abbot pointed out. "But that doesn't stop them if they suddenly go unbalanced. Who'd murder her?"

"Oh, my God!" Flik exclaimed. "How should I know? It's incredible. There wasn't anyone who could have borne her a grudge. But Arnoldson thinks I did it, doesn't he?"

"Does he?" I'm damned if I'll commit myself, thought Abbot.

"You look tired," Flik said. "I'll get you a drink."

Without waiting for him to say whether he wanted one or not she opened a dark red and gold Chinese cabinet, took out a siphon of soda and two glasses, put them on the table next him and went out of a door at the opposite side of the room. She moved silently, and Abbot saw she had taken off her gum boots and stockings and was in her bare feet; pointed, white bare feet with pink toenails. Her legs, in rough blue serge trousers, were long and straight. She wore a dark blue jersey like a fisherman's, which was tight enough to show off her figure, with its small waist. He was uncomfortably aware that his feelings reflected a little of Arnoldson's obvious wish to get as close to Flik as possible, to feel and touch her, and was furious. He then realized that he had not once looked straight into her eyes, or she into his; that in some way, she was trying to conceal what was in them, or behind them.

She came back carrying a bottle that glinted golden and inviting.

"Prewar whisky. I didn't think you'd want wine at this hour. I suppose, like everyone else, you know about the Chattock cellars?"

"No, I don't," Abbot said rather ungraciously. "What about them?"

"Laid down by great uncle Chattock when he built this place. You're sitting on top of some of the best and rarest wine in England." Flik smiled at him suddenly, and as suddenly looked right into his eyes. "Great uncle Chattock was exceedingly rich, which is more than Aunt Bee and I are. We have to sell a bottle now and then to live on."

"I see."

Flik poured out two large tots of whisky. The doctor had his neat, but she squirted a lot of soda into hers. Then she looked at him again, and he knew that he was only seeing the outsides of her eyes, and that behind them lurked lord knew what—some seething caldron of passion, or concealment, or secrets not to be told. Yet they were wary. They were probing him, trying to find out what he thought, what he knew. He wished she'd stop looking at him. And then she did, and he was sorry.

"Arnoldson thinks I killed poor Molly," she said. "I didn't. I don't know who did. I don't know why. But there's something that doesn't fit, and I can't think what it is."

"Are you shocked about it?" Abbot asked, also warily probing. "Has it upset you very much?"

Flik got up off the stool she had been sitting on, and began to prowl. "Shocked? I'm terribly shocked—I can't tell you how much. She was one of the family. Part of our lives. For her to die like that, all alone, perhaps frightened, is a sort of nightmare. I wish I could wake up."

"Well, you're a fool," said Abbot, "if I may say so. You ought to have howled and bawled and sobbed in front of Arnoldson. Instead of that, you wear a studied calm that you might've been practicing for weeks." The whisky was making him both talkative and indiscreet, but he didn't care.

Flik stopped prowling and came and stood in front of him. "But I'm not that sort. I don't howl and bawl. I can't howl and bawl to order. I never have. I'm past that stage."

"I see."

"Have some more whisky." She poured another tot in his glass, slopping it. "I ought to thank you for sticking up for me. I mean, for nobly lying that you were our family doctor. I'm very grateful."

"Why?" Abbot snorted, and added, "If you'll take me on officially as your family physician then I may be able to help you."

"Of course. But what help can you give? Do I want help? I suppose I do. Oh, God, yes, I suppose I do." Flik sat down on the worn and once lovely Persian rug in front of the fire, crossing her legs under her. Looking up at him, she gave the impression of being very young, only a child.

"Listen to me." Abbot put his glass down. "If there's anything you'd like to tell me, to get off your chest, then do. Sometimes it's a help."

"There's nothing," Flik said. "I don't know anything about Molly."

"I wasn't thinking about her," Abbot muttered. She was concealing something all right. Arnoldson was no fool. He was perfectly right. Flikka Ashley was afraid of something being found out. She was on her guard, almost as if she held a sharp sword in her hand.

Flik rolled up her sleeves, rubbing her arms. "I presume that Arnoldson gave you a few tidbits about me? He generally does when he can find a new audience."

This direct attack nearly put Abbot off his balance, and embarrassed him exceedingly. "He told me you were had up in court for swearing at a policeman in French. I may say that Norton sided with you."

Flik nodded her head slowly, so that her hair flopped over her face. Dark copper, and where the light of the fire caught it, almost gold. "Oh, yes? But I expect he told you more than that, didn't he?"

"All right, yes, he did. Something about this place catching fire. How did you manage to sleep through a bombardment of incendiaries?" he added inadvertently.

"I'd been on ambulance duty for forty-eight hours. It took a lot to wake me those days." Flik pushed her hair back, a gesture of defiance. "He hauled me out of bed. My— No one else noticed I was still asleep up there."

Abbot's frayed temper flew into shreds. "I've no desire to hear of your private affairs. They're not my business, blast them. I don't suppose there's a woman under sixty who—" He nearly bit his tongue. "I tell you, I'm not interested."

"But Arnoldson is," Flik smiled up at him, an unamused, crooked smile. "He'd love to know a great deal more about me than he thinks he knows."

"Well, I wouldn't, so that's that."

Flik's shoulders suddenly drooped. "Poor old Susan's going to be terribly upset about Molly," she said, changing the subject of her past.

"And who the hell," Abbot asked wearily, "is poor old Susan?"

"Susan Merridew," said Flik.

Abbot drained his whisky. "Is that the one you were watching to-night? Last night, rather? Why did you tell Arnoldson? It only added a bit more fuel to the fire."

"Why shouldn't I've told him?" Flik's surprise was genuine. "I'd have thought that on an occasion like this, everything's important. Haven't you ever been fascinated by watching someone when they don't know they're being watched? It's not snooping, or curiosity. I wouldn't have watched if she'd had a visitor, or anything like that. It was fascinating, a sort of dumb show. She's making new curtains for her cottage. She was like a little bird, first machining the hems of the curtains, then hopping on to a chair and seeing if they fitted the window. Then hopping back on to the floor and holding her head on one side. The fog made it all misty and unreal. It was pretty."

"You're really quite insane," Abbot said.

"Insane?" Flik repeated the word and looked away.

It was as if something cold and clammy had come into the hall. A cold draft. The wisp of an unseen, trailing shroud. The shadows in the corners seemed to deepen, and were answered by crawling shadows in Flik's eyes. It was impossible for her pale face to turn any paler, but somehow it took on a tint that was almost deathly. She swallowed, as though she was making some violent effort. Then Abbot heard, far away, the sound of the ambulance bell.

"I haven't known you ten years, or whatever the period is, but I'm going to poke your fire." He seized the poker, and began to belabor the burning logs with fiendish energy. If she heard the bell she'd go out and then she'd see Molly's corpse being taken away. She mustn't see that. She'd had enough. She'd had a damn sight too much, not only of this night, but of something else as well. He beat and hammered the logs, and suddenly the poker broke in half and fell in the grate with a crash. The bell had stopped.

"Blast it, I'm sorry. Now I've ruined your poker."

Flik began to laugh, and the sound was natural and unstrained. Abbot gave a sort of jibbering snort. "All at once I felt as if I was hammering Arnoldson on the head. My satisfaction was enormous and quite utterly bloodthirsty. I must be getting homicidal."

The fire crackled furiously, throwing up sparks and strewing the hearth with red-hot cinders. "I do wish," Flik said slowly, "I knew what it was that struck me. There was something wrong. Something that didn't fit." She rubbed her arms, thinking, then shrugged her thin, straight shoulders. "I don't know what to do about tomorrow."

"Tomorrow?" Abbot realized that he'd just been on the point of going to sleep. "What about tomorrow?"

"We'd asked some people in for drinks at six. It's Aunt Bee's birthday. I can put off people like the Ambroses, who live close, but some of the others live miles away, and haven't got phones, so I can't put them off in time. There isn't even a telegraph office in the village."

"Why put them off?" Abbot asked.

"It doesn't strike me," Flik answered, "as very pretty taste to throw a party when Molly's been murdered the day before. And of course the party's not tomorrow, it's today. How can I have a lot of people in here laughing like hyenas when Molly's being—when you're doing the—"

"Postmortem. No, I suppose not. But I don't see what you can do about it." What the devil's difference did it make? Abbot thought. Not hang a party wouldn't bring Molly back to life. "You'd better stick to your program."

The bell of the ambulance echoed hollowly in the hall.

Flik sat up on her heels, her eyes wide open. "They aren't taking her away? Now? All by herself?"

"Listen to me, my good girl, you can't help her by going with her. It's too late, anyway. They've gone." Abbot sighed. He wanted to go home to bed.

The noise of the bell receded into the distance. There was a dull banging on the hall door, and it began to open.

"Can I come in?" It was Arnoldson. He treated the doctor to a juicy smile and a half wink, and eyed the whisky bottle.

Flik stiffened. Abbot thought to himself that in front of the policeman she shed all signs of emotion in the same way a snake shed its skin at the appointed time.

"You can come in." Flik stood up, the picture of polite inhospitality. "Do you want a drink?"

"Not now, thanks. Just another word or two with you before I take the doctor home."

That's bad, Abbot decided. Arnoldson liked his drink. But the police didn't drink with suspects.

"I just wondered," Arnoldson said to Flik, "why you swept the bit of brick path after the first time you went into Molly's cottage to see her, and not after the second time."

Flik stared at him. Now she knew what it was that was wrong, what it was that did not fit. "I didn't sweep the path at all. I hadn't anything to sweep it with anyway. And why should I sweep it?"

"It was swept. Never mind." Horribly polite was Arnoldson now. "Now, if you wouldn't mind signing this statement. You can read it over first, and alter anything that's wrong, Mrs. Ashley." He handed her a notebook, held invitingly open.

Flik read what he had written. It was, she supposed, her evidence. Everything she'd said down in Molly's cottage. It seemed correct enough. She signed.

"And your address, too, please."

Flik wrote her address.

"You've left the door open," Abbot said to Arnoldson. "D'you want to freeze us?"

Arnoldson shut the door. It made a noise like an old-fashioned cannon going off. The acoustics of the hall produced echoes that were sometimes almost alarming:

Flik handed the notebook back. "Oh, and, just as a matter of form, Mrs. Ashley. Age, please?"

"Thirty-six," Flik answered without interest.

Even Abbot was surprised. She didn't look more than twenty-six at the outside. It was only her eyes that were experienced, and sometimes they, too, gave an impression of unsophistication.

"Thirty-six," Arnoldson repeated. Now he knew at last. "And your occupation, Mrs. Ashley?"

"Mainly carving and sculpturing."

"We all know that. Everyone knows about Flik's mermaid that's going to knock everyone flat when it's finished. That's where you were going tonight? To the mermaid?"

"Yes."

God, how could she stand this and not crack? Abbot wondered. The dead body of the old woman, the covert insults, the revolting familiarity?

"By occupation, we mean," Arnoldson said, "married, spinster, widow, and so on."

"Married woman."

"Former husband still alive then?"

"As far as I know."

"Married woman," Arnoldson muttered, writing. "Divorced?"

"Yes."

"Wouldn't you like," Abbot seethed, "to know what she has for breakfast?"

Arnoldson reddened, but before he could answer, there was an interruption. Someone was feverishly tapping on the hall door, little, frightened, urgent taps. Arnoldson went to the door, and opened it. A pathetically distressing figure fell in. A small figure wrapped in a dressing gown and over it a coat; thin ankles poking up out of worn galoshes, in one hand a large electric torch, in the other, as if for protection, an umbrella. A terrified little face peering out of a woolly shawl.

"Susan!" Flik exclaimed. "My dearest Susan, what on earth're you doing here?"

"Flik!" Miss Merridew tottered toward her. "I had to come. At first I was too frightened to go out in the dark by myself, but then I thought, I must go and see what's happened. I heard the bell, you see. The first time I thought it had gone past, then I heard a motor engine start up and the bell again, and I thought, that's at Shots Hall, so I had to come. Flik! Is it Bee? What's happened? Who are all these men?" She stared in alarm at Abbot and Arnoldson as if they were an army of toughs, armed to the teeth with lethal weapons.

"Susan, darling—" Flik put her arm round the shivering little shoulders. "Aunt Bee's all right. You oughtn't to have come out. This is Dr. Abbot and that's Sergeant Arnoldson."

"But why?" Miss Merridew wailed.

"Something's happened to Molly," Flik said gently. "Susan, dear, it's Molly. Poor Molly's dead."

"Murdered," Arnoldson put in with gusto. "So Mrs. Ashley thinks."

Miss Merridew screamed. In astonishment, Abbot wondered how such a large scream could come out of so small a body. At the same time, he foggily wondered at this new aspect of Flik, so gentle and so kind. He was all fogged up, anyhow. The whisky, he thought, had made him a little drunk.

"Oh!" cried Miss Merridew. "Oh! Oh!"

The baronial hall gave back her cries like the wailing of a banshee. A door at the far end of the room opened.

"What the hell's going on here?"

It was Bee Chattock.

CHAPTER 5

ABBOT, if he had visualized Bee Chattock at all, had seen her as an elderly, masculine female with cropped gray hair and tweeds. Therefore he was slightly surprised to see that she was nothing of the sort. Like the wine in the cellars below, she was of Victorian vintage. Her white hair, even at this hour, was dressed over a large pad in front, and a tight bun behind, half-hidden by a small lace cap with a lavender bow perched on it. Her crisp silk dressing gown was lavender, tight over her portly bosom, tight in the waist, flowing in the skirt, and trimmed with very good lace. From her neck dangled a lorgnette on a ribbon. Her voice was cultivated. The voice of a Victorian lady of good family. But her language was that of a Victorian gentleman when the ladies had left the room after dinner.

"Flik? What's all this? What the devil are you doing here, Susan, screaming like that? Who's that man with the spectacles, and what, may I inquire, are you doing here, Arnoldson? God almighty, what an hour to have a reception. Be quiet, Susan. Flik, have you been feeding these people the prewar whisky?"

Bee raised her lorgnette, and even Arnoldson quailed beneath the basilisk stare, while Miss Merridew reduced her shrieks to quivering sniffs. Abbot had an insane desire to roar with laughter, and knew quite definitely that he'd drunk too much.

"Well? I'm waiting for some explanation. Flik?"

Flik drew her breath in. "Molly's dead. I didn't wake you, as I thought it wouldn't do any good to ruin your night. Molly's dead."

"My God," said Bee. "Molly? Dead? What of? She was perfectly healthy, poor old thing. Why're you all looking so queer?"

"So far as one can say offhand," Arnoldson said, slightly cringing, but at the same time truculent, "she was poisoned, or took poison. Mrs. Ashley seems to be sure she was murdered."

"Then she's right. Molly wouldn't poison herself, not intentionally, at any rate. She hadn't been eating toadstools, had she, Flik?"

Flik moved her shoulders in a weary gesture. "Can you see Molly going down into the woods and picking toadstools?"

"No, I can't," Bee snapped. "Of course not. This is shocking. Poor, poor unfortunate Molly. What the devil's the use of paying the police if this kind of thing can happen?"

"D'you expect the police force should have a man stationed in every dwelling in England in case someone's murdered?" Arnoldson poked his head forward.

"Yes." Bee floored him, temporarily at least.

Miss Merridew cried quietly into her shawl, her hand in Flik's.

I'm sick of this, Abbot decided. I want to go to bed. Is this going to be an all night sitting, with a cold collation at the end of it? Poisoned coffee and baked toadstools with beards on them, and spots?

Arnoldson sucked his pencil. The lead made a black smudge on his wet lower lip. "You don't seem very surprised, Miss Chattock, to hear the old woman's dead."

"Surprise," Bee remarked acidly, "is hardly the word. What d'you mean, 'surprised'? Open your mouth and shut your eyes, and see what the queen'll give you. Surprised! A nice sort of surprise. I'm shocked, horrified. I'm sad to lose an old friend. More sad than you'll ever be about anything, because it isn't in you to be anything but greedy and curious. What d'you expect me to do? Scream like Miss Merridew? Wring my hands, with the tears pouring down my face? Sob, wail? What?"

Arnoldson swallowed, and his Adam's apple jerked up and down. Despite his longing for bed, Abbot enjoyed the performance. There was no doubt where Flik got her spirit. If she wasn't actually a Chattock, then association with them had produced the same toughness. Exterior toughness, anyway.

"We'd better be going, doctor." Arnoldson gave up the unequal battle for that night. "Just one thing, Miss Chattock. When did you last see Molly Pritchard?"

"When she came in to say good night to me before she went home. That must have been a minute or so before the quarter past."

"And at what time did Mrs. Ashley go out?"

"About half past. Why ask me? Ask her. I suppose you want her word corroborated? Now you can go to hell, and take the doctor along with you."

"Thanks," Abbot smiled, and was surprised to get an answering smile from Bee Chattock. He didn't shake hands with her when he went, nor with Flik. He looked at Flik through the whisky fog which was again obscuring her, and tried to convey a message that he'd get in touch with her. Like a ruddy conspirator, he thought, and, tripped over the back of Arnoldson's heels, for which he did not apologize. The door crashed shut behind him, and he was out again in the fog, the watchful darkness and the sloughing mud.

"Now then," Bee said when the door shut. "Susan, you'd better spend the night here, you can't go home in that deplorable state, gibbering like a monkey and sniveling like a brat."

"No, no," Miss Merridew weakly declined. "No, no, Bee, dear, I'm all right. I'll go home. I mustn't give way like this. I mustn't be such a coward. I'd rather go home. I'll be sure and lock the doors and see the windows are fastened. Oh, dear, oh, dear, poor old Molly."

She began once more to weep, and Bee, pouring out a tot of whisky, pushed the glass between the chattering teeth. Miss Merridew choked, gulped, choked again and stopped crying. "But I can't think—" she said, bewildered. "I simply can't think—"

"Don't," Bee said. "This isn't the time to think. No one ever had a sensible thought at this time in the morning. Flik, if she won't stay here, then you'd better take her home."

"No, no!" Miss Merridew clutched her umbrella and picked up her torch, which she had dropped when she first came in. "I wouldn't dream of Flik taking a risk for my sake. I'll go alone."

"Risk?" Flik repeated. "Risk of what? Darling Susan, what are you talking about?"

Miss Merridew's face crumpled up as if she was going to cry again. "Why," she dithered, "the murderer. He might kill you. It's awful! A murderer creeping about."

Bee snorted. "Don't be absurd, Susan. If anyone killed Molly, then they're miles away by now, running like the devil. Flik, you look fagged out, and I'm not surprised, what with finding Molly, and then that appalling creature Arnoldson hanging around like a bit of bad meat. Take Susan home, and then come back to bed. I'm going to bed now. We can't do any good sitting up till morning talking about it. We'll do that in the sane light of day. Take one of your sleeping tablets when you get in, and have some more whisky."

Flik nodded silently, and the business of taking Miss Merridew home started. First of all the old lady shed one of her galoshes in the mud outside the door. Then she dropped her umbrella. Flik, sorry for the little creature, curbed her weary impatience, found the galosh, picked up the umbrella, and half carried Miss Merridew back to her whitewashed sham olde worlde cottage.

And Norton, on guard in Molly's small living room, listened to the shuffling footsteps, the muffed voices, recognizing Flik's— "That's right, Susan, hang on to my arm…" Then the opening and shutting of a door across the road. Then silence.

Nearly frozen to death, he put a mat up against the crack under the door hoping to keep the damp and the fog out. The curtains were pulled tightly across the windows, and he had shut the door into the bedroom, trying to get some sort of fug up. Unimaginative, he still did not like this job one bit. The only comfortable chair in the room was the one from which the corpse had been removed, and there was still the imprint of Molly's head on the patchwork cushion. He stiffened. The latch of the wicket gate had clicked softly. The back of his neck crawled. Was the murderer creeping out of the fog to revisit the scene of his crime? Breathing through his nose, he turned the lamp out, kicked the rug away from the door, and flattened himself against the wall behind it. He did not really feel at all happy. He was not armed, and the unknown always rather alarmed him. The door began to open. He could tell that by the cold air that suddenly came in. The door opened right up against his chest, then slowly closed. He could hear someone breathing. They were standing still, as though taking their bearings, listening.

Norton held his breath till his lungs nearly burst. The thin beam of a torch lit on the fireplace, on Molly's chair, a wandering, vagrant light. Between him and the light someone was moving quietly. The door into the bedroom opened, swung half shut, and the light went behind it. Very cautiously, he let his breath out, waited till he could breathe comfortably again, and took his boots off. In his woolen-socked feet, he tiptoed to the bedroom door. Arnoldson had already searched the whole cottage, the living room, the bedroom, the small attic above, the scullery, and taken away with him the only things that seemed of interest.

Fascinated, Norton watched the light. Its owner wore gloves. The gloved hands touched this and that, very lightly, came to rest on a little walnut writing desk, pressed the bottom of it, and felt inside the hidden drawer that sprang open. Norton had seen many such things. His old aunt down in St. Arthurs had a little desk with a drawer just the same as that, except that it was in the lid. The owner of the hands took out a bundle of letters, tied up with blue ribbon, put the torch on top of the desk, and feverishly sorted the letters in the light of it. Pulled them out of the envelopes, glanced through them, put them back, searching, reading, sorting.

There was a soft sigh of relief. Evidently the intruder had found what it had come for. The gloves put the rest of the letters together, tied them up with the ribbon, and they vanished into a pocket. Still Norton waited. But he waited a little too long. There was the snick of a cigarette lighter, a burst of flame, and the smell of burning paper.

"Oi!" He turned on his flashlight. "Oi, Mrs. Ashley, you can't do that now!"

In the light of his torch, Flik's face turned first red, then back to white. She dodged behind a chair, holding the burning letter out of his reach. Stumbling, he made a grab for it, tripped on a rag mat, and by the time he had righted himself saw nothing more than a pile of black ashes on the floor, which Flik stamped on, grinding them with her heel till they were powder.

"Oh, now, Mrs. Ashley," Norton gulped, "you really shouldn't have done that."

"Well then, why didn't you stop me?" Only the corners of her mouth showed that she was trembling. "You scared the wits out of me," she added. "What're you doing here in the dark?"

"Well," he said rather uncomfortably, "Mr. Arnoldson put me on here to look after the place. It's quite usual, Mrs. Ashley, when anyone's died not quite right."

"I see." Flik gave him an odd smile. "Just in case the murderer revisits the scene of his crime?"

Norton fidgeted, not sure what the answer was. "After all," he hedged, "we don't know it was murder yet, do we? All the same, Mrs. Ashley, you shouldn't have done that. If there was anything you wanted here you could've asked."

Flik lifted her shoulders, and Norton thought, oh, Lord, what should he do now? There was a faint smell of wet leaves as she passed him and went into the small, cold living room. He followed her, and fumbling for matches lit the lamp again.

"Now, Mrs. Ashley—"

Flik waited, keeping her back to Molly's chair.

"Now, I'll have to ask you what it was you was burning," Norton went on, trying to do his duty as a policeman, and glad that Arnoldson wasn't there to see him and jeer. Arnoldson would have made one of his usual cracks about everyone falling for FlikkAH.

Suddenly Flik was on the defensive. "What I was burning, as you no doubt saw, was a letter." She began to talk very quickly, almost like a child making excuses for some misdeed. "It wasn't anything that could possibly've had anything to do with Molly being murdered. It was personal. Don't you see, I wouldn't try and hide anything that'd help to find whoever murdered her? It was simply personal—I didn't want Arnoldson reading my letters."

"Oh?" Norton caught up on her. "It was a letter of yours? Written to the deceased, was it? I'm afraid you'll have to give me the other ones— the ones you put in your pocket. I'm sorry, Mrs. Ashley, I am really. I'll always remember how good you and Miss Chattock were when I had to come up and see you about those ladders of yours what was stolen, and I told you my wife was ill and you gave me that bottle of port for her."

Flik moved impatiently. "D'you think I'd trade on that? I don't want to stop you doing whatever's supposed to be your duty, but I can't see how my old letters to Molly can have anything to do with what's happened. If Arnoldson thought so, then why didn't he take them?"

"Didn't find them, that's why, Mrs. Ashley." Norton, despite the cold, started to sweat, and he felt his face turning red. "He did take the old woman's bankbook, and her card of Christmas club saving stamps, but they were in the drawer of the dresser here— The saving stamp card was full," he added foolishly. Anything to go on talking, so that he'd put off the moment when he had to make Flik give him the letters in her pocket.

Flik's lips moved, as if she were saying something, or repeating something he had said; her eyes looked very large, and expressionless, like eyes that were turned back to front, so that they were staring inward at some idea. Groping for something. But she said nothing out loud, and Norton felt more and more depressed and uncomfortable. He cleared his throat.

"I'm really sorry, Mrs. Ashley, but you'll have to give me the rest of them letters."

He didn't quite know what he had expected her to do. But he hadn't expected her quietly to hand the bundle of letters over. It had not occurred to his usually logical mind that that was the only thing she could have done, except bash him on the head with a chair and then make a bolt for it. He mumbled a vague politeness and transferred the letters to his own pocket. Flik turned up the collar of her coat.

"Have a cigarette?" she said, and handed him a half-full packet. "I've more at home. Your need, as they say, is probably greater than mine. Why don't you relight the fire and make yourself some tea? Molly wouldn't grudge you using her tea. Or are you afraid it's full of poison?"

Her voice, thought Norton, was bitter as that stuff you put on the ends of kids' pencils to stop them sucking them. Well, all this was pretty bloody for her. "Mrs. Ashley? You wouldn't care to tell me what was in the letter you burned?"

Flik looked at him over her shoulder, her hand on the doorknob. "No, I wouldn't. It was purely personal. A letter written years ago. Go on, it's your duty to tell Arnoldson:" Then she went, shutting the door quietly behind her.

Norton listened. In due course he heard the muffled crash of the Shots Hall main door shut. "Hoo-bloody-rah," he muttered in disgust, and feeling more disgusted at the poking and prying that went with police work, took the packet of letters out of his pocket and, began to go through them. They were all addressed to Molly. The first one was dated thirty years before, in a faded, scrawling small-child hand.

> DARLING NANNIE,
>
> I wish Aunt Bee would tak me way from thise beastly school as the girls ar so stupid and when they have a fight they only fight sayeing silly things not with they fists like Uncle Hary tourt. I wonder how my tortoiuise is.
>
> With lots of love from your loving little Flik.

Oh, hell, Norton groaned to himself. This was something awful, like suddenly seeing someone with their clothes off. Arnoldson, rot him, would learn all this off by heart and spout it down at the station. He shuffled through the letters, one by one, filled with an abject apology toward Flik. She hadn't written often to Molly. There were two more letters, each a little less childish, from the school she hadn't liked. Another from some place in Scotland where she must have spent a summer holiday with an Uncle John. One from Paris, when she must have been about sixteen

> DARLING MOLLY,
>
> I haven't a thing to say against Paris. It's a lovely town, but the family I'm farmed out on for the good of my soul are as stuffy as an old featherbed. If I dare raise my eyes walking along the street they say it isn't proper for young ladies to look at young gentlemen...

And so on. A faintly scornful letter, the beginning of the many shapes that were the Flik to come.

Norton wondered when her mother and father had died, and supposed they did it when she was a kid, and then she'd been taken over by uncles and aunts. There was a letter written on her honeymoon. She must have married, from the date, when she was in her teens. The letter didn't say much, except that underneath the bald sentences there was an embarrassing streak of romance. The last letter but one was written from London ten years before, and he squirmed.

> DARLING MOLLY,
>
> I'm writing to Aunt Bee by this same post. I'm afraid you're

both going to be terribly upset, but I simply can't stand living with Mac any longer. I never told anyone, as I thought he might pull himself together, but after eight years of it he's simply getting worse. He's never sober now at all, and he's the filthiest drunk I've ever met, and I've met many. Only he won't let me divorce him. He says if I'm to get rid of him, then he'll divorce me, but he won't let me divorce him. So there's only one thing for it. I'll have to raise a tenner, bribe a young man to spend the night most respectably playing cards with me in a hotel bedroom, stage the usual scene when the maid comes in in the morning, and take the rap. I'm so terribly, terribly sorry, as I feel I'm letting you and Aunt Bee down. But I can't, I honestly can't stand it any longer. It's the pretending I don't care, and can stand it, and making out I'm perfectly happy that's so exhausting. I'll try and arrange everything so that there's no fuss or publicity, which won't be difficult as practically everyone in England's getting divorced, and after all I'm not a celebrity...

Norton conjured up Arnoldson before him, and made a rude gesture. "Stung again, you bastard," he remarked with loud, offensive satisfaction. "A divorcee, is she? Another man? Clever, aren't you?"

The last letter was written from Wales two years before. It related the history of the green rock. Norton lit one of Flik's cigarettes, and shook himself, trying to rid his flesh of the cold. The lamp gave out a puff of smoke, as though it had been caught in a draft. Where had the letter Flik had burned fitted in? Why had she burned that particular one, and tried simply to steal the others? Probably so important to her that she wanted to be rid of it at once, just in case. In case of what?

He bundled the letters up and tied the faded blue ribbon round them. If Arnoldson thought he was so damn clever, let him find them for himself. He switched on his light, groped his way into the bedroom, and put the letters back in the drawer Flik had taken them from. Leave everything as it is, Arnoldson had said when he went. All right, this was as it had been, with the letters still in the drawer. Grunting, Norton bent down and flicked at the burned ashes on the carpet, till they became part of the worn pile of what had once been best Axminster. A minute corner of white caught his eye. The corner of the letter Flik must have held as it burned. He picked it up, and shone his torch on it. It was the left bottom corner of a page. All that was on it were five letters of a word, but the writing was the same.

"Morph," Norton read out. "Morph. Morph. Morphine. Morphia."

He talked out loud, incredulous, distressed. For if he hadn't fallen for Flik in the way Arnoldson said everyone fell for her, he at least thought her very lovely. Lovely and, somehow, alone.

He went to the window and pulled back a bit of the curtain. The fog had lifted a little, and there was a gray light outside, the trees and hedges black against it. His breath made a cloud on the glass of the window. It was so cold that his breath was a cloud under his nose as well.

This is all damn nasty, he thought, and let the curtain fall again.

CHAPTER 6

THE Deputy Chief Constable's house was more than six miles outside St. Arthurs.

"I will not," he said, when he took over from his predecessor, who had tried to let him his own house on the sea front, "live with my work. I refuse to establish myself on the front and every time I look out at the channel see one of my own constables parading in the foreground."

So Major Mahew, accompanied by Mrs. Mahew, four dogs, a canary in a white cage, a lot of luggage and some very nice furniture, had taken Marsh House, which, so Mahew said, was thus called because there wasn't a marsh within miles of it. He was the first Deputy Chief Constable of St. Arthurs for thirty years who had not started life as a policeman. No one quite knew what he had started life as, but he had been in A.M.G. for part of the war, with the temporary rank of colonel. He had left with the permanent rank of major, which he disliked, preferring to be called plain mister.

On the morning of December 2nd, at 8.30 A.M., he stuck his head round the corner of Mrs. Mahew's bedroom door, and said, "Woman, you will stay in bed till your cold's better, and to hell with you. Even with a red nose you look more beautiful than the rising sun."

"I'm the red sky in the morning that's the shepherds' warning," she said. "Get out before you catch a germ. I didn't know what Lane'd like for breakfast, so I ordered a selection—sausages, grilled tomatoes, bacon, and lumpy porridge."

"What we'll get," Mahew sighed, "will be lumpy porridge, as everything else is off."

"Nothing is more likely. Good morning."

"Good morning, flower of the wilderness."

Mahew was forty-seven. Mrs. Mahew was forty-five. They had been married for exactly twenty years and accomplished the impossible. They still liked each other enormously, admitted it, and never quarreled. This fact still astonished them. They were quite convinced they had established a record and unbroken run of connubial bliss.

Mahew went down the short stairs, picking his way between dogs. Lane Parry was in the dining room eating, with relish, sausages and tomatoes, the morning's collection of newspapers spread over the table round his place. Mahew whipped the *Sunday Times* away and sat down at the other end of the table. His worst fears were not realized. Under the silver cover of his plate were also sausages and grilled tomatoes.

"But no bacon," he said to the *Sunday Times*. "No doubt the celebrated gentleman from the C.I.D., Scotland Yard, Inspector Parry, has got there first."

"I wish you wouldn't be so goddamn flippant at this hour of the morning," Parry said without looking up. "Hearty. All you need now is someone to come in and drag off your muddy riding boots and gory spurs."

Mahew and Parry had known each other for quite a long time. They went on with their breakfasts in silence. Presently the telephone bell rang.

"Pay no attention," Parry said.

The bell went on ringing. Mahew dragged himself away from the *Sunday Times,* the sausages and the tomatoes, fell over the same dogs, now in the hall, and went to the phone in his study.

His end of the conversation was brief. "Mahew here. I see. Right. I'll tell him. Oh? Why can't he wait till I get down to the town? Very well. I wish people would behave in a normal manner."

He planted himself in front of his breakfast again. "Your two heroes," he said to Parry, "of the razor-cum-snatch-cum-grab-come-racecourse gang have now been entrained for London, with escort."

"Good."

"Why they came down here, God only knows."

"Never heard of extradition orders. I'll be getting back by the latest possible train compatible with duty."

"Also there is a body."

"There always is."

Mahew and Parry finished their breakfasts in a comfortable peace and quiet. Then Mahew said, "That chap I was telling you about, Arnoldson, was on the phone. He has a body. It's the body of an old woman called Molly Pritchard. He appears to've started the ball rolling by neglecting to inform me about the body last night, having it removed from where it was found before I could have a look at it, and has now taken it upon himself to order a postmortem which is apparently already under way."

"Officious," Parry agreed. "Sack him."

"I wish I could. There's something about the man I dislike, but his present officiousness is scarcely a large enough excuse for me to have him thrown out on his ear. Blast him," Mahew added. "He's on his way up now, and he sounds pleased."

"He probably thinks," Parry said, "he's got the murderer, if it's a case of murder." He lit a cigarette and pushed his chair back from the table, stretching his long legs out in front of him. He was a long man altogether, including his memory. Ignoring the many strings he might have pulled, he had got himself into the police force by the regular way. Parry had done his three years as a constable, pounding his allocated beats and holding up the traffic to let perambulators and old ladies cross the road. On point duty he had been a great success. Never a female passed him without stopping to ask the way to some road or street the way to which they knew perfectly well. At forty he still had the same lean attraction that had fluttered the hearts of his erstwhile seekers of information.

"If this is really," Mahew said, "a case of murder, then I'm damned if I know how I'm to handle it. D'you know, Lane, we've never had a real murder down these parts?"

"What d'you call real murder?" Parry asked. "If it's murder it's real, if it isn't real, then it's not murder."

"I'm talking about killing someone with malice aforethought. I don't call a burglar getting in a panic and knocking a householder on the head murder."

"No?" Parry threw his cigarette end in the fire. "That's just a petting party, I suppose? Don't be a bloody fool, of course you could handle a nice, real murder. You'd love it."

"I'd hate it." Mahew, Parry saw, was suddenly very much in earnest. "Messy. A real murder's messy. Nasty human passions and desires, and greed or jealousy, or both or all. I'm all for a good, clean duel if it comes to settling scores, or a quick rage, and 'take this, you cad.' "

"Hoity-toity," Parry sighed, and pricked up his ears.

A car was coming up the inconvenient lane that led to Marsh House. As it came closer the sloshing sound of mud being plowed through by tires percolated into the room, disturbing the peace, making the dogs bark, pushing away the serenity and the secure comfort of a good breakfast.

Mahew got up and went into the hall. Parry, trying to make himself scarce, failed lamentably to do so, and became an unwilling audience to Mahew's ticking off of Arnoldson, which was brief but to the point.

"When I want you to take the law into your own hands," Mahew finished, "I'll tell you. I dislike red tape, but there're certain formalities which must be preserved, and certain rules which must be abided by. You'd better come into the dining room, Arnoldson, and thaw out some of your initiative."

Good for Mahew, thought Parry, and nodded Arnoldson good morning.

" 'Morning, Inspector," Arnoldson said, his face angry and beet red.

"Cold out?" Parry pushed his packet of cigarettes forward, wishing he could get to hell out of there. He had an unpleasant feeling that in some way he was going to be dragged into something he didn't want to be dragged into. The pale, wintry sunshine picked out the homely disorder of the breakfast table, so that it didn't look homely any longer. It looked untidy. Like a feast abandoned by feasters who had got up in a hurry to go out and do battle. Arnoldson was breathing quickly, his damp breath an uncomfortable steam; and the damp clung to his check overcoat, melting into small gray dewdrops. Parry realized that out of doors the sun was fighting a losing fight with a mist that hung over the clumps of trees, ready to descend and hide them.

"Light?"

"Thanks, Inspector," Arnoldson's face poked itself close to Parry's. "Got your boys off all right, all in good order, so you've nothing more to worry about."

"I never had," Parry said pleasantly. "I only came down for a change of air. No doubt you could've got tabs on them and rounded them up and sent them back to London without my aid. Petty crime's a nuisance, but it's always an excuse for a holiday."

"With you there." Arnoldson was self-confident again. "But murder, Inspector, is a different thing."

Parry, by nature not very malicious, forbore to agree that it was a little different, and studied the leading article in his paper. This was nothing to do with him. This was Mahew's bastard child, begotten of the Sussex sea fogs, for the special annoyance of Mahew and edification of Arnoldson, whose hair was too greasy. But as Arnoldson told his story, he found himself listening against his will, though he still kept his eyes fixed on the paper.

"That's the story the Ashley woman told," Arnoldson said, "and here's her statement, sir."

Mahew took the proffered notebook and read carefully. "Have you any reason to suppose," he asked when he had finished, "that Mrs. Ashley wasn't speaking the truth? And while you're about it, you might refer to her as Mrs. Ashley, and not the Ashley woman. She isn't a convicted criminal, nor a woman off the streets. I happen to've met her."

Arnoldson licked his lips and reddened. "It seems to me, sir, she wasn't speaking the truth. I'm just coming to that. Norton, who I left in charge of the cottage last night, can bear me out. He wasn't sure of the time, but it must've been about two A.M. this morning when he heard someone sneaking in the gate of the cottage, so he put the light out and got behind the door. Someone came in very quiet, with a torch, and he saw it was her— Mrs. Ashley—and what's more she was wearing gloves."

"I'm not surprised," Parry said. "In this weather no one but a fool would go out without them." Hell, he hadn't meant to interrupt or say anything, but Arnoldson had got into his hair.

Arnoldson gave him a vicious look and went on. "She sneaked into the old woman's bedroom and began poking about. Finally she opened a hidden drawer in one of those old desk things like you see so many of in the junk shops, and took out a bundle of letters. Norton watched her sorting them, and then before he could stop her, which was a poor show on his part, she burned one of them with her cigarette lighter."

"One moment," Mahew said. "Where's Norton?"

"I left him out in the car, sir."

"To freeze? Bring him in. You ought to have brought him in straight away. I'd like him to give his own version."

Reluctantly, Arnoldson, who wanted to keep everyone but himself out of the case, fetched Norton from the car and levered him into the dining room rather as if he was under arrest. The wretched Norton, unshaved, cold, hungry, angry and miserable, perched himself on the edge of a chair and accepted a cup of tea and a cigarette. He felt like some sort of sneak thief. Till he had been relieved at daylight, he had tramped round and round Molly's table trying to make up his mind whether he should tell Arnoldson about Flik's letters, or leave Arnoldson to find out for himself. In the end his sense of duty had got the better of him, and he kept thinking of the bottle of vintage port Flik and her aunt had given him for his wife. This seemed a poor thanks for their kindness.

"Now then, Norton," Mahew prompted.

Norton told his story, pausing every now and then to gulp uncomfortably; and Parry thought, he likes this Ashley woman, or girl or whatever she is, and he's feeling a heel.

"Mrs. Ashley," Norton hesitated, "assured me they were only personal letters, and so they are, because I read them, and she said the one she burned hadn't anything in it that could have had anything to do with the old woman's death. She said she didn't want Arn—she didn't want strangers reading them, that's all."

" 'Darling Nannie,' " Arnoldson grinned, " 'with lots of love from her loving little Flik.' "

"Thank you, Arnoldson," Mahew said coldly. "I shall read them for myself in due course. Well, Norton?"

"It was when she was gone that I found the bit of paper that wasn't burned. It must've been the corner she was holding, so it didn't get burned, if you see what I mean."

"I see," Mahew agreed. "Where is it?"

Arnoldson drew his breath in, and triumphantly produced the small white corner of paper out of an envelope. It was his trump card.

"See, sir? The beginning of a word. M-O-R-P. Morphia, or morphine. And by the looks of the old woman it was morphine that killed her."

"When Dr. Abbot has finished the postmortem," Mahew frowned, "we'll presumably know what killed her. At present we don't. Take a look at this, Lane."

Parry put aside the paper with a gesture of protest, and held his hand out. "It might be a part of many words. Morpheus, in the arms of same—Metamorphosis—Morphic— Has anyone asked Mrs. Ashley about it?"

"And put Mrs. Ashley on her guard?" Arnoldson's scorn was ill-hidden.

"Your case, not mine," Parry said very pleasantly, and lit another cigarette.

"What's more," Arnoldson went on, "I tested the whole cottage for fingerprints, and the only ones I found were the old woman's. So Mrs. Ashley must've worn gloves."

"Norton," said Mahew, "has already told us she was wearing gloves."

"Yes, but when she went into the cottage before."

"You mean when she found the old woman in there dead? She might very well have been wearing gloves on a night like last night. Did you ask her if she was wearing gloves when she found the body?"

"No, sir." The corner of Arnoldson's jaw began to work.

Mahew's baby, thought Parry. Let him rock it to sleep. He got up and went into the hall, patted one of the dogs and strolled across to Mahew's small study. There, a moment later, Mahew found him, and shut the door.

"Listen, Lane, I don't like the smell of this business in the least. It may turn out to be suicide, but it seems very unlikely. If an old cook was going to do herself in she'd most likely stick her head in the gas oven. But

I should say this is poison."

"Well?" Parry was not very sympathetic. "Suppose it's murder by poison? Then all you've got to do is to find the motive and the poisoner."

"All I've got to do? Thanks." Mahew lit his pipe, striking the match angrily on the side of the fireplace. "The whole thing's getting in a mess at the start. First, my only really good man with a fair, unbiased mind, Superintendent Willis, is down with a bad go of flu, so Arnoldson's the only chap to take his place. Second, for some reason I don't know, Arnoldson's biased against Mrs. Ashley, which isn't fair on her. Third, as she's a lady and I've met her, and she's one of our own kind, and I don't like Arnoldson, I'm biased for her, and that isn't fair on the law."

"So what?"

"I'd like an outsider to run the show. Someone who isn't biased and can attack the problem with an open mind. I told you, we've never had a real murder down here."

Parry groaned. "It mayn't be murder. The postmortem may show she died quite naturally of senile decay or fatty degeneration of the heart."

"On the other hand," Mahew pointed out, "the postmortem may show she died of poisoning. All right, all right, say that doesn't prove conclusively she was murdered, but I've got to prove who administered the poison, haven't I?"

"Yes, dear comrade, you have. So what again?"

"If it turns out to be poison, then it looks like being a complicated case. Arnoldson'll want to arrest Mrs. Ashley on the spot, and I shan't want to."

Parry shrugged his shoulders, and opening the French window that led out into the sopping garden, sniffed the air. Even though the sea was six miles away, he could smell the salt, mixed with the smell of decaying leaves. The mist still hung over the treetops, and the sun had lost the fight for the day. He closed the door behind him, and walked slowly across the lawn, whistling under his breath. Was someone, sometime, going to hang by the neck till they were dead?

Mahew watched the straight, disappearing back view and chewed at the stem of his pipe. He had met Flikka Ashley only twice. Once at someone's cocktail party; again, about a year ago, when his car had broken down just outside Shotshall, and she had come round the corner, swinging a stick she had cut off a hedge. She had recognized him, smiled, got her hands covered with grease tinkering with the carburetor, and somehow the car had started functioning again.

He could hear the mumble of Arnoldson's voice in the dining room.

He was evidently holding forth to the weary Norton. With a feeling of guilt, Mahew picked up the telephone receiver and sat down at his desk.

For once the local exchange was speedy. But he was still talking when Parry came back from his stroll. Parry's eyebrows rose into his hair, and he put out his hand for the receiver.

"No, you don't," Mahew said, fending him off. "Well, thanks very much, I feel it's the best thing to do under the circumstances. When we know the result of the postmortem, Inspector Parry'll ring you up. Of course if it's senile decay, then that'll be that and it won't be necessary fo—what—thanks…"

"You dirty dog," Parry said softly. "You snake in the grass. So I'm to nurse your baby for you, am I, you unnatural mother?"

CHAPTER 7

"FLIK? Flik? There's your phone going."

"Flik? Do answer, it may be the latest dope."

"Darling, why don't you have a proper phone bell fixed? Yours wouldn't wake a mouse."

Oh, shut up, all of you, Flik thought, wishing she could be as ungracious to her and Bee Chattock's guests as she felt. She edged past Phil Ambrose, who was talking to a young man who had left a leg in Normandy, and wriggled into the inconvenient corner where the telephone reposed.

"Hullo?" she said, unconsciously lowering her voice. Snatches of talk drifted into her unoccupied ear, foolish, meaningless. "So I got some more seeds from Suttons, and …No, these're the shoes I traded with Camilla for that red pullover…No, it was Reggie Wells who was my company commander then…Phil, honey…"

"Mrs. Ashley? This is Abbot here."

"Yes?" Flik answered. "Yes? Abbot?"

Abbot's voice said crossly, "Your party seems to be going strong, I hear noises like Bedlam let loose. Are you listening? I went for morphine straight away. She must have taken it in her tea. Evidently she had a sweet tooth and didn't taste it. About six grains."

"My God," Flik whispered. "Abbot? What time did she take it? She used to have her cuppa between quarter past and half past eight."

"All I can say is," said Abbot's voice, "that she didn't take it earlier than a quarter to eight, or later than nine. She can only have been dead a very short time when you found her. Did you touch her?"

"Yes," Flik said. "Yes. Only I must've had my gloves on. I can't remember feeling if she was warm still."

"I'm breaking all known rules and regulations telling you this," Abbot's voice said. "But I don't give a damn for rules and regulations. Mrs. Ashley? A Scotland Yard man's taken the business over."

"I'm glad. That'll mean something'll be done about it."

"Delighted you're glad, I'm sure. From what I heard he and the Deputy Chief Constable're about to pay you a visit."

"And Arnoldson?"

"I don't know."

"Thanks for telling me. I don't know why you should help me like this."

"Someone's got to." Abbot's voice was caustic. "And if I can do Arnoldson a bad turn, I will."

"Half a minute." Flik glanced behind her. They were still at it. Drinking the cocktails she had made from the bad gin she'd fetched from the pub. Talking rubbish. "But Phil, honey, you can't do that, peroxide'll make your hair fall out…But they didn't turn out apricot color after all, they were pink…Camilla'd trade the feathers off her hens…" Flik half smiled, picturing Abbot's scorn if he could listen to all that. "Abbot?"

"Yes?"

"If you're coming up this way, drop in." Then Flik rang off.

"Who was it?" Resplendent in rustling lilac silk, and a jet necklace, Bee shook off a persistent young woman who was telling her how to make homemade mothballs and joined Flik in the corner. "Well? Who the hell was that?"

"Abbot. Aunt Bee, Molly must have taken six grains of morphia in her tea, and there's a Scotland Yard man taken charge."

"Damn good thing too. Smack in the eye for Arnoldson. In the name of God, can't we get rid of this crowd?"

"They'll go," Flik said wryly, "when the drink runs out. It's only half past six. They'll think if they stay long enough they may get some of the famous 1860 brandy."

"Over my dead body," said Bee.

"Flik?" Phil Ambrose called, tossing back the brown hair she was talking of peroxiding. "Was that the police? Was it anything exciting?"

"It wasn't the police," Flik answered.

The police, however, were on their way. Parry, Mahew and Arnoldson, driven by a constable, bumped up the bad road that led to Shots Hall, while Parry inwardly cursed. The headlights of the car were ghostly streaks in the fog which had come down again. It was cold and raw. Somewhere a cracked bell summoned the faithful to evening service. Parry had forgotten it was Sunday. Perhaps, he thought to himself, the depression on him was simply the usual Sunday feeling.

"We're here," Mahew said. "Leave the car in the road, Mordant. Lane, you'd like to see the old woman's cottage first?"

"No, I wouldn't," Parry said. "But I suppose I'll have to."

The constable who was still in charge opened the door and looked pleased at the prospect of a little company.

"This is Inspector Lane Parry from Scotland Yard," Mahew told him, with a malicious glance at Arnoldson.

"This is where the old woman was found sitting." Arnoldson refused to take a back place. "As you see, Inspector, I haven't let anything be disturbed."

Parry stared down at the chair, picked up the cushion pressed by Molly's head, shook it, and put it tidily back. Having seen all that was left of Molly, he felt she would have approved his action as much as Arnoldson obviously didn't.

Mahew smothered a clucking laugh, and Arnoldson cleared his throat.

"And this is the bedroom, Inspector. This is the desk where I found the letters."

"I thought Norton found them? Or rather, found Mrs. Ashley finding them?" Parry stared at the desk, the floor, the ceiling, opened and shut the drawers of the dressing table, and strolled into the small scullery. No medicine cupboard and no medicines, he noticed. Evidently old Molly had either been very strong, or hadn't approved of medicines. Or had she, and they had all been taken away by whoever murdered her if she didn't commit suicide?

"I don't see that it's necessary to keep a man freezing in this morgue any longer," he said to Mahew. "What is necessary is to check up on everyone's movements in the village and round about between quarter to eight and nine o'clock yesterday evening."

"I've put a man on to that," Arnoldson said smugly. "I'll get his report later. We know what Mrs. Ashley said she was doing, we know Miss Merridew opposite was sewing curtains, anyhow."

They went out into the fog and the darkness again. The man who had been on duty thankfully got into the waiting car, and Parry turned the key in the lock of Molly's door and absently pocketed it.

"Oh, excuse me, sir!" The relieved constable suddenly stuck his head out of the window. "I forgot to say, there must be something going on at Shots Hall this evening."

"Why?" Mahew asked.

"I don't know why, sir," answered the literal man, "I'm sure. But I heard some cars driving in, and that door banging and crashing."

"Thanks," Mahew said.

"Perhaps the fathering of a reception committee in our honor?" Parry suggested. "Or a wake?"

"Idle curiosity seekers, very likely," Mahew grunted. "Arnoldson, you needn't come with us."

Arnoldson replied nothing. His silence, however, said a lot. Mahew turned on his torch, and he and Parry slushed through the mud up the road and in at the gate of Shots Hall.

"Not more than a couple of minutes' walk," Parry said. "Hell and damnation, what's this?"

There was a crash as he walked into the back bumper of a car. Mahew swiveled his light round and Parry rubbed his shins. The car was a big open sports M.G. In the light of the torch Parry saw that there was a hand accelerator on the wheel.

"Which tells us, my dear Watson," he remarked, "that the owner is gone in one hind leg. What's this? A very old Morris. And here we have an even older Buick, and, good God, bicycles galore."

"For Christ's sake, come on," Mahew fretted. "I'm frozen. If we're going to walk into the middle of a party it's going to be embarrassing in the extreme."

"Why?" Parry asked in genuine surprise. "We haven't come to arrest anyone. I simply wanted to meet Ashley and the aunt and break the ice, of which there must be tons. Where's the door?"

Mahew found it and knocked. There appeared to be no bell. Nothing happened.

"We'd better walk in," Parry said, and did so, Mahew beside him, muttering that he didn't like it.

The door crashed behind them, and they found themselves confronting the assembled company. The scene, thought Parry, was the most perfect example of suspended animation he had ever witnessed. Either everyone in some way knew who they were, or somehow guessed, and in consequence were stricken with a temporary paralysis. Phil Ambrose, in the act of bowing her head forward before tossing her hair back, remained bowed, her mouth open, staring through her hair like a Skye terrier. Tim, her husband, was most unfortunately frozen in the act of squeezing the trim waist of a middle-aged but very attractive woman in brown slacks, whose mischievous smile was fixed on her face as if it would never come off. The young man who had left his leg in Normandy was in the middle of pulling up one trouser leg to show the mothball girl his new tin leg, while the mothball girl had her mouth wide open like a cavern. A middle-aged man whose appearance shouted retired army,was poised with one arm high in the air, a half-empty glass in it. In some way, they all seemed to have been doing something ridiculous. All except Bee Chattock, who sat quietly in a wing chair, and Flik, who stood at the far side of a drink-laden table, her hands resting lightly on its edge.

Bloody funny, thought Parry, enjoying himself. Mahew, by nature shy, seemed unable to say anything. Very well, Parry decided, he too would say nothing until someone else did. There was nothing more nerve-racking to the guilty than silence. Not that any of these people might be guilty of anything at all. He started to make bets with himself as to who would break the silence first.

It was Flik. From Mahew's vague description of her, Parry knew at once which of the huddle was Flik. Only he had not expected anything so attractive. She had on a tight, plain black tailor-made and an immaculate white garment which he supposed was some sort of shirt.

She said, "Good evening, Major Mahew, do come in."

Mahew, who had been bordering on the verge of a nervous break-down, somehow got across the room and shook hands. The waxwork exhibition came to life. Phil Ambrose flung her head back and was just in time to see her husband hurriedly whip his arm away from the trim waist, and glare at him. If Parry had known the village habits, he would have also known that this was going to be the excuse for the Ambrose monthly row.

"Oh, and," Mahew said, "this is a friend of mine, Lane Parry. Inspector Parry, Mrs. Ashley. Er—"

"Aunt Bee? You haven't met Major Mahew, have you? And Mr. Parry—Major Mahew, Mr. Parry, my aunt, Miss Chattock. Phil—Tim Ambrose."

'We've met before," said the Ambroses to Mahew, and they introduced themselves to Parry. Phil immediately made eyes at him, defiantly, rather childishly getting some of her own back on Tim.

The retired major turned out to be a retired Captain Belairs. He had a dictatorial manner and was a bore, which accounted to Parry for the fact that he boasted of being a confirmed bachelor. The mothball girl answered to the name of Gwen Hunter. There was a nice but dull married couple called Jessen. The young man with the tin leg was amiable and intelligent. The attractive middle-aged woman was the owner of one of the bicycles. A small, vague group of quite ordinary people must be, Parry decided, the possessors of the rest of the bicycles and the Buick.

Everyone suddenly began to talk at once. Bee Chattock took Mahew aside.

"Say you've come on business and tell all these people to get out," she said to him. "I'm sick to death of them."

"I can't possibly do that," Mahew protested. "I can't throw your guests out." He took an immediate liking to Bee and wished his wife was there to enjoy her.

Parry found himself marooned in the middle of the fantastic pseudo-ancestral hall with Flik, who gave him a drink.

"I'm so sorry we butted in, Mrs. Ashley. We did knock, but nothing happened so we walked in."

"Everyone does. I wish these people would go. You must think it very bad taste to have a party on top of Molly being murdered. There was no way to put most of them off at such short notice, so the only thing to do was to have the party."

"It wouldn't bring Molly back to life to put off fifty parties," Parry said. "Why're you so sure it was murder, Mrs. Ashley?"

She looked up at him, and he had the same impression as Norton had had: that her eyes were turned back to front and were really looking at some inward idea.

"You didn't know Molly. She never went to church, but she was very conventional in her ideas about religion. The Lord giveth, and the Lord taketh away. She thought suicide was improper, cowardly, and an insult to whatever idea she had of God."

Lord, thought Parry, she smells nice. Not of scent but of something fresh, like grass. "I still ask, why murder? She might have died perfectly naturally of old age or a bad heart."

"But she—" Flik turned away. "Phil, one for the road?"

Phil, sulking, didn't answer. But Gwen, the mothball enthusiast, accepted eagerly. She had had rather too much to drink already, and was getting noisy and excited. "If only someone'd listen to me," she kept exclaiming. "Listen, if only someone'd listen to me—"

"I'm all ears," said the one-legged young man kindly.

"Inspector Parry?" It was the boring Captain Belairs. "Far be it from me to teach my grandmother to suck eggs, but my theory is that Molly's death was an inside job."

"Yes?" Parry had the patience of Job. "I dare say you're right."

"Someone who knew her habits, don't you see? Very well, why not question some of these people? Some of them mayn't have an alibi for last night. What I'm getting at is this—Molly left here alive and well at the usual time, and then Flikka finds her dead after she'd had her tea. I admit, some time after, but you see what I mean?"

"Perfectly," said Parry, and marveled at the way everyone in the country knew exactly what their neighbors did without even seeing them do it. "But this is hardly the occasion to question people, is it?"

"My dear chap, why not?" Captain Belairs, who had had a few nips on the quiet, and was therefore in the same state as Gwen, raised his arm, and shouted, "Silence!" in a resounding and compelling voice. "Inspector Parry would like to ask a few questions!"

"No, he wouldn't," said Parry amiably.

The captain brushed aside his objections as if they had been a swarm of flies. "Now then. Tim? Phil? What were you both doing last night?"

"Hit that bore on the head," Bee said to Mahew.

"Playing bridge," Tim said quickly.

With a small stab of surprise, Parry thought to himself that he said it a damn sight too quickly.

"Playing bridge," Phil echoed, pushing herself up against Tim, so that for the first time the once-a-month row was postponed. "With Gwen. We hadn't a fourth, so we played cutthroat."

Mahew caught Parry's eye, and Parry was aware that Flik was tautened up and a little anxious.

"In your drawing room?" asked the captain.

"Of course," Phil agreed.

Captain Belairs produced a stage ha-ha that echoed dismally. "In the dark? Well, I never! There wasn't any light in your drawing-room window, so you must've been playing in the dark."

Flik put an empty glass down on the table. "If we'd all had the sense to keep our old blackout screens and put them up in the winter, like Phil and Tim, then we shouldn't be so cold."

Good for Flik, thought Parry. So not only she, but some of the others were hiding something, a little afraid of the law's invasion on their private occasions.

"If only someone'd listen to me!" Gwen, after another drink, was now almost frantic. "I'll tell you who murdered Molly. It's so clear. Of course she must've been secretly married when she was young, and either her husband or son came back from goodness knows where and bumped her off, don't you see? Because she knew something about them? She had a past, and it rose up and bit her!"

"Be quiet, Gwen." Bee was furious. "You're drunk."

"She had a past!" Gwen persisted.

"Haven't we all?" asked the middle-aged beauty, showing her excellent teeth in an amused smile.

"She had a past, that's what it was," Gwen repeated with the dreary mulishness of the tipsy. "An illegitimate son. I feel sick—Flik, I want to be sick!"

"Now then," Bee took the floor and raised her lorgnettes. There was a lot of uncomfortable foot shuffling and someone knocked a glass over. "You can all go home and to hell with you. All, that is, but anyone who's got any business to talk over. Gwen, stop that disgusting sniveling."

"I'll take her home." The one-legged young man, who, Parry saw, was not quite as young as he had at first thought, and whose name, he had now gathered, was Clive Harris, grasped Gwen firmly by the arm and limped her to the door. Over his shoulder he said to Parry. "I live twelve miles from here, but if my car's ever any use to you, then let me know."

"Thanks," Parry nodded. "Thanks very much."

Gwen was removed. A minute later came the noise of the MG's engine revving up and the squelch of its tires as Clive backed it down the drive.

The bicyclists took their departure, apologizing very nicely to Bee Chattock and Flik for being such a nuisance, and they were so terribly sorry about Molly. Then the Ambroses went, both kissing Flik as though they were going back to Africa, instead of a few hundred yards down the road. The Jessens and the owers of the Buick said how terribly sorry they were about Molly and went too. The last was Captain Belairs, who made a determined effort not to go at all.

"I feel there's a lot I could tell you, Inspector," he said to Parry, "which may help you."

"I'm sure there is," said Parry. "Good-by. Nice to've met you. Good-by."

"Don't forget to shut the door," Bee nodded.

Thus summarily dismissed, the captain departed, a little unsteady on his feet and red in the face. But no sooner had he gone when the door opened again, without knock or ceremony. Framed in the darkness outside, his black hair shining in the light of indoors, Arnoldson stared at the table of empty glasses.

"Well?" Mahew said.

"Sorry to intrude," Arnoldson said in an unctuous voice, transferring his eyes from the table to Flik's legs. "But there seems to be some sort of shemozzle going on down the road at the pub. I heard someone scream, and then doors banging and another scream."

"Go and see what's wrong," Mahew ordered.

"My God," Flik said quietly. "What now?"

CHAPTER 8

NEITHER Parry nor Mahew knew that anyone could move so quietly and so unhurriedly as Flik, and accomplish so much in such a short time. One moment the Chattock's hall was a chaos of empty glasses, overflowing ashtrays, kicked up rugs, rumpled cushions and wet, alcoholic rings on the polished furniture; the next it was as orderly as if no one had been in there at all.

"Flik?" Bee asked. "What did you give those people to drink, may I inquire?"

"I found that bottle of gin wouldn't be enough to go round," Flik answered, "so I had to mix in what you might describe as other ingredients. I'm sorry, Aunt Bee. I'm afraid I used a little of the good whisky and what was left over from the bottle of Cointreau, and watered it all down with orange juice."

"God almighty!" Bee exclaimed. "Have you been drinking that filth?"

"Have you?" Flik went into a dark corner, and from behind a large vase of autumn beech leaves she had somehow preserved, produced a half-finished glass of whisky and soda.

To Parry's amusement, Bee Chattock did the same thing, except that her glass was almost empty, and she had secreted it under the footstool by her wing chair.

"Give these men a drink," she said to Flik, and Mahew and Parry thankfully accepted a whisky and soda apiece. "Well?" Bee went on. "I suppose you've come here to question us? If you have, then get on with it. I don't like shilly-shallying and beating about the bush."

"Which makes everything much easier," Parry smiled at her. "You needn't answer any questions if you don't want to. That's the law, though lots of people forget it."

"Such as Arnoldson," Bee said contemptuously. "We'll answer any questions you like."

Parry looked into his glass, then up at Flik. "I'd like to know what was in that letter you burned, Mrs. Ashley, and why you burned it."

If he had expected Flik to show discomfort, he was disappointed.

"So Norton did his duty? I suppose he was perfectly right. You've read all my letters to Molly?"

"Yes," Parry said. "I'm so sorry, but I had to. I may say that none of them appears to have any bearing on this case at all. None of them I read, that is. But I'm interested in the one I didn't read."

Flik lit a cigarette. Her lipstick made a red blotch on the end of it. "It was as entirely personal as the others," she said. "There was nothing in it that had anything to do with Molly's death, or could help in any way."

"I see." Parry felt in his pocket, took out an envelope and shook out a little corner of paper. "This is part of the letter that didn't burn, Mrs. Ashley. It's got one word, or part of one word on it, and the writing appears to be yours.

Bee leaned forward, and her stays creaked. For a few seconds that was the only sound in the hall. It seemed to Parry that the shadows deepened, waiting, and wondered how anyone could live in such a haunted atmosphere.

"Can I see?" Flik held out her hand. It was quite steady, but as she took the piece of paper from him, her fingers touched his, and they were as cold as ice. He was almost shocked when she laughed, then surprised, for it was a laugh of relief. "Morph," she read out. "Is that all? Morphia was the whole word."

Mahew blinked. The very word morphia ought to have made her shudder; but he remembered then that she didn't know that it was morphine that had killed Molly. Unless she—"

"I'd burned my foot with scalding water I was in town when I wrote the letter to Molly. I was in such pain the doctor I called in gave me morphia so that I could get a night's sleep."

"He gave you some morphia tablets to take?" Parry looked into the strange, inside-out eyes.

"No. No, he just gave me an injection. One injection the night I burned my foot."

She spoke lightly, but Parry knew she knew what his question had meant and that she was suddenly on guard. Poker face, he thought. She would make a brilliant poker player, if she wasn't one already. Or a champion fencer. At any rate, a worthy adversary, if she was going to turn out to be an adversary. He hoped not. She was so lovely. "I see," he nodded. "And the letter was nothing more than a description to Molly of your burned foot, and the doctor and the pain?"

Flik said nothing, but Bee Chattock made an angry noise in her throat.

"Stop trying to make Flikka say something she doesn't mean," the old woman snapped. "You and your Arnoldson seem to have put her in the dock, in your minds, already."

"He's not my Arnoldson," Parry smiled. "If Mrs. Ashley doesn't wish to answer, she needn't."

But Flik answered. "There was more in the letter than my burned foot. It had nothing to do with anything that's just happened. It was private—A personal letter I didn't want Arnoldson to gloat over."

"You don't like him, do you?" Mahew put in.

"No. Do you?"

Mahew looked embarrassed, but was saved having to say anything by the sound of someone outside trying to open the door and knock at the same time.

"Come in, can't you?" Bee hallooed impatiently.

The door opened, banged shut again, and Parry had his first view of Susan Merridew, who sewed curtains. Mahew had met her before at some appalling charity bazaar. They both stood up.

"Oh, dear," Miss Merridew apologized. "I didn't know you had company still, Bee, dear."

"They aren't company," said Bee. "They're policemen. Don't you know Major Mahew?"

"Of course," Miss Merridew twittered, shaking hands with Parry. "How are you, Major?"

"My name's Parry." Parry grinned.

"Parry? Then— Oh, Major Mahew!" Miss Merridew looked confused, and dropping Parry's hand took Mahew's instead. "I do hope Mrs. Mahew is quite well?"

"She's got a cold," Mahew said. "Otherwise she's in her usual form, thanks very much."

"So nice— Bee, dear, what I really came in to say was that I met Winnie at church this evening."

Bee sighed tolerantly. "Winnie? Winnie who, Susan?"

"Winnie the Pooh," Parry said under his breath. The swift changes of company, conversation, topic and atmosphere at Shots Hall were getting like some sort of transformation scene out of a pantomime.

"Winnie," Miss Merridew repeated. "Bee, dear, Winnie Marsh."

"Winnie from the pub, old Marsh's girl," Flik interpreted.

"Yes, dear. All day I've been thinking, how awful, poor Bee and Flik and that big house, and no one to even wash up a cup. So after church I said to Winnie, 'Winnie, it's time you did something except get in your father's way, so you'd better try and be useful.' I said, Winnie, you ought to think of others. Think of Miss Chattock and

Mrs. Ashley and all their trouble, and no one to even wash up a cup or clean out the grates: And what d'you think she said?"

The interested listeners waited for enlightenment. Parry felt, somehow, that Winnie had suddenly become of paramount importance, and could hardly restrain his impatience. What the hell had Winnie said?

"Winnie said," concluded Miss Merridew in triumph, " 'I will.' "

"Will what?" Bee inquired, bewildered.

"Why, Bee, dear, I just explained. Come up here and do for you till you find someone permanent. She said she'd just go home and get a warmer coat, and then she'd come up. She ought to be here now."

"Susan, dear," Flik said, "how sweet of you to think of it ."

"That'll be the end of the best glasses," Bee muttered.

"What, dear?"

Barmy, thought Parry, and avoided Mahew's eye, because Mahew was on the point of sniggering. This was a nice way to conduct a murder investigation. He pricked up his ears expectantly. A car was racketing up to the front door. Now what, and who? Was this the arrival of Harlequin and Columbine? Bee made an exasperated gesture toward the door, and he obediently opened it. There was a confusion of voices, one of which cursed fluently, while another wailed hysterically. Three figures formed in the fog. He opened the door wide and they all came in together. Abbot, Arnoldson; between them, supported by a hand under each arm, a young female creature whose legs dangled limply as if they hadn't strength to support the body above them.

"Be quiet," Abbot ordered, beside himself. "Shut up, can't you?"

But the young female only wailed the louder, the tears pouring down her face. When Flik exclaimed, "Winnie, what on earth's the matter?" Parry was not surprised. Nothing would surprise him again. Here, in the flesh was Winnie, making a right and proper entry accompanied by screams. He shut the door with a bang. This must be the shemozzle Arnoldson had heard down at the pub.

"What's wrong?" he asked.

Arnoldson raised his voice in an effort to make himself heard over Winnie's ululations and Abbot's swearing. "It's her father, old Marsh. She came back from church and found him dead in the chair in their sitting room. I've got Congreve down there. Marsh seems to've died the same way as the old woman."

"What?" Bee exclaimed. "Another?"

Flik's hand went up to her mouth and fell away again. Abbot temporarily silenced Winnie by smacking her head. Miss Merridew clasped her hands and began to cry, mercifully not very loudly.

"I stopped off for a quiet drink," Abbot complained, "and find the pub in an uproar, with this girl screaming, all the neighbors trying to crowd in, a body in a chair and Arnoldson laying down the law."

"I think it's about time," Mahew said, "someone did lay down the law. One body is one body too much, but two bodies in less than twenty-four hours are a damn sight too much. How did the man die?"

"D'you think," Abbot glared, "I've been holding a postmortem down there, with the cadaver stretched on the four ale bar, cutting it up with the kitchen knife? I can only say that there's a dead body which presents the same appearance as the body last night."

"Oh!" Miss Merridew sobbed. "Oh, oh, oh!"

Winnie started to give tongue again, but this time she was a little more coherent. She pointed a wobbling, accusing finger at Flik. "Mrs. Vale what lives opposite our back door, she came in and she—she—said she saw Mrs. Ashley go in the back door 'bout half past four, she said. Go in and come out, she said, 'bout half past four, she said. Urhur—urhur—ur—ur—" The accusation turned back into cries.

Parry automatically glanced at his wristwatch. It was just on a quarter to eight. "Did you go into the pub?" he asked Flik.

Flik nodded, then pushed her hair back behind her ears. "Yes. Yes, I did. Old Marsh had promised me a bottle of gin for this evening. I went down to fetch it."

"He was alive?"

Flik stared at him, surprised. "Of course he was. He'd left the gin on the kitchen sink. He was in his sitting room. I called out was that my bottle, and he said Mm-hmm, so I took it and went."

"You didn't see him?"

"What're you implying?" Bee demanded. "That my niece went in, murdered the man, took the gin and came home and gave a party on it? Eh?"

"I'm not implying anything," Parry answered. "I'm simply asking."

"Just a moment." Mahew shook the crying Winnie by the arm. "Where were you in the afternoon, before you went to church?"

"I went out with Bill—cycling. Two o'clock we started, and went to Witerlea—on the way back we went to church. I didn't go home till—till—"

"All right."

"It's dreadful, dreadful!" Miss Merridew cried.

"I think," Parry said, "we'll get down to the pub. Abbot, you'll come? Miss Chattock, can you keep the girl here for a moment? I don't want her screeching round my heels."

"Very well," Bee agreed coldly.

"Mr. Parry?" Flik's white face looked up at him. "You asked me if I actually saw old Marsh? I didn't. Not properly. I saw the back of his head showing over the top of his armchair. The sitting-room door was open. I thought, then, he was just going to have another nap."

"You're sure it was him?"

"Quite sure. And he was alive."

"I see. Thank you."

The fury that was the inward man of Abbot said, they've hung her already, by the neck till she's dead. He was too pleasant, this London policeman with his pretty manners and his good looks. To Flik he said, "I'll be back later on. I don't like the look of your blood pressure. It's too low."

He followed Parry and Mahew out of the door, the back of his neck aware that Flik was just behind them, seeing them off like a good hostess. He took no notice.

Arnoldson turned on the doorstep, and nearly trod on Flik. His mouth was very wet. He stared down at her. "Well, FlikkAH?" he whispered. "Now how about it?"

"Get out," she said, and flung the door shut so that he was nearly caught in it.

A mingled chorus of woe and horror still came from Winnie and Miss Merridew. For the moment they were ignored.

Bee glanced at Flik. "We'd better get some food together, darling."

Silently, Flik walked the long length of the hall and pushed open the swing door that led to the kitchen and the bathroom quarters. It was cold out there, and she shivered. Bee followed her, her silk skirts swishing, her jet necklace and lorgnettes making a small jingle. Her dignity was unruffled, her poise still upright.

"Flik, you don't think—?"

"No— No." Flik slipped her hand into the inside breast pocket of her tight black jacket. "No—it says quite definitely his hip was fractured. It couldn't mend in two weeks."

"He might have flown across?"

"In splints? No. And what reason would there be?"

"Someone had a reason for killing them."

"I know." Flik's eyes were somber. "I'd better burn this. If Arnoldson got hold of it, then the fat'd be in the fire."

"Over the sink," Bee said. "Then you can turn the tap on and run the ashes down the drain."

Another letter went up in flames, died into black ashes. This time Flik made sure there were no little bits left behind. The water gurgled in the sink as it ran out. She put the backs of her hands across her eyes, pressing them hard.

"You aren't feeling faint, are you?" Bee asked.

"We aren't a fainting family, are we?" Flik's red lips twisted a little. "I was thinking. There's something that doesn't fit. Something that policeman Norton said to me—it rang a bell, but I've lost the echo of the note. I can't place it. It's something that's wrong, somewhere. If only I could think what it was. I'll suddenly think of it when it's too late. And there's something else. Who did brush Molly's doorstep? Who brushed Molly's doorstep after the first time I went in to see her last night?"

"What's more to the point," Bee said briskly, "is where's the broom the brushing was done with? Molly broke hers a week ago."

Flik swept her hands away from her eyes, staring. "Good God, I never knew that!"

The kitchen door opened reluctantly. A sniveling face peered in.

"Miss Merridew said as how I was to do for you," Winnie gulped, eying Flik with suspicion.

"Hardly an apt phrase," said Bee. "I trust you won't."

CHAPTER 9

AT half past ten that night, just as Abbot was crawling into his bed, which was hard, lumpy and cold, his phone bell rang. He pulled the clothes over his head and took no notice. He was dead tired. In the morning he had to get busy on the postmortem on old Marsh. Molly was in cold storage, waiting for the Coroner's inquest, which, he knew, Parry was going to have postponed. The phone bell went on ringing. To his rage, Abbot heard the shuffling footsteps of his housekeeper going to answer it.

"Hi!" he shouted, uncovering his head. "Leave that pestilential thing alone."

But he was too late. A voice said through the keyhole of his bedroom door, "Doctor? Doctor? Are you awake? It's Mr. Craven— about his wife. He wants to know if you can go at once. She's in labor."

"All right, all right."

He scrambled into his dressing gown, fighting with the sleeves, and shot out of the room and down the stairs. "Yes? Dr. Abbot here. What? Oh, she is, is she? There's nothing to fuss about, my good man, lots of women have babies. I'll be along."

As he dressed, shivering in the cold, he described women in labor, their husbands and the cause of it, and their resultant children in precise and apocryphal detail, and felt a little comforted. Ten minutes later he was on his way to the village where Mrs. Craven labored. The fog was not as thick as it had been, and here and there a pale star showed. The salty air was still, the roads, once he left the town behind him, empty of cars. The Cravens lived down a side turning, rutted and pot-holed. A night animal scuttled across the headlight beams and vanished into the ditch.

A patch of light showed the open door of the small Craven house, where an agitated figure hovered.

Abbot braked, put the gear into neutral and switched the engine off. Then he collected his bag, and picked his way up the garden path.

"Dr. Abbot?" asked the male Craven, clasping and unclasping his hands as if he was praying, which he was not. "The midwife's here. I can't stand this, she's been groaning so."

"My good man, don't dither. Get yourself a cup of tea. Everything'll be all right. I want to wash my hands."

In due course, Abbot managed to get Craven out of the way, and went upstairs. Mrs. Craven lay on the bed, looking very well and rather smug. The midwife was attending to the baby, a boy. He hadn't been needed at all.

Half an hour later, Abbot was bumping back the way he had come. He was bitterly tired. It had been a hard day. The postmortem on Molly, the second body down at the pub, a sedative for the yowling Winnie, questions from Parry and Mahew, then two patients to visit before he got home to a cold supper at ten o'clock. The fog, the cold, the mud. Flik's eyes. Flik's danger. Tomorrow another postmortem and God knew what other trouble. The night was full of it, it was breeding trouble, secret, unknown. Suddenly he realized that he was on the wrong road. Instead of turning to the right when he got out of the Cravens' lane, he had turned left, and was heading for Shotshall, up the narrow, winding road that led to the hill and the village. He stopped the car, and lowering the window, looked out.

There seemed to be no place to turn. If he started backing and filling he would get bogged in the ditch, and the mud piled up by the side of the road. He went on. A light still shone from one window of the pub, the Shots Arms. With a feeling of furtiveness, he drove past it, up the last lap of the hill, and stopped his car by the stone gateposts of the unwieldy house, which he hadn't yet seen by daylight, except long ago, when he had driven past to visit a patient and not even noticed it. He had no idea what he was doing, or why, or what he was going to do. For some time he sat in the car. It was so quiet he could hear his own breathing, which sounded as loud as the panting of a steam engine.

"This is bloody silly," he said, and got out of the car. He had forgotten his torch, but somehow found his way up to the front door. It must, he knew, be nearly a quarter to twelve by then. He'd better go away. At that moment the door swung open and a torch shone on his face.

"Flik?" he said involuntarily.

"Abbot?" Her voice was soft, startled. "Abbot? What is it?"

"Nothing. I'm sorry, Mrs. Ashley, if I made you jump."

"You didn't. Come in. I heard a car, and then I thought I heard someone come up to the door." She hung on to the door as he went in, so that its bang was not as loud as usual. "I wondered who it was."

"Now you know. D'you usually dress up in an overcoat to answer the door?"

Flik turned up another light and poked the dying fire. "I was going for a walk," she said, without looking round.

"If you take my advice," Abbot said dryly, "you won't go for walks at this hour of the night. If you met, say, Arnoldson or Parry, they might think it a bit odd."

"Would they?" Flik turned round at last. "I often go for a walk at night. Do sit down." Her manner was formal, and Abbot knew she was guarding every word she said.

He planted himself in Bee's wing chair and held out his hands to the rather miserable fire. "Miss Chattock in bed?"

"Yes." Flik squatted on a low fender stool. "I'll get you a drink, shall I? You look very tired."

"So do you. I'm always drinking your drink—listen to me, don't do anything foolish, like, for instance, indulging in a few investigations of your own. Where were you going?"

"It's no damn business of yours," Flik said under her breath. Then she looked quickly up at him, her face contrite. "I'm sorry. You've been so kind, and now I'm being rude. Why did you come up?"

"God alone knows," Abbot said irritably. "I had to go out on a maternity case where I wasn't needed, took the wrong turning on the way back and practically found myself on your‚doorstep. Has Parry been in? He, or someone, still appears to be down at the pub."

"Still there?" Slowly, Flik unbuttoned her overcoat and shrugged her shoulders out of it.

"So that's where you were going, was it?" The bloody little fool,

Abbot thought. "After last night's excursion to Molly's cottage, I should've thought you'd have known they wouldn't leave the pub empty for anyone to walk in."

Flik got up, and he heard the clink of glass. The decanter, when she put it down on the table next to him, threw off flecks of rainbow color as its facets caught the light.

"Help yourself. No, I wasn't going to the pub."

He helped himself, and drank the whisky straight, in one gulp. It burned as it slid down his gullet, and he realized he must have poured himself out a damned big tot. But it loosened his tongue a little. "What's on your mind?"

Flik sat down on the stool again, near his knees. "Plenty," she said.

"Any fool can see that. For one thing, you're groping after some suspicion you can't place, for another, you're hiding something up on your own account. Something—"Abbot leaned forward. "Something you'd hate like hell for Arnoldson to find out."

"Is it so obvious?" Flik asked. "I must be more careful with my face."

"If it'd help you to get anything off your chest?"

"No. No thanks."

"Then you'd better look out for storms, my child. You'll have Parry up tomorrow with a string of questions. He was just getting his bits of evidence nicely sorted out and tabulated when I saw him last."

Flik jerked her head round. "Parry—He doesn't think I killed them, does he? Not Parry?"

"He didn't tell me." To hell to Parry. So she'd taken a fancy to his *beaux yeux,* had she? That was a nice business if she'd fallen in love with the man who, at this moment, might be getting together evidence to hang her. "I'd watch your step with Parry. He's clever. What about the Ambroses? He mentioned them. They live in the village, don't they?"

"The Ambroses?" Flik repeated. "What'd he say about them?"

"I can't remember." Nor could he. He wasn't in the least interested in them. "What've they done, anyway?"

"Nothing." Flik's voice was very positive. "Everyone'd had a bit too much to drink at the party. It wasn't fair to judge them from the idiotic way they went on. They're just a perfectly ordinary married couple— plenty of money. Tim Ambrose was in the Air Force."

"I'm going," Abbot said abruptly.

As he got up, Flik got up too, and touched his arm.

"What killed old Marsh? Morphia again?"

"Damn your eyes," Abbot swore. "I don't give wild opinions before

I've found out for certain. But it looked like it. Anyone in the village take morphia?"

"I don't give wild opinions either," Flik laughed curtly. "I should think nothing's more unlikely."

"Murder isn't likely, either. By the way, where's Winnie?"

"Sleeping at Mrs. Vale's."

"Mrs. Vale?" Abbot frowned. "Oh, yes, the lady who said she saw you going in the back door of the pub."

"I suppose I'd better look out for her, too?"

"I'd just look out," Abbot warned. "You might get a dose of morphine in your tea too."

Flik looked at him as he stood in the door, a strange, probing look— seeing him yet not seeing him. "I don't think so," she said, and eased the door when he went out. It thudded dully behind him. The side lights of his car were dim blobs. A little breeze had got up and was sighing in the trees. He stumbled through the mud and got into the car, shut the door quietly and let the brake off. Down the road a cart track turned into a field. He could let the car slip backward into it, then start the engine. He didn't want anyone to hear a car going away from Shots Hall. The wheels slushed down the hill, making a soft hissing noise. When he started the engine, it seemed to his jangled nerves to make enough racket to waken the whole neighborhood. He put his foot hard on the clutch pedal, and bumped down the hill in neutral, past the pub and the pale light, through the village, then got quickly into top gear and fled.

Holding her breath, Flik listened to the getaway. She put on her over-coat again, then did what she had been about to do when she had heard Abbot arrive. From behind a cushion she took a thick pair of socks, and pulling them over her shoes, turned the two standard lamps off and switched on her torch. The hall was a limitless cavern of darkness, for the fire had died to nearly nothing. A draft whistled under the front door, a sibilant whistle like a groom hissing in the stables. Only the noise was less pleasant. Flik picked her way carefully to the kitchen. From there a tradesmen's entrance led on to the drive near the road. She drew back the bolts, and going out into the darkness closed the door silently behind her. Odd, she thought, how seldom anyone used that door. She switched off her torch and stood still till her eyes had become more accustomed to the darkness.

I must know, she said over and over again to herself. I must know. I've got to find out

The breeze was rising and the branches of the invisible trees creaked and thrashed. The telephone wires whirred, strumming in time to the trees' complaint. Or was it the telephone wires making that noise? She stood perfectly still, her heart unsteady. If she were caught—

The whirring stopped. A light sprang out of the darkness, wandering till it shone full on her face. Somehow Flik summoned her voice, steadied it.

"Is that you?"

"Yes, Mrs. Ashley."

It was Norton. Flik had no idea what had prompted her to make the one remark that could sound perfectly normal and harmless.

"I've been put on to patrol the district, Mrs. Ashley. I wondered who it was. I thought I saw someone standing there." His voice was hopeful, hoping she would make some excuse, so that he wouldn't have to get her in the soup again.

"I know. I came out to see if you were anywhere around and'd like some tea, or something, before I went to bed. It's such a foul night."

"And the lamp on my bike's bust. I won't come in, thank you, miss— madam, as it's how Inspector Parry said I was to keep outside. Silly I call it."

He sounded almost tearful with relief.

"A rotten job," Flik agreed. Thank God he hadn't asked who had told her he was going to patrol all night. For no one had told her, and she hadn't known. "My heart bled for you when I heard your fate. I looked out for you earlier, but I didn't see you. Good night."

"Good night— And, Mrs. Ashley?"

"Yes?" Had he seen the socks over her shoes?

"I'd like to tell you how sorry I am about having to tell about those letters of yours. I felt mean, that's what, but if I hadn't, someone'd have found out. I don't know I much like being a policeman, and that's a fact."

Flik laughed, and her laugh was blown back into her mouth by a sudden gust of wind. "You had to do your duty, hadn't you? You can't let personal feelings interfere with your job. It's quite all right. Good night."

Norton's final good night drifted after her as she let herself in. Very quickly she put on all the lights in the hall in an effort to banish the shadows that lurked in the far corners. But the room still seemed dark, as though the night had invaded it, refusing to be kept out. She crouched over the dying fire, her back against the arm of the wing chair. She didn't want to go to bed, taking her thoughts with her as bed companions. If only Bee would snore, so that there would be other noises but the noise of the wind and the strange noises of the night; the creakings and the rustlings, the stealthy footsteps of nightmare.

She sat up suddenly, startled. "Parry? Parry?" But he wasn't there. No one was there. It was two o'clock. She had been to sleep, dreaming.

One of the lights flickered and went out, the bulb gone. She put her cold hands round her throat. What would a rope round one's throat feel like? Frightened, fearful, she fled up to her bedroom, leaving the lights to burn, pursued by wild thoughts and taunting, horrible suspicion.

CHAPTER 10

WHILE Abbot worked on the postmortem of old Marsh, Mahew and Parry finished their breakfasts. At one end of the table Parry, his long, well-shaped hands moving quickly, sorted report forms and various bits of paper into a tidy sequence, passing the results over to Mahew.

"One," Mahew read. "Report from Arnoldson. All chemists in St. Arthurs interrogated, and all say have not had prescription for or including morphine handed in by anyone in or near Shotshall, nor have supplied them morphine in any form. No doctors or the hospital in St. Arthurs have supplied morphine in any form to anyone in or near Shotshall except (a) Dr. Prout, who gave prescription to Mrs. Maunder, No. 2 Hill Cottages, Shotshall, two bottles cough linctus both containing minute quantity of morphine. Note—Dr. Prout says ten bottles of said linctus could not kill. (b) Dr. Saunders, who gave Mrs. Fewsey, Sea View, Shotshall, one injection of morphine about one year ago when she tore ligament in ankle.

"Two. Report from Dr. Abbot. Although Dr. Bannard, from whom he bought practice just before Dr. Bannard's death, attended a few people in Shotshall and vicinity, Dr. Abbot has so far had no occasion to be called in. Dr. Abbot tore up all files to do with patients of Dr. Bannard who were deceased when he took over practice, so is unable to say if Dr. B. prescribed morphine to anyone in Shotshall or vicinity."

"Pity," said Mahew, looking up. "Bannard might've given morphine to someone in Shotshall."

"He might," Parry agreed.

Mahew read on, silent again.

"Three. Report from Arnoldson. During time Dr. Bannard practiced, the following died in or near Shotshall. 1. Mrs. Green, aged 80, senile decay; 2. Mr. Joseph Green, widower of above, aged 85, senile decay; 3. Mrs. Jim Meopham (baker's grandmother), aged 72, pneumonia; 4. Major Andrew Merridew (Miss Susan Merridew's father), aged 82, heart failure following arteriosclerosis; 5. Mrs. Hannah Willard, aged 39, childbirth; 6. Mr. Will Arnot, aged 45, pneumonia following embolism. Note, all above people died over three years ago except the last one, who died just before Dr. Abbot took over Dr. Bannard's practice, and who was attended by Dr. Prout. See Report One.

"Four. Report from Arnoldson. The death certificates of the persons mentioned as dying in or near Shotshall have been checked up with the local Registrar of Births, Marriages and Deaths and tally."

"So what?" Mahew asked.

"So nothing." Parry looked up. "If old Bannard were alive, he might throw some light on the dark problem. But he isn't. I suppose Abbot's okay?"

"Good God, yes!" Mahew exclaimed, shocked.

"The only other way," Parry said, "of finding out if any of our people ever got their hands on large doses of morphine, is to check up with every doctor, hospital, chemist, dentist and so on in the whole of England."

"Rather a tall order, isn't it?"

"A damn sight too tall. There remains only the alternative of finding out every place and town all the people who may be concerned have stayed in in the last God knows how many years, and checking up with all the doctors and chemists in those places. Blast."

"That seems like a life's work, too," Mahew pointed out.

"Not only that," Parry said with a rueful smile, "but if anyone's feeling guilty about anything, they'll lie. If they went to town on August Bank holiday three years ago, for a week, they'll swear they were camping in the Lake District. Hell."

"It might be an outsider," Mahew suggested. "After all, why not?"

"Plenty of why nots, also plenty of nots. No strangers've been seen around for Lord knows how long, and whoever did the dirty work had an inside knowledge of the habits of the village. An outsider wouldn't know Molly always had a cup of tea at a quarter past eight every evening, or that she took so much sugar in it it'd drown the taste of everything else. I'll bet a hundred to one on that when Abbot's done his postmortem and analyzed the dregs of Marsh's teacup that we'll find the morphine was put in the tea. And old Marsh laced his tea with sugar too. And he always had a cup of tea round about half past four. Everyone in the village seems to know that. But a stranger wouldn't."

"What about," Mahew said, "someone who'd stayed in the village some time ago, and got to know its habits?"

"And returned, after the passing of time, like a shadow in the night? Taking a chance on it that the village habits hadn't changed by five minutes?" Parry shook his head. "It's an idea, but somehow it isn't very feasible. Even Flikka Ashley's American friend of the blitz only, so Arnold-

son said, tarried a very little while and then was gone. History relates he
spent two nights at Shots Hall, and then hopped it. History also relates he
was a G.I. Joe." He frowned, as if he didn't like that idea, which he didn't,
obviously, Mahew decided.

Mahew thought, I hope to God it isn't Flik Ashley. So does Lane. He
went back to the reports and notes.

"Five. Report from Sgt. Congreve. All except the following, in and
around Shotshall, had alibis for the night of December 1st between the
hours of 19:45 and 21:00: Capt. Belairs, who said he was in his house
reading. Miss Chattock, of Shots Hall, who said she was in her house
doing nothing. Mrs. Ashley who said what she was doing but it is not
proven. Mrs. Vale who said she was asleep in front of her fire which had
gone out. Harry Fewsey the butcher who was cutting up meat in his shop
and said anyone ought to have been able to hear him doing it only no one
did. Winnie Marsh who said she had gone round the corner, which one
she would not say, to meet a boyfriend she won't say either as it is not her
regular one Bill Ellison, and she said not to tell about it as Bill Ellison
would be mad."

Mahew gave a snort of laughter.

"Congreve's effort?" Parry grinned. "It's prime, isn't it? He paints an
almost perfect picture of village life. I like the bit about the indignant
butcher, and the wicked Winnie. Is Congreve a bloody fool, or has he a
sense of humor?"

"He's got a sense of humor. That's as far as we've got with Molly.
The next thing is the alibis for whatever time Marsh was poisoned yesterday. Let's see, Congreve's doing a tentative check up on everyone's movements between four and six, isn't he? That's the best we can do till we get
Abbot's report." Mahew rubbed his eyes, which were tired after two nights
of driving about in the darkness.

Outside, the trees were tossed by a southwester, which roared in from
the channel, salt-laden, relentless, bringing with it spurts of rain and wisps
of sea mist.

"I'll have to check up on every alibi myself," said Parry. "Check and
recheck. God, how I hate routine work. Why did you let me in for this,
you skate? This isn't my stamping ground. I'm a stranger in a strange
land. Mrs. Vale's few words make it look damn black for Flik Ashley."
He lit a cigarette and flipped the match end in the fire. "Damn black. The
old woman swore Flik was the only person to go in that back door. Not
that the old woman's oath is anything to go on." He was talking more to
himself than to Mahew, who was all ears. "Motive. Motive's what we

want. Did Molly know something about Flik that Flik didn't want to come out? She's got something on her mind. Her eyes're secret. And old Marsh— Flik knew him well, so the village says. Often went in there odd hours and played cards with him. Why? To amuse him? To amuse herself? To propitiate him? Did they secretly gamble, and she owed him a packet she couldn't pay?"

"What a damn fool idea," Mahew burst out. "Why not say she was secretly married to the old man, and call it a day?"

"Of course it's a damn fool idea, you miserable old bastard. But I'll tell you an idea that isn't a damn fool one. The kingpin, the hub, the why of all this mess, is Flikka Ashley. I'd like to know what was in that letter she burned."

"So'd I," Mahew agreed reluctantly. "But it doesn't mean she's a poisoner."

"Of course it doesn't. All the same—"Parry got up, fell over a dog, apologized to it, and looked out of the window. He didn't want any of this. He didn't like it. As a case, it was interesting, but there was too much evidence, and yet none. Too much secrecy. The whole setting, the whole atmosphere was too theatrical.

"I suppose we'd better get going," Mahew sighed, wishing he could stay at home and talk to his wife. He went out into the hall and shouted. The driver of the police car, who had been having a cup of tea in the kitchen, hurried out by the side door, wiping his mustache, and stood by the car waiting. He was intensely interested in Parry. He had never seen anyone from Scotland Yard before. He supposed the classy inspector had solved the mystery already. He little knew that Parry felt as bogged as any country constable hoofing his beat.

Parry nodded him good morning, and got into the back of the car beside Mahew. "Station?" he asked.

"I suppose we'd better," Mahew said. "In case there's anything new there—"

Immersed in his unpleasant occupation, Abbot chanted an inward ode of revolted dislike for everything.

"Yes?" he said, looking up at a white-overalled figure which had suddenly appeared next him.

"There're remains of morphine in this teacup," said the figure. "Same as the one yesterday. I went straight for morphine, as you instructed. Shall I let it go at that?"

"Go on testing for every ruddy poison under the sun," Abbot said through his mask. "One can't be too careful."

CHAPTER 11

THE blustering, tearing wind rattled the shutters of the Shots Arms, and gave Parry the impression that the pub was human, and its teeth were chattering. The brewery had sent over a man temporarily to take charge. Still decorously closed, partly so that the police could hunt its many corners undisturbed, partly in deference to the dead landlord, the two bars, saloon and public, were to open again at six that evening. In the meantime, the place served as the local police headquarters, and there, in the back parlor, Parry and Mahew found Arnoldson and Congreve having a warmup by the fire.

There was a look of lip-licking satisfaction on Arnoldson's face, which boded, thought Parry, ill for someone.

"Morning," he nodded, taking an instant liking to Congreve, whose bland and innocent eyes were windows through which peered an unholy and permanent mirth.

"Congreve's just doing a bit of routine checking up on everyone's movements," Arnoldson said contemptuously, as if such a matter was beneath his own dignity.

"At the moment," Congreve said, "I'm warming me 'ands. And as for everyone's movements, they don't seem to've moved much yesterday except when they went to church at 'arf past six, there then being what you might call a rush for the tabernacle."

"Why?" Parry asked, interested. "Is the community so holy?"

Congreve grinned. "What it was, was that last Sunday—that is, the Sunday before yesterday, the parson announced that 'is next sermon was to be on the diseases of sin."

"Oh?" Mahew stared. "Well?"

"What the villagers thought was they was going to 'ear a nice, fruity talk on venereal diseases, so they went in a body to be enlightened."

Parry let out a snort of laughter. "And were they?"

"They was sold again," Congreve explained with relish. "All it was, was a very old sermon re'ashed, about greed—eating too much and drinking too much, which the parson said was diseases."

Arnoldson made impatient noises in his throat, and Congreve, taking the hint, removed himself to continue his investigations. Both Parry and Mahew regretted his departure and resigned themselves to inwardly disliking Arnoldson more than ever.

"Any news?" Parry asked—unnecessarily, he thought, for it was obvious the detective sergeant was bursting with something.

With slow deliberation, Arnoldson took an envelope out of his pocket, and carefully tipped its contents on to the table. Two cigarette ends, smeared with lipstick. "There you are, sir. Found them this morning first thing, when I had another rake round in the ashes under this fire grate."

Parry and Mahew eyed the cigarette ends with considerable mistrust.

"Mrs. Ashley hasn't been in since we took over yesterday evening after the body was found. That's certain, as I've had a man in here ever since then—all night, too. What's more, the girl, Winnie, told me this morning that first thing yesterday she cleaned out this grate and threw all the ashes away. So they must've been chucked in under the grate sometime since then and when she found her father's body."

"I suppose so," Parry agreed. "Yes. Well? Let's hear your elucidations."

Arnoldson didn't like the tone of his voice, but continued to elucidate. He took another envelope out of his pocket, and withdrew from it, gloatingly, another cigarette end. "I picked this out of an ashtray yesterday evening when we went up to Shots Hall. Mrs. Ashley'd just stubbed it out. She didn't see me."

"I don't suppose she did," Mahew said coldly. "If she had, she'd probably have—" He was going to say, given you a running kick in the pants, but altered it to, "Made some remark."

"If you'll look," Arnoldson went on, "you'll see they're the same brand of cigarettes—Maston Majors. No one else in the village smokes them, and the lipstick's identical. *Looks* identical," he added quickly.

"From which you deduct?" Parry prompted, knowing the answer.

"That Mrs. Ashley was lying when she said she only came in for a few seconds, took the bottle of gin off the sink and went, without coming into this room. She must've stayed here long enough to smoke two cigarettes. Or at any rate finish one and smoke the whole of another, both of which she chucked in under the grate."

"Almost too kind of her to leave so many clues," Parry remarked.

Arnoldson's mouth twitched, his annoyance ill-concealed. "I've interrogated the old Vale woman again this morning, and it appears she was a bit muddled in her statement yesterday, what with all the excitement. She says now she comes to think of it, she didn't see Fl—Mrs. Ashley go in this back door, she only saw her coming out, which was about half four in the afternoon."

"I see." Parry pulled at his lower lip.

"Have you questioned anyone else as to whether they saw Mrs. Ashley come in here, or come out again?" Mahew asked.

"Been round the whole village. No one saw her at all, only Mrs. Vale. Anyway, Mrs. Vale's cottage is the only house you can see the pub back door from."

"Coming down the hill from Shots Hall? Did anyone see her?"

"No one saw her," Arnoldson said with satisfaction. "They were mostly having their Sunday afternoon naps between dinner and tea. Anyhow there're only three cottages between Shots Hall and the pub. I've done a plan of the village if you'd like to see it."

"Thanks." Parry took the plan idly, Mahew looking over his shoulder. "Ambroses down a side turning with Belairs opposite, and Miss Gwen Hunter this side of the Ambroses—Hmm—Mmm—Mrs. Vale facing pub back door. Three cottages Shots Hall side of the pub, six cottages the other side of the pub. The church right along the road— Hmm—Tom Barker's farm stuck away in the fields to the south—Shots Hall, then Molly's cottage, the stone shed, Miss Merridew's opposite it. What's this?"

"That's Harry Foster's cottage. He's Miss Chattock's gardener."

"I see, right past Shots Hall and then along what looks like an interminable lane. Lonely place to live. I take it there're outlying houses scattered about?" Parry asked.

"Yes, Inspector. Only I didn't put them in. They're all some long way off, and don't belong to the village itself."

Arnoldson fumed inwardly. He'd expected them to be struck all of a heap by the cigarette ends, and they weren't. To hell with the amateurish Mahew, and the stuck-up man from London. He'd enough evidence against dear FlikkAH to hang her, and they weren't bloody well interested.

"Well," Parry said. "Thanks. I'll now be getting about my lawful occasions. Think this chap from the brewery can fix us with some lunch later on?"

"I'll arrange it," Arnoldson said, as if he were used to working miracles. "I've got some work to attend to myself," he threw at Parry and Mahew as they let themselves out.

"Kee-rist," Mahew muttered, "but how I do dislike that oily man. I don't like this cigarette end business a bit."

Parry shivered, and buttoned up the collar of his overcoat. He never wore a hat, except on very official occasions, and the wind raged in thick, dark hair. "I don't much like it either. Either she isn't as clever as she appears to be, or someone's dumped a fine, stinking red herring in our path. I'm going up to see her."

"Mind if I drop in on Belairs?" Mahew asked.

"Mind?" Parry stared at him in surprise. "Of course I don't. What d'you expect me to do? Order you about as if you were a policeman? Take the car, old man. I'll walk. If we don't meet before then, we'll see each other lunch time. Time, I said. God knows if there'll be any lunch. 'By."

He started up the hill, while Mahew got into the car. A squall of rain caught him. When it died down, the morning was suddenly, for a brief moment, still and clear. The village itself was not beautiful, but the country round was. From where he stood halfway up the hill, he could look down on the grays and purples of the leafless woods, on plowed land and green fields, valleys and hills, in the distance the high, bare downs. The sea was a turbulent pale brown; by it, four miles away, the huddled town of St. Arthurs. For the first time he saw Shots Hall in its grandiloquent horror of gray stone, and found it had an odd attraction. Then the rain came down again, in gusts.

A nice winter resort, Parry thought, and wondered why anyone had ever settled in this bleak and dismal spot. He looked back over his shoulder and saw Congreve on the road below, standing in the middle of it while he scratched his nose ruminatively.

"Hoi!" Parry shouted, and Congreve began to wheel his bicycle up the hill. "Anything new?"

Blowing a little, Congreve came to anchor beside him. "It's the Ambroses," he said. "Squadron Leader and Mrs. Also Miss Gwen 'Unter."

"What about them?"

"Just what I'm wondering," Congreve said. "I went along to the Ambroses place—nice place it is, too, old converted farm'ouse—just to ask what they were doing round about the time Marsh was 'aving 'is tea, and to check up about their playing bridge at the time Molly must 'av taken her poison, and found them in a bit of a flap."

"Flap? What about?"

"I left my bike in the 'edge, and went along to the door and banged. I thought I 'eard someone yell come in, so I went in. Only they can't 'av invited me in, as they didn't seem to be expecting me. I stood in the 'all, and they was in what must be their drawing room, with their backs to me. And there was Mrs. Ambrose scrubbing some marks off the floor, and there was the Squadron Leader and Miss 'Unter arguing about some book. They was all arguing. Not that that's queer, it was what they was saying."

"And what were they saying?" Parry asked.

"Something about they'd better burn it. And something about Captain Belairs guessing what they'd been up to, and 'e might get them into trouble. That's about all I 'eard. I thought they'd better not see me, so I walks backward out the door and down the path and out the gate, and got on my bike, and 'ere I am."

"Why walk backward?" Parry goggled.

Congreve treated him to a coy smile. "So's if they looked out of the window they'd see me frontways on, and think I was coming, not going."

Parry began to laugh. "What a lovely story. And you do notice things, don't you? Have you ten pairs of eyes and ears?"

"There was a nasty smell in the 'ouse, and I think they'd been burning something in the fire," Congreve ruminated. "From the cross way she was going on, I 'ad the idea it was something belonging to Miss 'Unter."

"Possibly," Parry suggested, "some more red herrings? This place stinks of them. Do something for me, will you, Congreve? Go and see old Mrs. Vale again and jog her changeable memory. See you later."

"Yes, sir." Congreve hesitated, a faraway look of amusement in his eyes.

"What is it?" Parry asked hopefully, wondering what Congreve would pull out of the hat now.

"I was just thinking," he pondered, "supposing another stiff turned up a bit further down the road, say near the church?"

"What of it?"

"Only that just before you get to the church, you get out of the St. Arthurs borough, and the Pelsey district starts."

"Oh, and—?"

"I was just imagining the St. Arthurs police and the Pelsey police between 'oom no love is lost, gawping at each other across the demarcation line, like cows looking at each other over a 'edge. Good-by, sir."

And Congreve went, leaving the delighted and enlightened Parry to contemplate his freewheeling back view before he turned up the hill again to be nearly run down by Clive Harris in his M.G., shooting out of the entrance of Shots Hall.

"Hullo?" Clive shouted, braking violently, so that the car skidded.

"Hullo?" Parry said. Now what? What would be unearthed here? What would Clive have to say for himself? Anything? Nothing? Something to conceal, too? Or was his life an open book?

"Just ran over to see Flik and Bee," Clive explained. "And damn nearly ran over you."

"And how are they this morning?"

"Sweating their guts out. That bloody girl, Winnie Marsh, says she won't do for them. She's too upset, so she's gone out bicycling with a girlfriend. Upset, hell. Biking while father, presumably, is being degutted. I'm just off to the town to see if I can rattle up a lady to oblige."

"If Winnie's not really upset," Parry said, "then why won't she do her doing? Lazy, or what?"

"Partly lazy, I suppose," Clive frowned.

"And partly what else?" Parry knew what else, but he wanted Clive to say it, so that he could watch his expression.

"You know what these blasted villagers are," the young man exploded. "Muckraking and so on."

"G.I. Joe rearing his ugly head, in fact?"

"Yes. That and—well, Winnie seems to be going round saying Flik killed the old man, and Molly."

"Wasn't that liable to happen? After all, in each case Flik seems to've been the last to see the murderees alive."

Clive raised his fair eyebrows. "So you've definitely decided it's murder, not suicide? I think you're right. My God, who can it be?"

It dawned, suddenly, on Parry, that Clive Harris was in love with Flik, and he felt sorry for him. The wind blew Clive's hair in wild disorder over his forehead. It was soft hair, like a little boy's.

"You've known them a long time? Miss Chattock and Flik?" Without thinking, Parry fell naturally into the way of calling her Flik instead of Mrs. Ashley.

"An age." Clive smiled suddenly. "Ever since I can remember. Flik often stayed with Bee before she came to live here permanently. My father had the house that I've got now. He died in 1940, and after I'd parted company with my leg I settled in—do a bit of farming. It doesn't pay, but I've enough dough without that. It's something to do. One can't do nothing."

"How old're you?" Parry asked.

"Thirty," Clive answered. "I don't feel it."

"You don't look it," Parry said. "You know all about Flik's unfortunate marriage? It was unfortunate, wasn't it?"

"Christ, yes. She was still in her teens when she fell for Mac Ashley. He was an utter bastard. She didn't let it out till it came to the divorce. But he gave her hell, blast him." Clive's vehemence was like the wind's, wild and furious.

"I see. Funny she never married again."

"Why funny? Why should she if she doesn't want to? I wish she would."

"Marry you, you mean?" Parry suggested.

"Well, yes." Clive reddened. "Only she won't. She isn't in love with me. We're good friends, but she's not in love with me. She wouldn't marry anyone she didn't love. She's—romantic. Why not? I'm so really in love with her there's nothing I'd like to see better than Flik married to some really decent chap who'd look after her."

"Very magnanimous of you," Parry said. "Was she in love with the G.I. Joe?"

"Oh, blast it," Clive swore. "Do you think I poke my nose into her affairs? I don't know anything about him. It's her business. People did all sorts of crazy, reckless things at that time. Bombs and blitzes, and your next moment may be your last, so what the hell? Go to blazes—" He suddenly flinched, and his hand went down on the place where his stump joined his false leg.

"Pains, does it?" Parry asked, genuinely sorry.

Clive looked up at him, his rage gone, grinning. "It's nothing. It's only when it's cold and wet. Then I get an occasional jab of rheumatics in the old stump. Nothing to what it used to be when I had my first leg. The damn thing didn't fit properly, or something."

"Can't you take something for it?"

"No need. The pain doesn't last now. Not like it was at first." Clive was suddenly miles away, in the past with its pains, with the leg that didn't fit. "At first I did, sometimes. When it got too bad."

"Morphia?" Parry said softly.

"Yeah— What?" Clive jerked his head up, and stared at Parry. "How— Yes. Yes, I did. After I was invalided out. The local G.P. where I live gave me a prescription. If I don't tell you, you'll find out for yourself. Only a tenth of a grain. After a month or two I found it getting a habit, so I chucked the bloody little bottle of tablets in the fire and took to aspirin. I've never touched it since—didn't even bother to get the prescription back from the chemist who had it. I suppose now you want to know the name of the doctor and the chemist?" His voice was malicious. "The doctor's name was Vassard—I say was, because he's dead. The chemists were Jones, Wane and Wade of Dover Street. You can ring them up. They're in the London phone book. Did I ever give any to Flik? No, I didn't. Good morning, Sexton Blake."

The brake squeaked off, and the M.G. slid down the hill. At the bottom, Clive turned round and waved, making a rude gesture at the same time, laughing.

Parry, liking Clive enormously, returned the compliment. Rather to his embarrassment, he then found that Flik was watching him from the gate, her mouth wide with amusement.

CHAPTER 12

"GOOD morning," Parry said. "I hope Clive'll be successful in his search for a lady to oblige. "

"I very much doubt it," Flik answered. "Though he's a great scrounger. How's crime?"

She looked better this morning, Parry thought. Less strained, less curt. A nut-colored woolen handkerchief was tied under her chin and her hair was very bright and rich against the gray of the sky.

"Done the chores?" he asked.

She nodded. "I suppose Clive told you Winnie's decided not to do for us, and why?"

"Yes, he did." Her frankness was disconcerting, and he still felt slightly embarrassed that she should have seen the exchange of compliments between him and Clive. For he had also made a rude noise as well as a rude gesture. He felt himself growing a little hot.

"What lovely raspberries you can make," she congratulated him. "Do do it again."

"Bpprph," Parry said, pursing his mouth in a feeble attempt. He was, he knew, getting entirely demoralized. His office at Scotland Yard, viewed in his mind's eye from this distance, seemed quite unreal. He drew in his breath and pulled himself up with a jerk. "Were you going for a walk?"

"I was going to see what'd happened to Harry, our gardener."

"Happened?" Parry echoed. "Why should anything happen to him?"

The guarded look came back into Flik's eyes, and he knew that behind them a sudden alarm had risen like a gust of wind.

"Why—I don't mean anything awful. It's just that he hasn't turned up to work today. He had a bit of a cold Saturday and yesterday, so I thought I'd go along and see if he was all right. I mean, if I ought to put him to bed and cosset him." She moved her head in the restless way Parry was beginning to know and recognize. "He's so old. We keep trying to persuade him to give up work, but he won't."

"Needs the money, I suppose," Parry said. "Like everyone."

"We've enough of an Imperial Tokay that can't be bought now to keep him in affluence till he dies," Flik said impatiently. "That's our capital. Did you know? Rare wines and liqueurs. We've got an 1870 port we're keeping up our sleeves till it rains so hard the roof won't keep it out. I'll open a bottle for you some time."

"Thank you." Parry treated this news with the reverence due to it. "But I couldn't drink your roof. Are you going to see Harry now?"

"Yes." Flik tightened her handkerchief. "I've just got to see first that there's no rain coming in on my life's work."

"Life's—oh, the famous mermaid?"

"The famous mermaid."

As she turned away from him he said, "Just a moment," and laid his hand on her sleeve. "I've been looking at Molly's account book and savings bankbook. They tally up very neatly. The items in the account book check up with the sums paid into her savings bank account. What were you paying her for?"

Flik rounded on him. But her face was perfectly calm, not angry. "When I die," she said, "everything I possess in the world's going to be burned."

"So that meddling policemen can't poke and pry. Quite. Well?" He felt a heel. But it was his job to be a heel.

"If it'll satisfy your curiosity, I'll tell you." The wind pushed Flik about so that she swayed with it. "Every time I sold an order—one of my carvings—I gave Molly a present. She didn't want to take it, but I made her. I wanted her to have what's so prettily called a nest egg to fall back on when she really couldn't work any longer."

"And you had a job to make her take your presents?"

"Yes."

"I see." Parry pulled out a packet of cigarettes, tried to light one, failed and threw it away. Flik had just flipped a dead end from her gloved fingers into the road. "Would it amaze you to hear that along with Molly's account book, her savings bankbook with the Western Bank, her card of Christmas club savings stamps, or whatever it is, there was a will? A last will and testament, properly made out by a solicitor, signed and witnessed?"

Flik said nothing.

"Would it amaze you?"

"Surely you mean surprise? Amazement is rather an exaggerated word, isn't it? Or should one say exaggerating?"

Will I ever find the chink in her armor? Parry wondered irritably. Or hadn't she one? She damn well had, of that he was certain.

"Very well. I bow to your choice of words. Would it surprise you, then, that in her will she left you everything? That she'd somehow saved £500? And that it's all yours?"

Now it wasn't the wind that swayed Flik.

"Actually," Parry said, "Arnoldson had no business to help himself to Molly's will. Nor her bankbook. Nor her card of savings stamps. They should have gone to her solicitor, or rather, he should've been informed and come and fetched them. As it is, I rang him up this morning early, and he's got them safely."

Flik looked at him, and again he saw the inside-out eyes, groping and fumbling for errant thought, some illusive idea. Her lips moved, and he bent his head down to her, thinking the wind had carried her words away with it.

In the end all she said was, to him, meaningless. She said, "Was it completed? Full?"

"Was what?" he shouted, using the noise of the wind as an excuse to shout it down. "Was what what?"

He looked behind him as a steady roar came up the hill. Arnoldson, on his motor bike.

Flik said, "Of course it was. Norton said so."

"What? What're you talking about?"

Arnoldson's motor bike came to a standstill. A crash helmet hid his greasy hair. The wind had dried his moist mouth, and the upturned collar of his leather coat concealed the beginnings of fat under his chin. Viewed thus, he looked, in a florid way, almost handsome, and very nearly well bred. He was evidently conscious of the fact.

"Just ran up to tell you, Inspector, lunch's ready," he said.

"Lunch?" Parry repeated, looking at his wrist watch. "Now? At twelve o'clock? D'you mean lunch, or what's called elevenses?"

"I mean lunch." Arnoldson's voice was a mixture of servility and cheek. "The brewery chap said he lunched at twelve, so we all lunch at twelve. If I hadn't gone on at him there wouldn't be any lunch at all, except for himself."

"I'll be down. Keep something for me," Parry nodded curtly.

Arnoldson, looking at Flik, turned his motor bike and roared down the hill again.

"Aunt Bee and I could've given you lunch," Flik said. "If you're not afraid of being poisoned."

"Don't say silly things like that," Parry caught her up. "Such a damn silly thing to say. It's very kind of you," he added, "but I'd better eat down below with the others. I've a lot to do."

He felt extremely annoyed at Arnoldson's interruption. He had been, he was sure, on the point of getting under Flik's guard. Now she had shut down on him again, master of herself, and, indeed, the whole situation so far as she was concerned.

"Might I see your mermaid before I descend to the depths of the Shots Arms?" he asked.

Flik pulled her mouth down, half amused. "No one's ever seen it but me," she said. "It's one of my rules never to let anyone set eyes on my works of art till they're finished. I shan't have done with my green rock for another couple of months or so. Maybe I never will."

"What d'you mean by that?"

"Nothing," Flik shrugged. "All right, if you really want to—"

Without waiting to see if he followed or not, she swung round and picked her way through pools of mud and water along the road. He fell into step beside her, curious. They passed Molly's cottage, and he said, "Was the old gardener, what's-his-name, Harry, upset about Molly?"

"Naturally he was," Flik answered. "He didn't know, of course, till yesterday afternoon."

"Why of course?"

"Because that was the first time he came out after she'd been murdered. He came along yesterday afternoon to see if there was anything we wanted such as more logs brought in for the fires."

"Used he to go and see Molly in her cottage?" Parry asked, wondering why he hadn't thought of the question before.

"No. He respected her privacy, even if the murderer didn't. He's a queer old man. His head's full of jumbled ideas, some of them rather charming ones." Flik turned down a rutted path, and taking a key out of her pocket, unlocked the door of the small, unprepossessing stone building. "Come in," she invited, and shut the door after him when he did so.

For a few seconds they were in pitch darkness, and for no known reason Parry was violently aware of Flik close beside him. He put out his hand to touch her, and found himself holding her hand. She had taken her gloves off, and her fingers were warm and firm. Then there was a snick, and the place was flooded with light, bright unscreened light that came from four bulbs hanging from the ceiling, so placed that there were no shadows cast anywhere. He let go Flik's hand, and saw her face was flushed.

In the middle of the bleak and dismal room, there was a mound covered by a canvas drawsheet. With a gesture half careless, half defiant, Flik pulled it back, and Parry looked on the famous mermaid everyone seemed to have heard about, but had never seen. He hadn't given much thought as to what he expected to see, but had vaguely visualized something very modern, something wild and odd. Something that reflected a part of Flik's secretiveness and smoldering fire.

"My God, how beautiful," he said, involuntarily. "How beautiful."

She lay there, the life-size, sea-green mermaid, part of, yet not part of, the pale sea-green rock she was carved from. She lay on the rock asleep, her pillow a young, sleeping seal, relaxed, innocent and sleeping sweetly, her sea-green hair spread out in tendrils that seemed wet from the sea, her tail curled half under her, her arms drooping by her sides, her breasts curved and perfect. One arm was only half finished. From the forearm downward it was still part of the rock, unformed and unshaped by the chisel. Like a light dawning in the darkness, Parry knew that he was looking on all that Flik craved for in her strange, troubled soul. Peace and quiet, a dreamless, unafraid sleep. Then, horribly, he thought of the peaceful, eternal sleep of morphine.

"I'm sorry," he said slowly. "I didn't realize you were a genius. I won't tell," he added, and knew that he had said the right thing.

"Thanks." Flik pulled the canvas back in place. "If you'll go first, then I'll put the lights out."

He went, wishing he could linger, and look and look again. Almost roughly, Flik gave him a push, and he was out in the dank and disgusting December midday. The door banged behind him, Flik locked it, and put the key into her pocket. Against the wind, they struggled back to the road. Then the wind, with what seemed its usual unexpectedness, died down to nothing.

"What's that row?" Parry asked.

Flik listened. "That? Susan's sewing machine. She'll never be done. She's making new curtains for every window in her cottage, and they've all got ruffled frills round the edges." She crossed the road and leaned over the low, clipped hedge, which separated the little front garden from the road. "Susan? Susan?" she shouted.

The noise of the machine stopped, started again, then stopped for good. A front window next the door opened, and Miss Merridew's small, inquiring face looked out.

"Oh, Flik, dear!" she exclaimed. "I hear that horrid child Winnie won't do a hand's turn. I'm so sorry. Mr. Fewsey told me when he brought my chops. Such nasty ones too, all fat and gristle. I said to him, 'Mr. Fewsey, it's really too bad she won't,' and, I said, 'Mr. Fewsey, when my dear father was still alive you wouldn't have brought chops like that,' and he said, 'That's what modern girls are coming to—out bicycling when their father's lying dead—' "

Parry listened, in a state of some mental confusion, to Miss Merridew's prattle, which was as inconsistent as a kitten chasing an imaginary mouse. Flik, he however noticed, appeared to be quite used to Miss Merridew's form of conversation and made all the appropriate answers. It struck him that she was very fond of the silly little old creature.

"Oh, and Major Mahew too," Miss Merridew cried. "Good— Oh, dear, no, it's Mr. Barry."

"Parry," he smiled.

"Flik, dear? I wonder if old Harry could possibly chop a tiny bit of wood for me before he goes home tonight? Could you ask him, dear?"

"I will when I see him," Flik promised. "Only I haven't. He hasn't turned up today. I'm just going to see if he's all right."

"All right?" Miss Merridew's eyes widened. "Flik! You don't think-You don't think—?" The eyes filled with agitation. "It's all so— Now, after two of them—"

"He's only got a cold, or something, Susan. He wasn't looking too grand yesterday."

"Not looking too grand yesterday?" Miss Merridew repeated. "And he hasn't come today? Could it be flu?"

"Maybe," Flik said. "Yes, yes, of course, Susan, he's only got a cold, or flu. Don't let your imagination run away with you." Her voice was soothing, the kind of voice you'd use talking to a child. "Why don't you come over to lunch?"

"Flik, dear! How kind. I'll do all the washing up and then you and Bee can have a nice rest."

"You'll do no washing up, my dear. Look—Susan? Here comes Harry, so you see it's all right."

Harry himself, however, didn't look, thought Parry, a bit all right. As he doddered toward them his steps were uncertain, and his face was pinched and gray. But he seemed fairly cheerful.

"Sorry, Miss Flikka," he mumbled. "I didn't feel too good nor yesterday nor today."

"I told you yesterday," Flik remonstrated, "you looked as if you were going to be ill. You don't look any better today. Harry, do go home and stay home. You aren't to do any work."

"I got some work to do," Harry said doggedly. "And I'll do it." He peered at her, then at Parry. Then at Miss Merridew.

And with that, taking no more notice of anyone, he doddered up the road and in at the gates of Shots Hall.

Parry sighed inwardly. Now Flik would be concerned with Harry, then with lunch and stopping Susan Merridew from washing up. There was no more to be got out of any of them for the moment.

"I'll be off," he said, "and see what the Lord's provided down at the pub."

"Oh," Miss Merridew cried. "Wouldn't you care for a little home-made cordial and a biscuit first? Such nice cordial. Dear Gwen makes it every year—out of elderberries, I think? Or is it blackberries?"

Parry hurriedly excused himself and knew that Flik was laughing at him. As he slushed down the hill, the wind got up again, though without such violence. He'd got nowhere. Nowhere at all. He'd seen what, to him, seemed a work of genius. But that was about all. Or was it? At the back of his mind little prickings and promptings were like the echo of pins and needles. There was a pattern to all this, if only he could piece it together.

Never a man to jump to conclusions without evidence to prove them, he was yet quite certain that the murderer, with or without accomplices, was right under his nose. In the village. There spread in front of him a dreary vista of interviewing every man, woman and child in the place, writing down everything they had to say, everything they had seen, everything they had heard. Miles of paper and routine work, of checkings-up on everyone's statements. The fact that he'd such a small cast of players to choose from, only seemed to make things more difficult, for where intimacy crept in, logic crept out.

He was relieved to see Congreve going into the pub. At least lunch would not be too dull.

CHAPTER 13

THE brewery's man, with much reluctance, had provided a tin of very nasty soup and some sandwiches filled with something else out of a tin. There was, however, plenty to drink, which was only natural. Old Marsh had somehow managed to scrounge a pretty good supply of hard liquor, and as nearly all the villagers drank beer, mild and bitter or stout, his supply of the real stuff had accumulated.

They lunched in old Marsh's sitting room, the table littered with crumbs, glasses and the contents of a box where Marsh kept his own money and most important possessions. After going through his few papers, Parry decided the old man had no solicitor, and that therefore the police would have to take charge of his petty cash, his savings bankbook, the inevitable card of savings club stamps and his account book, which was of peculiarly little interest compared to Molly's.

"I suppose Winnie'll get anything he had?" Parry said. "That is, when she's proved she's his only child and rightful heir. There doesn't seem to be a will, and precious little to be gleaned in the way of information; if he had any letters, then he must've torn them up and got rid of them. Pity."

"What about fingerprints?" Mahew asked. He had indigestion and was rather bad-tempered.

"Marsh's and Winnie's all over the kitchen, this room and the bedrooms above," Arnoldson said. "And the fingerprints of the whole blasted village all over both bars. Nothing to be got in that line."

Arnoldson got up and kicked his chair away, muttering something about if no one else had any work to do, he had. "I'll ring up the chemists in London, sir," he said to Parry. "With your permission, of course," he added.

"I told you to, didn't I?"

"Dear God," Mahew groaned, "what a bloody awful lunch. What a bloody awful pub, anyway. I've got a bellyache."

Congreve looked at him with affection and respect. Mahew was enormously popular with the St. Arthurs police force. In his office he was businesslike and formal, out of it he was almost too human to be true.

"The gent from the brewery," Congreve sympathized, "is the man we're after. 'E's a poisoner by nature, intent, upbringing and 'abit. I don't feel too 'appy under the belt neither, sir," he said to Parry. "That old Mrs. Vale won't change 'er mind. She sticks to it she saw Mrs. Ashley come out the back door 'ere at about 'arf four, and didn't see 'er go in:"

"So that's that," Parry said.

Sounds of Arnoldson using the very old-fashioned phone came from the passage where it was located in a dark corner between the kitchen and the public bar. With some relish his audience listened to his increasing rage as he got two wrong numbers in succession. Congreve, especially, was appreciative when the angered detective sergeant dropped an *h* and then picked it up again with emphasis.

"If I stopped," he whispered to Parry, "to pick up all my aitches what I dropped, I'd get a crick in my back, and grow roots in the bottom of me regulation boots from staying so long in the one place."

Mahew, suddenly feeling better, stifled a laugh. "What role d'you want me to play now?" he asked Parry.

"Just be your own sweet self," Parry said. "I think we might go and visit the Ambroses. In the meantime Arnoldson can go and run Gwen

Hunter to earth. She appears to dabble in herbs and homemade cordials. I'm not suggesting she concocted morphine from poppyheads, but she bears investigating."

It occurred to him that amongst other people, the principal of which were Flik and Bee, he must also have a talk—he quailed at the thought—with Miss Merridew. She seemed to be more familiar with the inhabitants of Shots Hall than anyone else, and she lived within spitting distance of their gate.

Arnoldson came back from his telephonic inquiries, smoothing his hair and looking commendably cool. "Checks up neatly," he said. "The chemists, Jones, Wane and Wade still have Harris' prescription for morphine given him by Vassard. They supplied Harris with one tube of morphine tablets, twenty tablets in all, each one a tenth of a grain. That totals two grains."

"Mm—" Parry mused. "He might've got another prescription from another doctor as well."

"And donated some to the suffering Fl— Mrs. Ashley?" Arnoldson put in.

"What's she suffer from?" Congreve asked with wide-eyed simplicity. "I 'ad an aunt once what suffered from 'allucinations. Every time a man walked past 'er little snuggery, she used to say, 'Know 'oo that is? That's the rate collector, and 'es not calling 'ere and never will.' Actually, 'e was always calling, and every time she opened the door to 'im she said, 'Funny, I thought I 'eard someone knock, only there ain't no one 'ere.' Then she'd bang the door and lock it."

"A close relative, I take it?" Arnoldson remarked sarcastically.

"By marriage only, sir. And not long then, my uncle being removed in a plain van, where 'e passed peacefully away, beating 'is 'ead on the 'igh class padding, crying, 'Jehovah, Jehovah.' "

Mahew and Parry got up and hurried to the gents' lavatory, which was situated in a brick building resembling a sort of miniature slaughterhouse outside the back door.

"If you want to give me a Christmas present, old boy," Parry said, "then may I have Congreve wrapped up in tissue paper with a red ribbon round him?"

"No." Mahew was quite definite. "Lane? This is an appalling mess. Talk about fiddling while Rome burns. All we're doing is enjoying Congreve baiting Arnoldson, while there's a murderer crawling about."

"I know." Parry sobered up. "Only there're so many ends, I don't know which one to pick up first. So much to do, so little ruddy time to do it."

"What the hell d'you mean?"

They were outside the slaughterhouse now, leaning with their backs against it, much to the interest of old Mrs. Vale, who was always interested in the traffic to and from the back door. During the hours of daylight, so few in winter, so many in summer, she kept a sort of tally, thereby knowing just how much beer everyone had drunk.

Parry half shut his eyes. "Two poisonings in forty-eight hours. That's a terrible risk, isn't it? Either the poisoner is mad, or he or she's trying to achieve some end. In the first instance, if they're mad, they'll have got the lust for killing in them by now, and go on. If there's some end to achieve, so desperate a need to polish off two people in forty-eight hours, the chances are the end isn't: achieved at all. In most murders, the killing of one person achieves the end in view—gain, revenge. But here we have two. The first wasn't sufficient. So there was a second. Either because of that end, or because the second murderee, so the murderer suspected, was a potential danger to their safety. So they were bumped off in the most merciful way possible. Both of them. That gives one to think—"

"You mean," Mahew said, rather appalled, "there're going to be some more bodies lying around?"

"If there's a lunatic knocking about, there might be. Killing, with an unbalanced mind, almost becomes a hobby."

"But to kill because it's necessary?"

"It must be damned necessary, when it comes to two in two days. I do hope not, however, though it'd make our job very much easier."

Mahew detached his back from the gents' lavatory, where it had got quite warm for the first time that day. "Then I hope we don't have the easier way foisted on us. Have you any ideas?"

"A whole lot. Too many, in fact."

They walked the not very long distance to the Ambroses. With reluctance, Arnoldson walked too, and they left him banging on Gwen Hunter's door. Evidently she was in, as the door opened and he vanished inside.

"How d'you get on with Belairs, by the way?" Parry asked Mahew.

"I don't like him. I don't know why, but I don't. As well as being a bore, he's got a nasty sort of mind. Kept throwing out hints."

"Wants to make himself seem important," Parry said, banging on the Ambroses' front door. "I know the type. Travels in red herrings."

Tim Ambrose opened the door, radiating a false heartiness, which was also reflected by Phil, hovering in the background. There were dark rings under her eyes, and she was painfully jumpy.

"Do come in," she shrieked over Tim's shoulder: "Lovely to see you all." She tossed her hair back, feverishly pulling at a cigarette:

The drawing room was charming. It was also very hot, as an enormous fire blazed behind a needlework screen.

"What a delightful room," Parry said, tactfully ignoring the remains of a very nasty smell.

"Yes, it is, isn't it?" Phil exclaimed, hair tossing again.

"Drink?" Tim invited. "Do have a drink?"

"We've had some, thanks," Mahew said. "At the pub."

"Oh, well then—do sit down."

They sat, Congreve perched on the edge of his chair, looking innocent.

"Were just checking up," Parry said, "on everyone's movements during the times when Molly took, or was administered, poison. What were you two doing between a quarter to eight and nine on the evening Molly must have taken the poison?"

"We told you," Phil squeaked in an anguished voice. "Phil and I and Gwen were playing bridge here—cutthroat."

"Of course we told you, at Flik's party," Tim echoed, fidgeting. "With the old blackout screens up to keep out the cold."

"Yes, of course I remember." Parry moved the cushion behind him, and Phil darted at him, her mouth open.

"That's such an uncomfortable chair," she almost screamed, hair tossing. "Do sit in another one."

Parry put his hand behind the cushion and brought out an ancient tome on which was inscribed in faded gilt lettering, *Ye Black Arts and Magicke Accordinge to Luigi.*

"I told you we should have burned it," Tim croaked at his wife.

"We traded it with Camilla for a cat, our cat—" Phil was now in tears, which struck Parry as odd, for she didn't seem the crying kind. "It made messes—the cat did—only it came back yesterday and had kittens in the kitchen. We— Oh!"

"Tst-tst," Congreve remarked. "Don't upset yourself like this, Mrs. Ambrose, it's bad for the little one what's coming along so nicely."

"Oh—oh!" Phil sobbed furiously. "How did you know, you stinking policeman? I haven't told anyone, except Tim, of course. Everyone staring. Watching you swell. Oh, God!"

"How on earth," Parry said rather crossly to Congreve, "did *you* know?"

"I'm the eldest," Congreve said untruthfully but with pride, "of a family of sixteen, so I know the signs."

"Shut up!" Tim raged at him. "Phil, honey, take no notice."

"May I ask," Parry interrupted, raising his voice, "why you're at such pains to conceal such an excellent alibi for the times during which Molly took morphine?"

"Morphine?" Phil and Tim chorused.

"Morphine."

"Oh, my God!" Tim stared. "Is that all? I mean, we just knew she was poisoned, and that was all."

"What you mean," Parry said with the patience of job, "is that you thought you'd make some childish experiments with this book, and having done your cabalistic writings on the floor, you did the necessary by burning some of your friend Gwen Hunter's herbs?"

"But they were all deadly poisonous," Phil squealed. "And we were scared stiff when that damned old Belairs started chucking hints about as to what we were doing on Saturday night. We burned the rest of the herbs this morning—they were dried ones—deadly nightshade, and lords and ladies, and stuff like that. Besides, it's illegal."

"What is?" Parry asked wearily. "Burning dried herbs, scrawling on the floor and reading an old book? The last executions for witchcraft in this country were in 1718. A lady called Mrs. Hicks and her small girl were hanged. You'll forgive me, I'm sure, when I tell you that you're a couple of silly young fools—the third being your friend Gwen—and that you've quite needlessly taken up the time of the police. Now, what were you doing yesterday afternoon and evening? I take it you know old Marsh is dead, and may have been poisoned too?"

"We walked over to the Jessens for tea," Tim sulked.

"You saw them at Flik's party. Go on, check up on that, and be damned to you."

"Hoity-toity," Congreve murmured.

"I see. You know Fl— Mrs. Ashley very well, don't you?"

"Yes, we do!" Phil cried. "And if you think she did it, then you're damned well wrong. Yes, you are!"

"Phil, honey—"

Parry signaled silently to Mahew and Congreve and prepared to escape before Phil indulged in another outburst of prenatal jimjams. "By the way," he asked as they were about to make their exit. "Who's Camilla?"

"You saw her at Flik's party," Phil exploded. "Blast her. That woman Tim was cuddling. Middle-aged. I hate her—Camilla this, Camilla that. She loves to be talked about under her nose. Everyone saying Camilla'd trade the pants off her bottom, so she would. Free publicity under her nose. I suppose she can't do without it, even after all these years."

"Phil, be quiet." Tim took her by the arm and shook her. "It's unfair. Why rake all that up when everyone's forgotten about it?"

"I won't be quiet!" Phil shouted. "Camilla Pain-Wentworth. Don't you remember? I was only a small kid then. She's supposed to've re-formed years ago. She must be fifty by now. Camilla Pain-Wentworth, don't you remember?"

"Sure," Parry said slowly. "She used dope. Morphine. Thanks. Where does she live?"

"Look her up in the phone book, you nosy policeman," Tim jeered, and turning his back, went on, with commendable patience, trying to soothe the expectant mother.

"Well, well, well," Parry sighed as they tramped back along the lane. "What a community. So soon as we eliminate one lot, someone else crops up. Ambroses out, Camilla in."

"Pain-Wentworth—I ought've known," Mahew said. "She can't live in the St. Arthurs district."

"This is like driving a car along the road and every corner another passenger 'ops on board," Congreve decided cheerfully.

"All I can say is," Parry grunted, "that I hope the springs don't give way from the strain."

CHAPTER 14

HAVING found Camilla's address in the local phone book, Parry went off in the police car to find Camilla herself. She lived a mile or so from Pelsey, out of, as Mahew had surmised, the St. Arthurs district. Her house was small, modern and cheerful. Camilla herself seemed delighted to see him, and said she'd been expecting him, and wouldn't he come in.

With her were two of the bicyclists who had been at Flik's and Bee Chattock's party the evening before. They were playing rummy. Apparently it was the continuation of a game that which had started at teatime on Friday, gone on till midnight on Friday, recommenced again on Saturday night, got under way once more on Sunday afternoon, and continued till the three of them had started off on their bicycles to Shots Hall at a quarter past five for the party, had yet again recommenced on their return, and had been going on ever since. As for alibis, not only Camilla but her friends were plastered with them.

"Don't you get a little tired of playing rummy so much?" Parry asked.

"Not at all," the players chorused. "We've got to go on with this game, because you see poor Camilla's lost, on paper, ten thousand pounds, her house, all her clothes and her bicycle."

"So you see," Camilla smiled, "they're giving me a chance to win a little of it back."

"Very sporting," Parry said. "Have you lost a cat?"

"My dear! Yes. Poor old Muffin, and she was going to have kittens at any moment."

"She's had them," Parry said. "At the Ambroses. You traded a book for her, didn't you?"

"Camilla'd trade her knickers in the middle of the road," said the rummy-playing bicyclists, "if you offered her a nice hen in exchange."

Camilla looked pleased. "Book? Yes—some stupid old book the Ambroses took a fancy to. Do you mind?"

"Not in the least," Parry reassured her. "It wasn't that I wanted to see you about."

"I didn't expect it was," Camilla said dryly, rather taking the wind out of his sails. "You wanted to know if I still take morphine? Well, I don't. I'm nearly fifty, and I've never touched the stuff since I was about thirty-four. They put me in a home, where I was more or less cured. What finished the cure completely was overhearing someone say, 'Camilla used to be so lovely, and now she's a bloody old hag of ninety.' And I looked in the glass, and sure enough, I was. You see, I'm very conceited."

"Are you?" Parry laughed. "I think you're very nice."

"You ought to've known me in the old days," Camilla said complacently. "I was pure hell. If I wasn't doped, I was tight or both. Talk about painting the town red. Now I keep hens and play rummy, and flirt."

"She'd flirt with a broomstick if it wore trousers, Camilla would," cried the admiring friends.

It was obviously all too true that Camilla had given up doping. Not only that, but after her cure, the Home Office hadn't allowed her any ration, for the simple reason she hadn't wanted one.

"My dear," she said, "if I wanted to get hold of anything like that now, I'd have to change my name, put on a wig, a false nose and a false bosom and emigrate to a country where no one knew me. And I simply couldn't be bothered," she added. "One's reputation dies hard, even after all these years."

"Yes," Parry agreed. "I suppose it does."

So that was that.

When he was going, Camilla said, "The postman said this morning
something about trouble at the pub at Shotshall—old Marsh. Is he really
dead too?"

"Yes."

"I wondered why you were so interested about what we were doing
on Sunday. How dreadful. Such a dreary old man, and such an appalling
pub. Do come again, won't you? You've got such fascinating eyes, and I
do like your smile."

"I'm so glad," Parry thanked her. Then he added, "Do be a dear and
lay off Tim Ambrose. His wretched little wife's so upset."

"All right," said the obliging Camilla, "I will. Thanks for telling me.
'By, ducky."

On the way back in the car, Parry thought, that's settled her. Or had
it? Was it really all right, her end of the many loose ends? Could she
possibly have hoarded some morphine, just in case, sealed up in a bottle—
apparently she'd taken it in tablet form—so that it had in some way kept
for years? Only if she had, she hadn't killed Molly or Marsh with it. Her
alibis were as watertight as any alibis could be, which was saying a lot,
for most of them leaked like hell once they were launched into the stormy
sea of police investigation.

He stopped at a public phone box in Pelsey,and rang through to the
St. Arthurs police station. Abbot's report had just come in. Marsh had
taken from five to six grains of morphine in his well-sugared tea, not
earlier than four on Sunday afternoon, not later than five o'clock. He
must have died at approximately a quarter past seven, only a quarter of an
hour or so before Winnie got back from church and found him.

Parry then rang Abbot's house and was told he was out, and had not
left instructions as to where he could be found. He's gone to see Flik,
thought Parry.

He was quite right. After a hurried bath, Abbot had got into his car
and made straight for Shots Hall, irresistibly drawn there by some instinct
like that of a homing pigeon. It was an instinct that made him exceedingly
angry, so he was not in the happiest of moods when he stopped his car
outside the front door and extricated his long, tired legs from behind the
wheel.

It was getting dark. The wind howled no longer. From the sodden
ground a mist rose to a fellow mist that descended from the sodden skies.
Shots Hall looked gloomy and forbidding, secret, and hiding something,
which undoubtedly, Abbot thought, it was. He shivered, tired and utterly
fed up. For the first time he caught sight of Harry's rubble rock garden

and saw Harry himself crouched in the middle of it, apparently sticking labels, skewered on wire holders, in amongst the nasty mess of dead fire-flowers, some of which he had cleared away into a pile. It was a depressing sight. The old gray man, the fallen, overgrown ruins which bore so little resemblance to the garden Harry had seen in Sutton's catalogue. December, the unhappiest time for any garden, was peculiarly unbecoming to the garden of Shots Hall on a misty evening.

Abbot was just going to the door when a light appeared from somewhere and threw a faint and ghostly radiance on Harry's rubbish heap. It seemed to come from round the corner of the house. Wondering from which of the few remaining rooms it shone, Abbot banged on the front door and noticed that there was, after all, a knocker to bang with. It was placed very high up, so that no one under nearly six feet could possibly reach it.

"How damn silly," he said out loud. "What a lunatic asylum of useless contrivances." He reached up and, lifting the knocker, let it drop. The noise was nearly deafening, but had the result of attracting someone's attention.

The door opened and Flik looked out at him. As it had done the first time he had met her, and ever since, her loveliness struck him like a blow in the chest.

"Hullo," he said ungraciously and straightened his spectacles.

"Come in." She held the door wide and let it slam behind him.

"What's the matter with that pestilential door?" he demanded. "Why does it always do that?"

"It was not properly hung. In summer nothing'll keep it open but brute force or a row of flatirons. We like it that way. It's familiar."

"I see. All part and parcel of the dear old place that means home?" Automatically, Abbot found himself jeering. "Doesn't the noise of incomings and outgoings disturb your aunt?"

"She's not easily disturbed," Flik said, also jeering in return. "As you may perhaps have perceived. Come into what we call the drawing room. There's a fire in there today."

As she led the way across the hall, Abbot saw that the door into what he supposed to be the study was open. In the evening's dim light, Flik's wood carvings were vaguely outlined against the pale paneling of the room. They gave a rather uncomfortable impression of heads recently severed from living bodies, staring with eyes, now dead and sightless, at nothing. The drawing room, however, dispelled the dreary and haunted atmosphere of what he'd seen of the rest of the house. The mid-Victorian pine paneling had been scraped of its varnish, its decorations attended to with a plane and entirely removed. There were one or two pleasant pictures, dulled with age; the mid-Victorian fireplace had been replaced by an Adams one which, Abbot found later, was genuine. Flik had picked it up somewhere in a junk shop. Above it, mellow and warm, hung a gilt mirror, a thing of curlicues and long-tailed birds and little Chinese pagodas. Here, as in the hall, the few bits of furniture were old and well arranged; as in the hall, the curtains, the covers, the rugs, once luxurious, were worn almost threadbare.

If Abbot was capable of approving of anything, he approved the way no attempt had been made to camouflage worn arms and backs of chairs by horrible bits of needlework or brocade arm and head rests. Nor were the thinnest patches in the rugs hidden under tables and chairs which got in the way and which mustn't be moved.

It was from this room that the light must have shone on to Harry's rock garden, for it stuck right out from the main structure of the house, its far end bow-windowed. He could see Harry groping and poking amongst his weeds, still sticking his bits of paper into the wire skewers. Something in his back view showed his intense concentration and that, to him, what he was doing was of the utmost importance.

"Well, Abbot? Done staring?"

"What?" He hadn't seen Bee Chattock sitting serenely dignified by the fire. "Sorry. Yes. I like this room."

"We're overcome by your admiration," Bee snapped, her eyes small pinpoints of amusement. "You've got the manners of a hog. Sit down, can't you, and stop stamping about?"

"I wasn't aware I was stamping." Abbot sat, choosing the most comfortable chair.

"You're continually stamping," Bee said. "Inwardly. Also swearing with, no doubt, the greatest obscenity."

"Aunt Bee's partial to bad language," Flik said, and laughed one of her rare laughs, "Have some tea? It's freshly made with nice fresh poison."

"Be quiet," Abbot exploded. "Don't say things like that. It's morbid to make a joke of something that's not a joke at all."

"I'm not joking—" her eyes turned, dark. "What d'you expect me to do? Have a good cry? Oh, for God's sake—" She broke off and pressed her lips together. "Well? What about Marsh?"

Abbot told her. Neither she nor Bee showed any apparent surprise.

Flik muttered, "Poor old devil, how bloody."

"It's revolting," Bee agreed, and made the noise which can only be spelled, "Faugh."

"What about my tea?"

The look Flik gave him, he was amazed to see, was almost one of gratitude, and he thought, to hell with it. I wish she wouldn't do that—like a dog that's beaten and then forgiven. She's actually grateful I think she won't poison me. "No, sugar;" he said. "And very little milk. Parry been up? Or Arnoldson? Anyone?"

"At midday. I'm all dressed up to be grilled. Why doesn't Parry come and do it?"

Abbot said nothing, thinking she was all dressed up in that lovely wool dress not to be grilled but to kill. It was the color of her hair, and very tight in the waist, and plain. She'd a fancy for Parry, all right, and Parry, might the devil take him, wouldn't hesitate to hang her if needs be. Then, less unjustly, he decided it was all pretty bloody for Parry, unless he was unmoved by her loveliness, which seemed impossible, even for a policeman.

There was a long silence, which was neither particularly comfortable nor particularly enjoyable. To sit in silence, wondering who was the murderer in their midst, was not exactly a happy pastime. He glanced at Flik over the top of his cup. She was looking straight in front of her, that guarded, secret, concealing, look in her eyes.

"Haven't you any idea who might've had a grudge against Molly and Marsh?" Abbot asked, unable to bear the silence any longer.

"Nobody bore them a grudge."

The definiteness with which Flik said this staggered him. It was as good as admission that she knew who had killed them, and why. That she should know anything about the murders, and not tell what she knew, had the effect of making his flesh creep. It wasn't human, unless she'd done the murdering herself, and that wasn't human either.

"Don't say a thing like that to Parry," he found himself saying.

Flik didn't answer. She got up and went to the window, looked out, and opened one of the casements. Bee's eyes followed her; the expression in them struck Abbot as odd—as if she'd suddenly realized that Flik knew something and hadn't told her, and wasn't going to tell her, and was alarmed in consequence. What awful mess had he gotten himself mixed up in? he wondered with distaste, and his mind darted to the man Arnoldson was so fond of talking about. The man who'd apparently been Flik's temporary lover. Only that wasn't a secret.

"Harry," Flik called, leaning out the window. "Time to go home.

Would you like a cuppa?"

Dim and muffled, his answer came back. "No, Miss Flik, thank you. You ought to know I don't drink tea this time of the day, so you should. It's getting mighty dark, what with the fog."

"Then go home, Harry, do go home—you look poorly."

"All right, Miss Flik. I'll come round the front—" Ghostly, his voice added something about a bottle.

"What the hell's the matter with him?" Bee asked. "In God's name why can't he give up work, or just potter when he feels like it? You're supposed to be a doctor, Abbot. What's wrong with him?"

Abbot pulled his thoughts away from Flik and transferred them, without much interest, professional or otherwise, to Harry. *"Anno Domini—a prevalent disease."*

Outside, in the fog and the falling darkness, Harry's labels were like the white flags of a surrendering army. Flik shut the window and went out into the hall. Her shoes had very high heels but they didn't click and patter like high heels usually did. Feeling he ought to try and show some interest in the ancient gardener, Abbot followed her. The hall seemed emptier, larger, lonelier and more full of shadows than ever.

Flik opened the door, letting in the cold and the damp. It was a quite horrible evening. The howling of the gale had, at least, been alive; now it had dropped, the world was dead and watchfully silent. Harry stood on the step, and Abbot saw that there was more than *Anno Domini* wrong with him, for his face had a haggard, gray look that was not born of old age alone. He peered up at Flik, blinking in the little light that shone out on him, holding out his hand, as if begging for alms.

Flik's fingers groped on the table inside the door, and Abbot saw she was looking for a small, long bottled filled with almost white fluid.

"Medicine for Harry?" he asked, his voice curt..

She looked at him over her shoulder. "I didn't know you were there. Phospherine. Harry says it suits him. I got Clive to bring it up from the town this afternoon when he went on his unsuccessful hunt for a lady to oblige. Harry, I've taken it out of its wrapping. You're so fumble-fingered with anything but flowers—don't come tomorrow: I'll be along and I'll do your chores."

Harry pocketed the bottle, still peering up at Flik.. Why, Abbot thought, he worships her as if she was God. Then, with unreasonable irritation, he saw that Parry and Congreve were coming up the short drive, both absorbing, in their different ways, the picture of Flik and Harry, of himself hovering, a bloody fool, in the background.

"Evening," Parry said, and nodded, including Abbot and Harry in the nod.

"Evening," Flik said, tightening her back. "This is Harry. Or have you met before?"

"Them's the police," Harry remarked, his scorn ill, if at all, concealed. "They're looking for the murderer, so they are. Restless. If they'd sit down quiet, they might find out. Everyone's restless, even you, Miss Flik, hammering at that there rock of yourn. Home, you ought to be, with a man to mind."

"Harry—" Flik's eyebrows raised in a gentle hint to the old man to pipe down in the presence of company. But Harry had something to say, and no one, not even Flik, was going to stop him saying it.

"There's too much running around, so there is. No one does enough thinking, or if they does, they do too much, and in the wrong direction. Live in the present, that's all, and no making preparations for to meet their deaths, which is what'll come to everyone and you can't stop it." He threw a baleful look at Parry and Congreve, who were, quite evidently, enjoying themselves at Harry's expense. "Miss Flik? One never knows when one'll be carried off, as I'm always saying to you. So I've labeled every thing what's underground in the rockery. You might take on and weed, and dig up something what ain't showing this time of year. So I labeled everything. That's what's called foresight. See? If I died tomorrow, you'd still be able to find out just by looking at the labels. And don't you forget it—restless and higgly-piggly, and no sitting down quiet by the fire."

Without a good evening, without more ado, without a backward glance, Harry shambled off down the drive, and the mist and the grayness claimed him.

"A little cuckoo, I take it?" Parry inquired. "Poor old chap."

"I don't know," Flik said, "if he's such a poor old chap."

"Nest well feathered?" Parry went on, hoping for more information.

Flik turned, ran right into Abbot, and held the door open wide. "Sorry," she apologized. "I'd forgotten you were there."

"The monotonous regularity with which you forget my existence," he remarked, wishing he were a female and so could scratch her face, "is almost boring."

"It's because you don't get in my hair, so I don't notice you. Do come in, Parry. Congreve, isn't it?" She let the door go, and the house seemed to shiver as it crashed to.

Abbot, who had wanted to escape, finding himself shut in again instead, mentally tore his hair in abortive fury.

"Stamping again?" Bee stood there beside him, a large, old-fashioned key in her hand. Parry and Congreve had gone with Flik into the drawing room. "There's only one place in this house that seems to be free of policemen, murderers and victims, and that's the cellar. I've a fancy for some '70 Marsala. It's quite excellent. Are you coming, Abbot?"

"All right, all right," he raged. "It'll make me sick, but what's that? At my age one may as well die happy, in one's cups, and to hell with everything."

"I do so agree with you. When I was your age I thought the same. Now I just taste and savor the bouquet. To you the full bottle."

Rather staggered by Bee's sententious speech, Abbot asked, "Bottle, what of?"

"Damn sour grapes," Bee answered, "by the look of things."

CHAPTER 15

WHILE Bee and Abbot crouched on a packing case in the cellar, sipping Marsala out of two crystal wine glasses by the light of a candle, the grilling of Flik proceeded above their heads. Bee's turn would come in due course.

Mahew, very thankfully, had gone home, and was sending the car back later, with another driver, for Parry. Determined that he would make things as painless as possible for Flik, Parry had sent Arnoldson off on some wild goose chase on his motor bicycle. The detective sergeant's interview with Gwen had been fairly unproductive. She had had so many theories, each one more absurd than the other, to expound, that he hadn't been able to get a word in edgeways. He, personally, thought she was far too stupid to nominate as a suspect, though her alibi for the times between which Marsh might have taken the overdose of morphine on Sunday was very vague. She was a plain and plobby girl, but any girl was better than no girl at all, so Arnoldson had started making mild advances to her and Gwen had seemed to be liking it. He put her down as being oversexed, and he was quite right. This had made him wonder, as she obviously hadn't a boyfriend, if she was mentally unbalanced, and therefore had gratified some desire or other by committing murder. But he had, if not put the thought from him, then pigeonholed it for the time being. She was such an entire fool, or so it seemed to him. And whoever had murdered

Molly and Marsh wasn't a fool. If they were, then all he could say was they'd had the luck of the devil not to have yet been found out. He still pinned all his faith on Flik.

Congreve, who had once met Flik down at the pub when he had gone in there while making inquiries about a valuable dog someone had lost and had been treated to a pint by her, felt, at the moment, very sorry for her. He wished Parry'd left him behind, but Parry had insisted that Congreve should come along and use his ten pairs of eyes. Awful, Congreve thought, to have to drag your past up in front of two men.

"Your American friend," Parry said. "Can you tell me his name? And, by the way, now that I come to think of it, how very odd that an American army man should've been here during the blitz. America wasn't in the war then."

Flik tapped her cigarette ash into the grate. "We use blitz in rather a loose way down here," she said. "We got raids—sneak raids—down on the coast right up to 1943. We lump all of them under the heading of the blitz."

"Another little mystery solved," Parry said amiably. Poor Flik, this was horrible for her. "And his name?"

"Jim, I think." Flik's voice was admirably careless. "Yes, I think it was Jim."

"Jim what?" Parry prompted.

"How can you really expect me to remember all that long time ago?" Her mouth turned down in scorn.

"I 'ad a girlfriend once," Congreve put in, hoping to ease the tension. "'Er name was Lucy, but I'm blessed if I can remember what 'er surname was. 'Er teeth stuck out."

"That," Flik smiled at him, "must have been a disadvantage at times, I expect."

"Well, it was, in a manner of speaking," Congreve agreed. He had never had a girlfriend called Lucy with teeth that stuck out. Now that he had invented her, however, he was quite pleased to go on talking about her. "It was rather like being butted by a nanny goat, if you see what I mean. Not, that she wasn't quite a nice girl—" He caught Parry's eye and trailed off into silence, feeling duly reproved.

"And before Jim, I think you had another admirer?" Parry felt sick inside him, but somehow he must get a more definite line on Flik. "Please don't think I mean anything by that. It'd be very extraordinary if you hadn't. Correct me if I'm wrong, but according to the village gossip which is thrust at me whether I want to hear it or not, which is generally not, there was some chap used to stay down here you went around with quite a lot. I think, didn't he, he used to stay at Miss Merridew's before her father died?"

"Her cousin." Flik got up and began to pile more logs on the fire. "Mervyn Crawford. I used to go for walks with him, if you call that going around with him quite a lot."

"He's dead, isn't he?"

"Yes. In the blitz, the real blitz." She crouched down on her heels, sweeping up the ashes in the grate, avoiding his eyes.

What's wrong here? Parry wondered. She doesn't want to talk about him. There seemed no excuse, however, to pursue the subject. He had been a cousin of Miss Merridew's, his name had been Mervyn Crawford, and he'd been killed in the blitz. He really couldn't start asking questions like, "Did you ever kiss him? Did you ever sleep with him?" For that, most definitely, would be exceeding his duty as a policeman. Besides, he didn't want to know.

"Now," he said, "let's go right over Sunday afternoon again. That is, if you don't mind. You do realize, don't you, Flik, that you needn't answer any of these questions? Not at this stage of the proceedings, anyway."

"You told me before." She screwed herself round so that she was facing him, and sat down on the stone curb that edged the hearth. "Ask away."

"First of all, let's get the time you went down to the pub quite definite."

"The nearest I can say is that it must've been about half past four," she said. "I know Aunt Bee told me to hurry up, as she wanted to have tea, and we have tea about a quarter to five."

"All right," said Parry. "Let's say it was half past four Now, do try and think back—did you see anyone on your way down to the pub, or on the way back?"

"No. No, I didn't. Not a soul. They mostly snooze Sunday afternoons in the village. One of our olde worlde merrie English customs." Her face, looking up at Parry, was suddenly impudent, and it made her look he thought, absurdly young.

"No one at all—" he echoed. "All right. Tell me as clearly as you can just what you did when you got to the pub. Yes, I know, you told me before, but there may be some small detail you've forgotten, which might be an awful help."

Flik stopped looking impudent, frowning, concentrated. "I can't remember if I knocked on the back door. I think I did, and then went straight in. Old Marsh never locked that door unless he went out, and when he packed up for the night. I saw the bottle of gin on the sink—or rather, on, the drying board by the sink. The door into Marsh's sitting room was open, and I saw the top of his head. He was sitting as he usually did, in that big chair with its back to the door." She broke off, thinking backward. "There was a teacup on the table by him. He always had a cuppa at half past four."

"Always? Did you know all his habits, then?"

"Haven't you yet discovered that everyone in this village knows everybody's habits? Don't you see, that's what made it so desperately easy for the murderer? This is the first time in, I should think, living memory, that the usual routine's been upset and disorganized."

"I know," Parry nodded. "That's just what did make it so easy for the murderer. And so difficult for us chaps. All right. He always had a cuppa at half past four, and everyone knew it. Was the cup empty or full? Do try and remember. So much hangs on it."

"Hangs." Flik repeated the word as though it tasted horrible. Then she drew her breath in and slowly let it out again, much to the interest of Parry and Congreve. "No. No, I can't pretend I remember if the cup was full or empty. I wish I could. But I can't, I honestly can't. There was a teacup there on the table by him, and that's all I can remember about it. It was there, full or empty, I don't know."

Surely, Parry thought, if she'd poisoned him, she'd have jumped to it and said the cup was empty. Or was that too unsubtle for the very subtle Flik? "Very well, we'll have to skip that point. Just tell me what you said, what Marsh said, what you both did, and how long you were there."

"I called out, 'Oh, Marsh, is this my bottle of ruin on the sink?' And he said 'Uh-huh,' or 'Mh-hm.' Then I said, 'Well thanks, I'll be down later after I've poisoned our guests off.' " Flik bit her lip, and flushed. "How awful that sounds—those silly things one says without thinking. Anyway, I picked up the bottle, stuck it under my arm, called out good-by, and went. I shut the door behind me," she added.

"And you didn't go into the sitting room at all? You didn't actually see Marsh's face, and he didn't say more than 'Uh-huh' or 'Mh-hm' or a similar sort of noise?"

"Correct," Flik agreed. "I thought he was dozy, and didn't want to disturb him. If you're thinking it mightn't have been Marsh sitting in the chair, but someone else, then you're wrong. It was Marsh. He was bald, and he had an old scar on the top of his head in the middle of the bald patch."

Parry pursed up his lips and delivered what he thought was his bomb-shell. "Why did you throw gravel at Mrs. Vale's window either before you went into the pub, or after you came out of it?"

The bomb failed to explode. Flik stared at him in blank incomprehension which appeared to be perfectly genuine. "Gravel?" she repeated, as if she wasn't sure if she'd heard aright.

Parry jerked his head at Congreve.

Congreve said, "Yes, Mrs. Ashley. It's old Mrs. Vale again. I must say, 'er memory's what you might call tricky. Yesterday she said she saw you going into the pub as well as coming out of it, today she says that now she's quite sure on second thoughts, which according to 'er must really be the best ones, she only saw you going out. Oh, Lord, I spent what seemed hours with the old thing, and talk about talk. Anyways, she joggled up 'er memory like someone what's shaking a medicine bottle, and the next dose is that she says, now she comes to think it all over, she was snoozing by 'er fire Sunday afternoon when something wakes 'er up, and she says, what it was, on second thoughts, was someone chucking gravel at 'er window. So she gets up to see 'oo it is, and while she's looking out the window, you comes out the back door of the pub and goes round the corner and up the 'ill."

"But who threw the gravel?" Flik's eyes were saucers of astonishment. "There wasn't anyone there, and I certainly never threw any gravel. There wasn't any to throw."

"How d'you mean?" Parry asked. "None to throw?"

"It's all tarmac and mud at the back of the pub," Flik explained. "There simply isn't any gravel to throw. And there wasn't anyone there to throw it."

"Did you see Mrs. Vale staring at you out 'er window?" Congreve put in.

"No, I didn't; and I didn't because I never even looked across at Mrs. Vale's cottage."

Parry and Congreve looked at each other, into the minds of each coming the same, strange thought, the same question: Who, if it wasn't Flik, had armed themselves with gravel, picked up God knew where, hidden in the only hiding place, the gents' lavatory, and after they'd seen Flik go in the back door, drawn Mrs. Vale's attention to the fact by darting out, throwing gravel at her window, and then hiding in the lavatory again till Flik had gone, Mrs. Vale had finished her stare, and the coast was clear for them to depart? And why? In his mind's eye, Parry saw again the tiny slit of a window in the slaughterhouse, through which anyone could see who was coming down the road from the Shots Hall direction, and see them go in at the back door. He had cried for a clue, and here it was, and he didn't know in the least what it meant. Then he thought of Mrs. Vale's memory, which, as Congreve had put it so nicely, she joggled like someone shaking a medicine bottle, and his heart sank. The gravel might exist only in the imagination of Mrs. Vale; for Mrs. Vale, convinced she might herself be poisoned at any moment, was getting more and more imaginative. Only, Congreve had said, she'd been very definite about the gravel.

"Listen, Congreve?"

"Yes, sir?"

"I know it's dark, but you've got your flashlight. Go down to Mrs. Vale's, look around her front garden, and see if you can find any stray bits of gravel which might have bounced back from her window. You'd better tell the old girl you're there, else she'll have fits thinking it's the murderer come for her. And Congreve? When you've done that, drop in at the pub and keep your ears open. If I don't see you down there before Norton relieves you, then leave a report with him, and any gravel you may find."

"Yes, sir. Am I allowed, in the course of my duty, to 'ave a drink?"

"I'd be very surprised if you didn't," Parry grinned.

"Sorry." Flik stood up. "I was forgetting—I'll give you a drink now, Congreve."

"That's very nice of you, I'm sure," Congreve thanked her, "but if I don't get along to Mrs. Vale's now, I'll be fogbound. Honest, the notion of being fogbound along with Mrs. Vale makes me feel queer—like being stuck in a rowboat in the Atlantic with a radio playing the same tune over and over again, and you can't turn the rud— the thing off."

Congreve went, and Flik drew the curtains across the drawing-room window. She didn't press the subject of drinks, and Parry knew that she wasn't going to risk him refusing to drink with her as well. In a few minutes he'd damn well ask her for one. He wasn't there with a warrant for her arrest in his pocket. If only she'd come across with whatever it was that was on her mind, that was nothing to do with the poisoning of either Molly or Marsh. But she wouldn't. He watched her as she went into the hall, listened to her light footsteps as she went from window to window drawing the curtains. He waited for her to come back, and when she didn't, strolled into the hall. She had changed her high-heeled shoes for gum boots, and was putting on an overcoat.

"Hullo?" he said, surprised.

Her hands dropped to her sides. "I'm sorry. I thought you'd done with me."

"Where're you going to?" Parry tried to make the question sound light.

"I was going to work on my rock," she said. "That's all."

"I thought you did that after dinner always?"

"You forget," Flik answered a little bitterly, "that our routine has at last been disorganized. If it hadn't happened in such a horrible way, I'd say, thank God. D'you wish me not to go out?"

If he said he didn't wish her to go out and went on with his probings and questionings, she might crack. Then he looked at her again and knew that she would do nothing of the sort. There was in her some quality of strength which was not the usual strength of hardness. Hers was of pure nylon. For the greatest strength was only in the finest and the best, the purest; soft, light, but enduring.

He picked up her right hand and turned it round and round in his, curiously. It was so slim and tapered. There seemed, looking at it, no strength in it at all.

"How on earth d'you hack at the bloody great hard rock with those?" he asked.

"I just hack," she said, as he dropped her hand again

"Well, go and hack. Perhaps your aunt wouldn't mind talking to me for a bit."

He went with her to the door, opened it, and held it open as she walked past him, her torch turned on, its beam hardly piercing the mist and the darkness. There was someone else out in the drive. Parry let the door bang behind him, and followed her to investigate. It was Abbot.

"To hell with Marsala," he said to Flik as she stopped for a moment.

She began to laugh. "Not the '70, surely? Aunt Bee's the limit. D'you feel bad?"

"Bloody awful."

Still laughing, Flik went on her way to the mermaid.

"Now what do you want?" Abbot said to Parry as Parry turned his torch on him.

"God, man, how long've you been out here? You're dripping with fog."

"I've been out here for, I should say, at least half an hour, and I still feel as if my head was splitting. God and his holy angels put a curse on Marsala, Madeira and all their brothers and sisters. Buzz-buzz-buzz."

"Is that what your head's doing?" Parry inquired.

"Yes and no. Listen to her. She was machining when I arrived an hour ago, she's been doing it ever since. She never stops. May her curtain rings drop off and her frills shrivel. May the rods come down on her head and bash it in— I won't say bash her brains in, as she can't have any."

Parry listened, heard the cause of Abbot's rage, and realized that he had heard it himself when he and Congreve arrived. Miss Merridew's activities reminded him that after he had had a talk with Bee Chattock, Miss Merridew was on his schedule. He wondered when, if ever, he would get anything to eat that night.

Abbot began to stumble up and down the drive, and Parry automatically stumbled with him. Between the two men, so utterly dissimilar in every way, a lopsided friendship had sprung up, a mutual liking tempered with, on Abbot's part, a quite violent resentment of Parry's mere existence on the face of the earth.

Abbot began his mutterings again. "Of all the sins of the devil, domesticity is the worst. There ought to be a law against it."

Parry, delighted by Abbot's flights of fancy, said what would men do if women refused to be domestic? "How'd you like it, if you had a wife, and she refused to provide you with food or mend your socks or look after the little ones?"

"I haven't got a wife, and I shan't ever have a wife. But if I had, and I had to watch her sitting there, her tongue firmly clenched between her teeth, year in year out, surrounded by yards of mending wool, knitting wool, needles, thread, pins and foully diseased paper patterns, being domestic, I'd kill her. I've seen some of my patients, and the wives of other of my patients— How are you today, my dear Mrs. Bloggs? Purl one, pick up two, drop three, excuse me—I'm very—baby darling, don't eat that pin—I'm very—pick up ten, knit six together, plain one, drop one, purl one—one, two, three, four, five, six, this is my husband, seven, eight, nine—now I must go and see if the butcher sent the meat. That's domesticity, Parry. Obscene. And when they're knitting little garments, looking coy and girlish, or proud and blatant—" Words, for the time being, failed the maddened and rather tipsy Abbot, who didn't possess Bee's well-trained head for vintage wines.

"Well then," Parry suggested, "if you had a wife, I suppose you'd expect her to be purely ornamental? Wouldn't that be a trifle disappointing when she got older and wasn't ornamental any longer?"

"It wouldn't in the least," Abbot said more reasonably. "Because she'd be intelligent as well. She'd be so intelligent I'd never know she was any older. She'd be amusing and entertaining—"

"And she'd smell nice, and she'd be warm and understanding, and she'd make love to you, and flatter you, and she'd be secret and exciting,

and she'd have soft hands that caressed your weary brow—and sometimes she'd fight with you and pull your hair out by the roots, and put it
back again, and make you jealous, then comfort you—when you wanted
to talk, she'd talk with you and entertain you, when you didn't want to,
she'd be as silent as velvet—she'd be as deep as a well, but as pure as well
water, a stormy sea that could calm down to the unruffled surface of a
mountain lake. And of course, from time to time, her defenses'd break
down, and she'd be all yours, and you'd feel most exceedingly strong and
masterful—"

"Who the hell're you talking about?"

"I thought perhaps you were in love?" Parry was now as delighted
with his own flights of fancy as he'd been with Abbot's. Especially as he
hadn't been down in the wine cellar, and Abbot had. "Aren't we all?"

"What?" Abbot was suddenly appallingly sober.

Parry, lighthearted for the first time for nearly three days, shone his
torch on his watch. "What with one thing and another, we've been out
here for damn nearly half an hour. Or rather, you've been out for nearly
an hour to my nearly half."

"At my age," Abbot said with self-loathing, "that's a calamity. I'll
probably get pneumonia. That'd be too bad. Some unfortunate'd have to
queue up at the registrar's office for my death certificate and get pneumonia himself. Poetic justice. The patients I haven't killed off in my lifetime
I'll kill off after I'm dead:"

"If you aren't going home, then in hell's name come inside out of this
miserable dump of wet and darkness. D'you know Clive Harris, the young
man with one leg who's in love with Flik?"

"Clive Harris?" Abbot paused in his way up to the door. He spoke
almost roughly. "Why should I know him? I've heard of him, that's all.
Farms over the other side of Pelsey. What else about him?"

"Nothing much. I wondered if you'd ever attended him. He once took
morphine."

Abbot made an impatient noise in his throat, and opened the door,
fumbling. "Come in, can't you?"

"I'll just get some of the mud off my shoes. Go in yourself." Parry
began kicking his feet on the step. The door swung shut in his face. He
whipped round, and ran lightly down the drive and into the road, past
Molly's dreary, empty cottage. Through the mist, Miss Merridew's lighted
sitting-room window, thinly curtained with its new pair of curtains, the
only relief in the darkness, the droning of her machine the only noise.

Parry tried the door of Flik's shanty, and he felt a glow of relief. She really was working, then. But he did not feel quite so pleased when he pushed the door open and saw her sitting on the mermaid's tail, her hands idle, her coat still on, her gum boots muddied. She looked up at him, calm, cool.

"Time I went home," she said, "and started mucking something up for dinner."

"Yes," he agreed. "I think it is."

CHAPTER 16

FLIK was in the kitchen, doing her mucking up for dinner. Unashamed, Abbot slept off the last fumes of the Marsala in a chair by the hall fire.

Down in the pub, Congreve made a tidy little parcel of a few bits of gravel, put it in a large envelope along with his report to Parry, and waited for Norton to relieve him. While he waited, he leaned on the bar in the public bar, drinking beer and listening. The place was crowded, and everyone was holding forth about Molly and old Marsh. After he had listened to the theories everyone propounded to him, he shifted himself to the saloon bar, an even gloomier apartment. Here he found the Ambroses, mellowed by two whiskies apiece. They greeted him without rancor and insisted on ordering him another pint. Phil had perked up, and there were no signs of the earlier tears. She was full of Muffin and the kittens, which, she said, were very weakly.

"Personally," Tim said, "I think they ought to be put down." He ordered two more whiskies and another pint for Congreve. He was getting rather wildly talkative, as he had already had a very large whisky before he had left home. "I don't mean drown the poor little bastards in a bucket of water, as that's a lousy way of putting anything down. Just shove some dope into them. You know, open their mouths, and shove some dope in. Like I did Flik's old cat, you know, the white one that went blind—if you don't want your drink, Phil, honey, I'll have it."

All ears and eyes, Congreve ordered another round of drinks and made Tim's a large one. At all costs he must get him back to the subject of putting Flik's cat down. "I always thinks it'd be far kinder to put 'em down when they're past it. Only I don't like the idea of shooting 'em, which's the kindest. So messy. A dose of something's the best, like what you said. The vet generally 'as something 'andy."

"Only the vet isn't always handy," Tim nodded owlishly. He had rather a weak head for drink. "There's only one vet for miles round here, so I said to Flik, 'I'll do the deed for you, old girl.' "

This, Congreve decided, was almost too good to be true. "That's right," he said soothingly. "I always, says, that ain't no job for a lady. That's a man's job, that is."

"'Sright. So I wrapped the tablets Camilla gave Flik up in a bit of juicy meat, and I said, puss puss, lovely, and shoved it down her gullet, and the old girl went off to sleep and never woke up."

"Fancy?" murmured the gratified Congreve, and was sorry to see that Phil was kicking Tim in the shins, and that Tim was scarlet, at last realizing that he had been plunging about with both feet in it.

"Medinal," Phil babbled, incoherent with embarrassment. "Medinal sleeping tablets."

"Sure, sure, that's right. Medinal—I couldn't think of the name. Same again, landlord, or whatever the hell you are. Does anyone know when the draw's going to be? Phil, honey, when's the draw going to be? You know, Congreve—" the unhappy Tim stammered. "The Christmas savings club business, that we buy stamps for—this week we can get our last stamp to fill up the what-d'you-call'ems cards, you know. Then there's a draw, and everyone gets their dough back, and a bit more, and the lucky ones get a sort of extra bonus—you know, for Christmas. If you default, you know, don't buy your full quota, then all you get's your money back. Oh, hullo, Belairs? What's yours? Where's that bloody brewery man got to?"

Congreve, in the ensuing muddle of calling for drinks, escaped, and made his way by devious routes to the kitchen at the back. There he opened the envelope he had addressed to Parry, and tearing a leaf from his notebook, wrote an accurate account of Tim's conversational efforts. As an N.B., he wrote, "Of course, it might really have been Medinal." Then he did his package up again, and proceeded to wait for Norton to relieve him. He knew that if he rejoined the Ambrose party they would shut up like clams.

Sitting on the kitchen table, he suddenly realized that behind the shut door of old Marsh's sitting room there was company. He held his head on one side and listened. There were female giggles and a male voice. Though he was unable to hear what they were saying, as the door was old and thick, he recognized the too fruity tones of Arnoldson, who must have arrived back from the wild-goose chase. Unashamed, Congreve put first his eye, then his ear to the keyhole. Unfortunately the key was in the lock. While he debated his next move, he reviewed Arnoldson impartially in his mind. That man, he thought, didn't ought to be in any police force anywhere. Snake in the grass. All politeness to Mahew and Parry, and behind their backs he'd jeered at them. Now he was in there carrying on with, presumably, Winnie.

Congreve pulled down his tunic, assumed a face like a block of wood, knocked and walked right in. Arnoldson stood in front of the fire, refreshing himself with a large whisky, warming the seat of his pants. It was quite evident, by the way that Winnie was dithering about, that she had just jumped away from the fire. She was red in the face, and writhing with silly giggles. She was only sixteen and a half.

Father's death, thought Congreve, had not much upset her. True, she had on a fancy black dress, but she hadn't left out the lipstick—slightly smeared—nor the dried-blood-colored nail varnish.

"Well, Congreve?" Arnoldson wiped his mouth on a large, white handkerchief, and looked superior.

"I only wondered," Congreve said in a humble voice, "if you 'ad any further orders for me before I go off duty."

"I don't think so. No. Anything to report?"

He was playing to the gallery. The gallery consisting of the still writhing, giggling Winnie.

"No, I don't think so." Congreve looked earnest and vacant.

"Old mother Mahew gone home to his old woman? I suppose Parry's basking in the sunshine of Shots Hall? These dudes from the Yard know which side the bread's buttered."

Blimey, Congreve thought. Arnoldson was plastered. He caught sight of a whisky bottle pushed under the table. Winnie began to pat her hair into place and Congreve retired to the kitchen.

In due course Norton appeared, sweating and out of breath after his uphill ride.

"Anything new?" he asked Congreve.

"Not as you might say. Unless you count Arnoldson getting tight in there with Winnie. She's asking for trouble, that's what she is. Not but what Arnoldson ain't asking for trouble too."

"He shouldn't ought to drink on duty," Norton said disapprovingly. "Where's Inspector Parry?"

"Up at the 'All." Congreve buttoned himself into his overcoat and switched on his torch. "Give this 'ere envelope to Mr. Parry, will you? 'E'll be down soon, I expect. I'll be off now. I won't be low and wish you 'appy dreams and sweet repose."

While Norton listened to the exchange of pleasantries between Arnoldson and Winnie down at the pub, Parry labored with his attack on Bee. As an attack, it was a hopeless failure from the start. He felt like a one-man army laying siege to a fully garrisoned fortress bristling with guns.

"I haven't the slightest intention," Bee said, as cool as a cucumber, "of discussing Mac Ashley, Flik's husband. He's one of the subjects one doesn't discuss, like lavatories."

"But at least," Parry said, "you can tell me if he's dead or alive. I ask you in preference to Flik simply because I feel it'd be less painful for you to talk about him than her."

"Very well. Mac Ashley's alive. But you can't blame the murders on him. He happens to be in prison. Now are you satisfied?"

Parry was not only satisfied but amazed. "Good God, not that Ashley? Was that swine her husband? The chap who got six years last year for being tight in charge of a car, running it onto the pavement, killing two women and a kid, and then half killing the constable who tried to arrest him?"

"I'm gratified," Bee said maliciously, "that you're capable of showing some slight emotion."

"But his name was Simon Ashley "

"We always called him Mac, I don't know why. Damn your curiosity."

Rather shaken, Parry levered himself out of his chair and wandered into the hall. He kept thinking of Flik's letters to Molly about the man who was now doing a stretch which, he thought, wasn't half long enough. Then he thought, is this the secret they've been trying to hide? It can't be. There's no disgrace as far's Flik's concerned. He looked up. Flik was standing by the fire, leaning over the sleeping Abbot, a curious expression on her face. She hadn't seen Parry; she was absorbed in the contemplation of Abbot. All Parry could see of the doctor was his long legs, relaxed in front of him, for the big chair hid the rest of him. He stood quite still, and presently Flik straightened herself and went quietly back to her cooking, still without noticing him. Parry tiptoed to the fire, and also bent over Abbot and stared, trying to imagine why she had been so strangely absorbed. He couldn't place the expression on her face at all. Abbot had taken his glasses off. In sleep, he still looked angry, but the bitterness and irony had gone from the anger. Without his glasses he seemed ten years younger. He looked, in fact, the age Parry knew him to be. Having a flair for women, he decided that this was what must have intrigued Flik; and the fact that Abbot possessed, now that they were revealed, very thick black eyelashes which looked soft.

Queer, odd Flik, Parry thought. He went back into the drawing room.

"D'you think Miss Merridew'd be busy now if I go over to see her?" he asked Bee.

"What you mean is, do I think she'll be just going to have dinner and offer you some? I don't think anything of the sort. She has some disgusting supper of snippets and tidbits at a quarter past seven, or thereabouts. D'you want me to ask you to dine?"

"I'd love you to. But I'm afraid I'll have to be a little gent and share some revolting garbage out of a can down at the pub with Arnoldson and Norton."

"I wish you luck. And don't worry poor Susan too much if you can help it."

As Parry was putting on his overcoat, Flik appeared at the door of the kitchen quarters. Most women, he was aware, when they were in the middle of cooking, looked like it. They were either half hidden by an apron, or rather aggressively—as much as to say, look how hard I work—they wielded some implement of their toil: a dish mop, a cloth, a large, dripping spoon. But Flik showed no signs that she had ever been near a kitchen in her life. He almost woke Abbot up, just to show her to him.

"Going?" she asked.

"I'm going to pester your poor Susan," Parry explained. "I'll try not to upset her:'

Flik half opened her mouth, then shut it again and said nothing.

"By the way—" He turned back from the door, his hand on the knob. "You used to go down to the pub and play cards with old Marsh, didn't you?"

"Yes."

Parry tried a direct attack. "Why?"

"Why?" Flik repeated, surprised.

"Yes. Why?"

"He liked playing cards. He was lonely after his wife died eight years ago. Winnie wasn't any good to him. There was a two-handed patience he liked playing, and none of the villagers seemed to be able to cope with it but me."

"D'you count yourself as one of the villagers?"

Flik laughed softly—softly, Parry knew, so as not to wake Abbot up. "Yes, of course. I live in the village, don't I?"

"I suppose you do. Play for high stakes?"

"Terribly high." Her smile was mocking. "I was thousands in his debt. There's your motive for you. I suppose you're looking for a motive?"

"To hell with you." Unreasonably peevish, Parry let himself out, and, preceded by the thin light of his torch, weaved his way between puddles to Miss Merridew's gate. Like Molly's, it was a wicket gate, only much neater. The short, flagged path to her door was innocent of even the smallest weed. Everything tidy, well ordered, well kept. He looked for a bell, found none, and knocked with his knuckles on the white door.

The door opened a crack, and he saw that it was on a chain.

"Who's that?" Miss Merridew was evidently taking no chances.

"It's me, Miss Merridew. Only Inspector Parry. Might I come in and warm myself up?"

Thus disarmed, Miss Merridew let him in, bobbing round him like a little, friendly poodle.

"Oh, dear, yes! Do come in—poor man, such a horrid night. So muddy and damp and horrid, isn't it? Now, if only I hadn't finished my supper— I wonder if I could find you anything? I eat so little, really, that there never is. Now, when my dear father, was alive, there always was—do come in. In here. This is my drawing room. Really it's a living room. When there isn't a dining room, then it's a living room, isn't it? Not a drawing room, as there's nothing to withdraw from but the kitchen."

Holy Moses, thought Parry, shall I ever get any sense out of her?

Contrary to his expectations, the room wasn't cluttered up with dozens of faded family photographs in fancy frames, useless knickknacks, whatnots and a hundred horrid little ornaments and pictures. True, there wasn't much room to move, but this was simply because the room was so small the necessary furniture would only just fit into it. Otherwise, Miss Merridew's taste was excellent. A bright fire burned in the duck's nest grate that had been imported into the comparatively modern cottage. The sensible walnut dining table was bare of a cloth, and spread in orderly array were an old-fashioned writing case, some papers, account books, an inkstand and a pen.

"I'm afraid I interrupted you? You were busy?"

"I'm only too glad to be interrupted!" Miss Merridew cried. "I was getting in such a muddle, I really didn't know how I was going to get out of it."

"You don't look as if you could ever be in a muddle about anything," Parry complimented her tactfully. "When I'm writing, I strew the whole place up."

"Muddle in my mind. The accounts you see, Mr. Barry, the Vicar's indisposed—flu. So I'm trying to—you see, he does the accounts part of it all, and I do the collecting—I just can't remember who's had what. I've got an idea that Mr. Fewsey—he's our butcher, such a nuisance, isn't it?—hasn't bought any savings stamps for three weeks, only I'm not sure if it's him or Mrs. Sharpe."

Miss Merridew gazed up at him with doggy eyes, as if he could both disentangle what she was talking about and her accounts at the same time. Light dawned on him slowly.

"I see what you mean. The Christmas savings club stamps? Well, why not just ask them? Mr. Fewsey and Mrs. Sharpe, that is?"

"I never thought," Miss Merridew pondered. "How clever of you to think. Of course I could do that, couldn't I? You see, the vicar went to bed today. I got a message from his wife. I must say, I thought his sermon a little disappointing yesterday, and that's what it must have been."

Parry, thinking of Congreve's remarks about yesterday's sermon, nearly laughed. .

"I'm almost sure, though," Miss Merridew went on, "that Mrs. Sharpe is up to date with her stamps. Because I seem to remember her saying something about, 'Well, that's nearly that, isn't it, Miss Merridew?' Such a nice woman. Last year she drew the goose. And this year—"

She began to show symptoms of tears.

"Might I sit down?" Parry asked hurriedly. "This is very cozy compared to the hall at Shots Hall, isn't it?"

"Dear Bee and Flik—" Miss Merridew's mind appeared to have wandered from her accounts. "What would one do without them? I will say that hall is rather drafty, but still, very dignified."

"Most." If I ever get a fit of hysteria, Parry decided, it'll be right now. "It must be very cold for Flik working down in that stone hut of hers every night?"

"I always say, 'Flik, one day you'll get pneumonia. Is it worth it?' "

"Nothing," Parry said sententiously, "is worth it, is it? Does it worry you to hear her hammering and hacking away, Miss Merridew?"

"Indeed, no. I'm so used to it. It only worries me to think of her there all alone in the cold, poor darling. And it must be so tiring."

"Now, for instance—" Parry's mouth, opened in speech, remained open.

Inspiration is a staggering thing: the sudden parting of the clouds that shows the clear sky beyond. So, too, rather staggering, is the sound of someone stumbling past in the road gurgling incoherent cries of horror.

"What's that?" Miss Merridew exclaimed, her eyes nearly starting from her head. "Oh, Mr. Parry—" she got it right at last—"Oh, what's that?"

"Don't worry—someone drunk, probably. I'll just go and see. Everything's quite all right. Stay here, and I'll be back and tell you, and we'll go on with our pleasant talk."

Parry shot out of the door, down the path and out of the gate, and didn't realize, till he was in the road, fumbling with his torch, that Miss Merridew was clinging to the hem of his coat. He stopped for a moment, to try and shake her off, but she wouldn't be shaken. His torch wavered between her and the figure that stumbled in at the drive of Shots Hall. Miss Merridew clung. Parry ran. He caught up with the creature that was crying its animal cries just as it fell over the doorstep of the Chattock ancestral home.

"What the hell's wrong now?" he asked. "Be quiet, can't you?"

"I won't—I won't! It's happened again—Harry—dead." Gwen's face was twisted in pure, stark fear. "Harry—dead—sick all over the place— sick—and blood—oh, God!"

Miss Merridew began to scream.

The foggy night, so unpleasantly silent before, was now dreadfully filled with the noises of human terror.

CHAPTER 17

ABBOT, accustomed to waking quickly and at once, sat up, fumbled for his glasses and listened. Muffled by the thick walls and the heavy door, Gwen's and Miss Merridew's screams were still recognizable as those of fright.

Damn it all, now what?

"What's happened?"

Simultaneously, Flik came through the door from the kitchen, and Bee out of the drawing room. Abbot staggered to his feet, shaking off the last dregs of sleep and Marsala, and opened the front door. Like a kind of football scrum, Parry, Gwen and Miss Merridew fell in on him, Parry still trying to shake Miss Merridew off.

"For heaven's sake, Miss Hunter, take it easy and try to tell us what's wrong," Parry fumed, grabbing Gwen's arm and shaking her. "Now then, what's all this about Harry?"

"Oh!" wailed Miss Merridew. "Oh, oh!"

"I told you!" Gwen moaned, a little more calmly. "Harry—dead— sick all over the place, and blood—in his cottage."

"Blood—?" echoed Miss Merridew, clinging to Parry. "Blood—? *Blood?*"

"Be quiet, Susan." Bee detached Miss Merridew from Parry and tried to pacify her. "Don't make such a goddamn row. Gwen, be coherent, if you're capable of it."

Parry glanced sharply at Flik. Her face was the color of chalk, her mouth a straight, appalled line.

He said to Gwen, "What did you go to Harry's cottage for?"

"He'd promised me some herbs—some herbs. He promised them to me, so I went to get them."

"In the pitch dark?"

Flik was putting on her overcoat and her gum boots. Miss Merridew broke away from Bee, and attached herself again to Parry. Aggravated beyond words, he almost flung her away from him, then pushed Gwen backward into the hall, and made a bolt for it. Abbot, quick to think as to move, was already groping in his car for his bag.

"Come on," he said. "He mayn't be dead. Damn these women. Which way? Any good taking the car?"

"No—muddy lane. Got your doings?"

They began to run. Too late, Parry found that Flik was running beside him, and that Gwen and Miss Merridew were hot on his tracks, still wailing. There wasn't time to stop and send them all back. As Abbot had said, Harry mightn't be dead. In which case, every second counted.

"Go back," he however said to Flik as he ran. "And take those two with you."

"I'm coming. Don't waste time—give me your torch. I know the way better than you."

They turned right, off the road, past Miss Merridew's cottage, up the filthiest lane Parry had ever seen. The mist lay in wisps across their path. One moment the darkness was clear, the next a blanket. Their feet slipped and stumbled, the mud coming to their ankles.

"Hell, what a lane," Abbot swore. "The devil and all his devils take it—"

A faint light shone from Harry's open door. Gwen hadn't waited to shut it. Furious, Parry knew that any footprints there might be would be obscured by the tramplings of his companions, all of them except Abbot unwanted.

"Stay outside," he ordered Flik. "And keep those two out."

It was no use. They crowded in after him, though Flik did try to stop Gwen and Miss Merridew in the doorway. Her efforts were fruitless. Gwen, seeing Harry for the second time, burst forth into renewed yowls, while Miss Merridew stood there and shrieked. And even Parry and Abbot, used to nasty sights, were shocked.

Harry lay on the floor on his front, his face twisted round so that they could see one side of it. When Gwen had screamed about sick and blood, she had not exaggerated. But Harry's face, oddly enough, though it was a dreadful color, and contorted almost out of recognition, had a strange look of content on it the face of a man who'd done his damnedest not only in life, but in dying.

Then Gwen gave a gurgling cry, and Miss Merridew shrieked louder than ever.

"Get them away from here, Flik." Parry turned on her, authoritative, insisting on being obeyed. "Take them back to your house and keep them there. There's nothing you can do. He's gone."

"Yes."

Her eyes were black, turned inward, searching again. Very quickly, she pushed him on one side, and before he could stop her, whipped open the drawer in the deal kitchen table. For a long moment she stared down into it, then shut it again and turned away.

"Come, Susan—Gwen, come along—got your torch?" This time they allowed themselves to be led away. Parry called after Flik, "Please phone the pub at once and tell Arnoldson or Norton to come up here—or both of them."

"Yes."

Parry shut the door, shutting them out in the mud and the mist and the night; shutting them, for the time being, out of the front of his mind.

"Is this another poisoning, Abbot?"

"You know damn well I won't give loose opinions till I've done a postmortem," Abbot said. He bent over Harry, looking into his eyes, feeling him. "It looks to me, for your information only, that the cause of death was a seizure brought on by this appalling vomiting. The effort must have driven all the blood to his head and he burst a vessel. That's what it looks like. I won't say that's what it was."

"And the blood?"

"Maybe from the stomach. Maybe he burst a blood vessel in the throat, to put it in simple language for laymen. I'd say he's been dead the best part of a couple of hours, but I can't vouch for that now. His pupils are slightly contracted too."

"Look at this." Parry jerked his thumb at the table. "That's a queer lot. An empty teacup—a mug, a jug of water, and a packet of salt.'"

"And what," Abbot asked, "does that suggest to you?"

"It suggests that someone put something in Harry's tea, that he noticed it tasted queer after he'd drunk it, so he took an emetic, just in case. Do I take it the same idea suggests itself to you?"

Abbot picked up the teacup, stared inside it, then dipped his forefinger in the dregs and sucked it. "Not sugary, and a bitter taste." He put down the cup—Parry saw with approval that he'd handled it with his handkerchief—and picked up the mug. "This is pure salt and water by the taste of it, and more salt than water. I'll have to take samples of all this for analysis. Mind if I turn the old man over?"

"No. Go ahead."

Parry's agile mind darted here and there as his eyes ranged the small, bare room. He kept seeing a picture of Flik sitting on the mermaid's tail, in her overcoat and her muddied gum boots, doing nothing. In his ears he heard Miss Merridew's horrified echo, "Blood? Blood?" Blood, as if she couldn't believe her ears. Small details, scraps, superimposed themselves on more details and scraps. He opened the drawer in the table, and, just as Flik had done, stared down into it.

"Parry?"

"Yes?"

"Harry had some sort of growth in his innards. Look at this swelling. Wonder if he knew he had something fatal, took a dose of something and then thought better of it?"

"I don't think so. Do you?"

"No, I don't, to be candid. I'm not a policeman, but I somehow don't think so. It's a bloody queer business."

"Bloody queer."

There was a squelching of feet in the mud outside, and the door opened. To Abbot, sensitive and alert, there was something repulsive about Arnoldson's face as the pale lamplight shone on it. If anything so pink, moist and fleshy could be vulturine, then it was vulturine. He's seeing the rope round Flik's neck, Abbot stormed inwardly.

Flik, too, as she calmed Gwen and Miss Merridew with strong tea at Shots Hall, saw, in her mind's eye, the loop of a rope, felt its strands touching her skin.

"Flik?" Bee said imperatively. "Have some whisky at once. You look dreadful."

"It was dreadful, dreadful!" Miss Merridew cried. "Too dreadful."

Gwen, now considerably calmed down, her fear replaced by excitement and a sense of importance—for wasn't it she who'd found Harry?—

said, "I could do with a quick one too, thanks, Bee."

"I didn't ask you," Bee said. "So there's nothing to thank me for. Far be it from me, however, not to take a hint. Flik, give Gwen some of the whisky out of the remains of the other bottle."

"Why?" Gwen sulked. "What other bottle? Have you two bottles, one with poison and one without?"

"Your shockingly bad taste," Bee said in an icy voice, "is no more than I'd expect."

"Oh, Gwen," Miss Merridew sniffled, "how can you say such a thing at a time like this? Such a horrid thing to say—poor Flik."

Flik, silent, cold, gave Gwen a drink, not from the other bottle, which had whisky from the pub in it, but from a bottle of prewar whisky, which was running very low. Then she helped herself, and, still silent, poured a drink out for Bee.

The clanging of an ambulance bell filtered into the hall, at first far away, then close, then passing. Miss Merridew burst into a fresh outbreak of tears, and Gwen downed her whisky, looking defiant.

"I'd like to know," she said, "when you went to see Harry last, Flik?"

"Would you?" Flik had never liked Gwen. She liked her less now.

"Be quiet, Gwen," Bee snapped. "If Parry hadn't told Flik she was to keep you here, I'd throw you out. If you're going to soak up my whisky, then kindly keep a civil tongue in your head, damn you."

"Sorry," Gwen muttered. "Sorry, Flik. I'm upset—I feel a bit faint."

Flik took the hint and gave her another whisky, a very small one. The ambulance bell sounded again, passed, died away. They'd taken all that there was of Harry. There was something else she ought to think of, but she seemed drained of further coherent thought. She opened the hall door and, as she shut it behind her, ran into a broad back. A torch snicked on, and her heart missed a beat.

"Norton."

"Yes, Mrs. Ashley? Anything I can do?" He sounded profoundly uncomfortable, which, indeed, he was.

"No, thank you. Did you want to see me, or my aunt?"

"No—no, thank you, miss—Mrs. Ashley. It was only Arnoldson said to stay up here in case—well, in case any of you ladies felt scared, if you see what I mean?"

"I see what you mean perfectly, thanks. Mr. Arnoldson needn't be afraid we'll run away, not on a night like this. It's so foggy. Not a night for running anywhere." Flik was just going back indoors, when she heard feet coming up the drive. One pair. Parry? It wasn't Parry but Abbot.

He saw her in the light of Norton's torch, and Norton, disgusted with his job, tactfully began to stamp up and down, as if to warm himself, with each stamp getting a little further away from the house. He hadn't been told to ruddy well eavesdrop. Abbot opened the door of his car and got in, leaving the door open.

"Abbot?" Flik crept in beside him, suddenly thankful for his gaunt presence. His shoulder against hers was hard. She had the queer fancy that under his flesh his bones were fine and long. "Harry? What killed him, poor old boy?"

Abbot's voice was low. "They've taken him away, and the—well, the necessary. I seem to've had enough sleep to get along with for a bit, so I'm starting on the postmortem straightway. Then I'll tell you. Parry's going to get the inquests on the other two postponed again, so you won't be hauled up before the coroner to give evidence yet."

"Does he know anything? I mean, doesn't he have any idea yet who did it?"

"I don't know. He's suddenly closed up like a clam. Flik?" His shoulder moved with a jerk. "For God's sake, if there's anything you know, or want to tell, tell me. If I knew, then I could really help you."

"There's—nothing. And why should you help me?"

"You bloody little fool." He pushed her out of the car. "Why?" He started the engine, and the car roared backward, savagely driven, down the drive into the road. Then it was gone.

Flik opened the door, muttering to herself, "Let us join the ladies."

The ladies, however, weren't to remain long in peace, if the silence of the hall, with its dark corners and drafts could be called peace. In five minutes Parry arrived, Arnoldson behind him. Parry had read Congreve's reports and inspected the few bits of gravel, for Norton, tactlessly displaying the package, had had it taken away from him by his superior, who, in turn, had given it to Parry while they were up in Harry's cottage. Now Parry's theory, which had blossomed so unexpectedly, was somewhat shaken, but he showed none of this in his face. At the sight of him, Miss Merridew began to cry again, only not so loudly. At the sight of Arnoldson, Gwen, freshened by her two drinks, began to wriggle about on the sofa.

"Well, Parry?" Bee raised her dignified eyebrows in question.

"Did either you or Fl—Mrs. Ashley know if Harry suffered from some form of internal growth?"

The two women stared at him, then at the door. For from outside came a confusion of voices, male and female.

"Now what?" Bee said. "A deputation? A lynching party? What's going on, Parry? Are the vigilantes out?"

"I've no idea." Parry seemed just as surprised. "Arnoldson, go and see."

Arnoldson, however, had no opportunity, for the door opened without ceremony and the Ambroses, both pretty well pickled, Captain Belairs, who gave rather the same impression, and Camilla, very sober, made a concerted entrance, almost forcibly herded in by the captain, who looked triumphant.

"What the hell d'you all want?" Bee demanded. "Get out. Phil, you've no business to drink so much when you're going to have a baby."

"What?" Phil's voice was shrill. "How d'you know? I never told you. Tim, d'you tell her, you slob?"

"No, he didn't. But it's quite obvious. And you're taking it very badly, Phil. I pity Tim, you must be making life hell for him."

"I like that!" Phil squealed. "When he's practically living in Camilla's pocket!"

"But that's so much better, honey," Camilla pointed out, "than if he was practically living in my bed." She smiled at Parry, and he thought how nice she looked. She had on a dark brown corduroy suit made rather like battle dress, and, he noticed with amusement, a pair of old American army gaiters some admirer had no doubt parted with with the greatest pleasure. "Besides, sweetie," she went on to Phil, "I've laid off Tim. I think he's a little dull, to tell you the truth. I've fallen, temporarily, for Lane, haven't I, honey?"

This rather embarrassing overstatement was mercifully drowned by a flood of speech from Captain Belairs, who was extremely angry that Camilla had stolen his thunder, ruined his entrance, and taken his mind off the job in hand.

"I brought these people up," he shouted at Parry, "because they're trying to withhold evidence from you."

"Don't shout," Bee said. "Gwen, stop that wriggling about. You aren't a four-weeks-old puppy."

Jees Murphy, Parry wondered, were all these villagers like this all the time? If so, no one could say that country life lacked variety. "Well, Captain Belairs?"

"Don't take any notice of him," Tim jabbered, swaying a little. "He's a bloody old busybody. Listening, that's what he was doing. Eavesdropping, and so on. Even when I was on the phone the bl—"

Miss Merridew took her crumpled handkerchief away from her nose.

"How can you use such language? And Camilla saying such things—in front of poor Bee and Flik when—"

"Miss Merridew? Please," Parry remonstrated.

"I insist on being taken notice of," Captain Belairs declared, thumping a table with his fist. "If no one else'll do his duty, then I will."

"Hear, hear," Gwen chimed in, hoping to curry favor with someone or other, preferably Arnoldson.

"Don't all speak at once," Parry said with patience he didn't feel. "If anyone's got any statement to make, will they please make it singly, and one by one? Mrs. Ambrose? Have you anything to say?"

Phil took no notice. She was comforting Tim because Camilla'd said he was dull. True, her comforting was not very original. "There, Tim, my pet. There, there, my pet. There, there, Tim, my pet."

Parry, driven to the point which was nearly beyond endurance, looked across at Flik. Silent, serene, lovely, she contemplated Phil and Tim as a mother might contemplate her two children who, having fought, were kissing and being friends again. She's quite, quite incomprehensible, Parry thought.

"Squadron Leader Ambrose?" he prompted.

"Go t'hell. Phil, darling, you don't look fat a bit—"

"Inspector? If you would kindly listen to me. If I might take up but two minutes of your no doubt valuable time?"

"Yes, Captain Belairs? I understand you've been listening to other people's conversations. Well?"

Camilla sat down on the arm of Bee's chair, admirable in her calm and assurance. "Don't listen to him, honey," she smiled up at Parry. "He'll only run off the rails and tell you about Poona. I'll tell you, and it's all my fault— Quite unintentionally I told you a lie. You won't believe that, but still—a couple of years ago, at least, about then, Flik rang me up about her cat. She was an old white one. She'd gone pretty nearly blind, and besides that, she had something in her innards that hurt her. Flik couldn't get the vet. One never can get the local vet when one wants him—honestly, never. Flik wanted to know if I'd anything to put her to sleep with— I said I hadn't. And then I remembered I'd got some Medinal. Five grains each tablet. Tim came over and got them. I rang up Tim, because I thought it was a rotten job for Flik to have to do—be quiet, gallant captain. I gave Tim all I had. Four tablets—no, five. And he took them back and fed them Flik's cat. That's all. You asked me if I'd had any dope, and I told you I hadn't. I'd forgotten about the cat business."

"Medinal isn't dope," Parry said. "So why all this fuss?"

"Aah-haa." Captain Belairs took the floor again. "Why indeed all this fuss? You do well to ask that, Inspector. Why, if everything's above board, should Tim Ambrose take all the trouble to ring up Camilla Pain-Wentworth from the pub phone, tell her he's put his foot in it by telling a policeman he poisoned Flikka's cat, and beg for her advice? Why should Camilla Pain-Wentworth dash over on her bicycle immediately and hold a consultation, right there in the bar? Why indeed?"

"I'm so surprised, darling," Camilla said, "that you don't know all the answers. They're so simple. Poor Tim flapping like hell, and obviously suffering from one over the eight, so what should I do but come to the rescue? Actually, it was just an excuse for me to rush over in the hopes I might see you, sweetie—not of course," she added, "that I wish to be unfaithful to the charming Inspector, but the thing is, he won't be here forever, and you will. I've always had a passion for uniforms. Did you wear a sword, Captain? If so, do put it on one day, just for me."

This was all very funny, Parry thought, but he'd had enough of it.

"As there's just been another death," he said, "I'd be glad to know what you four people were doing between, say, a quarter to six and seven this evening."

The eyes of the four people concerned turned themselves on him, staring.

"Good God," Tim said, suddenly sobering up. "Who?"

"Harry, who was gardener here. Well, what were you all doing?"

"Phil and I were on our way to the pub at quarter to six," Tim said. "We got there at six, as anyone can tell you, and we've been there ever since. Phil, honey, you aren't going to be sick are you?"

She shook her head dumbly, her face green.

"Camilla?"

"I was playing rummy with those two you met. Tim rang up, and I dropped everything and biked over to the Shots Arms, where I've been ever since."

"Captain Belairs?"

"I was at home till I went up to the pub at about—I forget when. Some time round about seven, I think. This is monstrous!" he exploded. "Police everywhere, so-called expert from Scotland Yard, and a murder every day. Aren't you going to arrest anyone?"

Parry swayed backward and forward from his heels to his toes. When he spoke his voice was very distinct, each word clipped and clear. "No, I'm not going to arrest anyone. I'm not going to arrest anyone for the reason that I've no idea who the murderer is. No idea at all. I've no clues.

Nothing. But I'll tell you all one thing, which you can pass on if you want to—I do know that there's one person in the village, who I admit I don't know, that holds the clue to the murderer's identity. That person is therefore in danger. So everyone'd be wise if they did their eating and drinking when no one else is around who might slip some poison into their food or drink."

In the ensuing silence, Belairs dropped the card he'd been holding up his sleeve. "Damn funny, isn't it, that all three victims were old retainers of the Chattocks? Damn funny—not only Molly and Harry, but Marsh, knew Flikka since she was a child. Marsh was butler to an uncle of Flikka's in Scotland. Did you know?"

Arnoldson dug his hands into his pockets, furious. For he had made that discovery about Marsh just an hour or two ago, and had been biding his time to spring his trick at the right dramatic moment.

Parry looked over at Flik. Her lips moved, but no sound came out of her mouth. When at last she did speak, with what seemed a most dreadful effort, all she said was, "He was a very bad butler."

CHAPTER 18

AT last Parry got rid of them all, even to the clinging Miss Merridew. Bee had wanted her to spend the night at Shots Hall, but she refused. If, she'd said, she spent the night there, then she knew Flik would give her bed up to her and spend a sleepless night on the sofa. So she'd go home. Yes, she'd go home. So far as it was possible for Miss Merridew to be firm and coherent about anything, she was firm and coherent. So home she went, escorted to her door by the disgruntled Arnoldson.

Parry sighed. "And now I'm going home too," he said to Bee.

"You must be tired," Bee said.

"Tired and aggravated," he smiled. "Why didn't either of you tell me Marsh had been a butler in your family?"

"We never thought," Flik said. "Personally, it simply never occurred to me. I took it for granted you knew. It was years ago. He was a nice old thing, but a bad butler. My uncle pensioned him off, and eventually he landed down here with his wife, and Winnie—that must've been quite twelve years ago."

"Thirteen," Bee corrected her. "He used to hiss down the back of one's neck at table. He ought've been a groom. Parry, d'you mean to tell me you've no idea who's done these murders?"

"You all heard what I said, didn't you?" As he answered Bee, he was looking at Flik, right into her eyes. "Now I'm really going. Arnoldson'll be sleeping at the pub tonight. And by the way, Norton's going to sit up all night in Molly's cottage just to keep a lookout for anyone who might think of wandering round during the hours of darkness."

"By the way"— Bee smoothed the lap of her silk dress. "Have you found the broom Molly's step was swept with?"

"I haven't actually found it," Parry said. "By what Arnoldson told me, it must've been a very stiff broom from the marks it left on the bricks. A stiff broom with a chunk of bristles missing from the middle of it."

Neither Bee nor Flik made any comment on this gratuitous information. Parry thought that on the whole he hadn't expected any. He buttoned up his overcoat and pulled on a pair of ancient leather gloves.

"How're you going?" Flik asked, walking with him to the door.

"Mahew's sent the car back for me. It'll be down at the pub." He opened the door and peered out. The mist still hung over everything, dark and dismal. "You look all in. Do go to bed, Flik." He looked down at her, at her eyes that were hiding things, her polished copper head that held so much in it, her pale face—poker face, oh, poker face. "Good night. And don't forget Norton's close—just in case you want him." He held her hand for a moment and then let it go, and went himself.

When the door crashed shut, he realized that he'd got quite used to the row it made. He hadn't really noticed it all evening, and yet it had opened and shut, so it seemed, continuously. Switching on his torch, he rounded the corner and stopped outside Molly's cottage.

"Norton?"

"Yes, sir?"

Norton's head, a dim blur, appeared out of Molly's living-room window.

"I'm afraid you're in for a wretched night," Parry said to him. "I'm really sorry for you. Shall I get the gent from the brewery to bring you up something in a bottle to console you?"

"No, thanks, sir. Very nice of you to've thought of it, all the same. But I think I'd better keep my wits about me, such as they are."

"Your wits're all right. Listen, if you could possibly bear the idea of removing your regulation boots and creeping round in your socks, you might take a little stroll in the small hours."

"Yes, sir?" Norton shuddered audibly, and Parry laughed.

"To look for a broom. You know the broom I mean? You mayn't

have to go far. Only for God's sake don't make a noise about it. I tried to get an opportunity to have a look round today, likewise yesterday, but there was always someone about. Good night."

"Night, sir."

Half an hour later Parry was drinking hot grog in front of Mahew's study fire, eating a large supper off a tray. Mahew was snuffling, having caught Mrs. Mahew's cold.

"I simply can't see," he said, "the rhyme or reason of this wholesale killing off—now Harry. Good God!"

"You might very well say that one reason is that as the bodies were all old retainers of the Chattocks, Bee Chattock or Flik, or both, bumped them off to keep their mouths shut."

"Rather a long time to wait, surely, if they knew something to the Chattock discredit?"

"Yes, my dear Sherlock. Yes, indeed. Sweet bad luck to it, if only we could find the motive—the real motive for the motive. Hell."

"Hell, as you say—"

"Knows no fury like a woman scorned—" Parry finished. He jerked his head up, staring at Mahew. "A woman scorned—a woman scorned— would anyone scorn Flik?"

"Not bloody likely," Mahew decided. "Flik? Who on earth'd scorn her?"

"Then—" Parry shook his head. "A woman scorned—another woman scorned in preference to Flik. Oh, who the hell is this now?"

The phone bell had started to ring with loud insistence. Mahew groaned, hauled himself out of his chair; and dragged his aching legs to the telephone.

"Hullo? Oh, Congreve. Yes? If it's anything important, then you'd better talk to Inspector Parry. Hang on."

"Blast you," Parry said, taking over the receiver. "Well, Congreve? You ought to be in bed and asleep, there's a tough day ahead tomorrow. Did you know Harry's copped it?"

"Yes, sir." Congreve's voice came with admirable distinctness over the line. "I rang through to the Shots Arms, thinking as 'ow you might be there, and 'is—Sergeant Arnoldson told me about it. What a mess, ain't it?"

"Quite literally a mess. What is it? Anything new?"

"It's something what I've thought of, an idea that came into the wide open empty space what's my mind, sir. I don't suppose there's nothing in it, but one doesn't never know."

"Yes?" Parry prompted. "Go on."

"I've got the notes about it 'ere, sir, in an old notebook I just dug up at 'ome." There was a faint rustling of paper from Congreve's end. "On November 10th, 1942, the late Dr. Bannard reported that some time during that day or evening, while 'e was on 'is rounds, a new package containing, 'e said, some tubes of sleeping tablets, was stolen out of 'is car. 'E then gave a list of the patients 'e'd visited. Most of them living in the town, or on the outskirts. D'you want me to read out their names, sir? There's one at the end that's interesting."

"Go ahead," Parry said.

Congreve reeled off a list of names and addresses, none of which conveyed anything to Parry, and then paused. "And 'is last visit was to Captain Belairs, what was then living the same place as 'e does now. That was at 9 P.M. on, like I said, November 10th, 1942."

"So what, Congreve? What's on your mind, and what've you got hidden up your sleeve?"

"It's a bit 'ard to say. That time Arnoldson was away on a gas course for nearly two months, and the Superintendent we 'ad then, Lewis by name, left in 1943—so there ain't many, what with the changes we've 'ad, what remembers it except me and Norton. And of course Major Mahew wasn't 'ere in 1942. Well, sir, I was just thinking back on things—Dr. Bannard, when 'e reported the theft, said the stuff what was stolen was called Barbitone, or something of the kind, but suppose it wasn't? Suppose it was morphine?"

"Kee-rist," Parry whistled. "But he wouldn't lie. Or would he have lied?"

"It's 'ard to explain. Dr. Bannard was getting old, and there'd been a bit of a shine on account of 'is 'aving given too much anesthetic to some guy what was being operated on at the 'ospital, and on top of that 'e gave a wrong prescription to someone, and they'd 'ave died if the chemist 'adn't spotted it. So everyone was saying the old gent was past it, and 'is patients was beginning to drop off. Now, suppose it came out that 'e'd left morphine lying round in 'is car for anyone to steal, there'd 'ave been no end of a rumpus, and 'e'd 'ave been for the 'igh jump. And 'e was very proud of 'is reputation. As it was, we 'ad to put out an S.O.S. about this Barbitone stuff, and people said, 'Oh, wasn't old Bannard getting careless?' Only people soon forgot it, as we got a thousand-pound bomb bang in the middle of the town, and up went the cinema, and Wrights the chemists, and Figgets the greengrocers, and so on—"

"The chemists? So if he'd got morphine or Barbitone from Wrights, there was no one, and no books left to tell the tale?"

"Not a sausage," Congreve agreed. "What a mess it was. Cor'."

"It gives one," Parry said, "most furiously to think. But, Congreve, a reputable doctor couldn't tell a lie like that."

"To save 'is reputation? People'll do a lot to save their reputations, sir, and that's a fact."

"Let's assume then," Parry said, "Just for the sake of argument, that it was morphine that was stolen, and not Barbitone. Where does it take us?"

"Back to Shotshall, sir, doesn't it? At 9 P.M. on November 10th, 1942, with Dr. Bannard's car parked in a nice, dark lane, where there's hardly any traffic."

Parry grunted thoughtfully. "Surely, Congreve, this is all a bit much of the long arm of coincidence? No murderer in the world could ever have the luck to've had everything made so easy for him. And why steal morphine in 1942, and not use it till so long afterward? How'd anyone even know there was morphine in Bannard's car, supposing, that's to say, there was any morphine at all?"

"You got me there, sir. But look—suppose someone 'ad the idea they wanted to do theirselves in? Suppose they wanted to commit suicide? Suppose on the evening of November 10th, 1942, they'd seen Bannard's car parked there they might've thought doctor's car—doctor—drugs and poisons, let's 'ave a look. So they looked, found morphine, whipped it, and then changed their minds. Thought to theirselves, no, I won't do myself in, but I'll do in the one what brought all this trouble on me. Only they couldn't think 'ow to fix things, so it took them all these years to figure it out."

"You do know all the answers, don't you?" Parry said, his eyes snapping. "Congreve, keep all this under your hat, will you? And be ready down at the Central Police Station early tomorrow morning, and I'll pick you up. We can tie your bike onto the back of the car."

"Yes, sir. Good night, and I 'ope you didn't mind my ringing you."

"Mind? Good God, no. Good night, Congreve."

"Now what?" Mahew asked. "What the devil was all that about?"

Parry told him, and added, "There's no doubt the murderer's as mad as a coot. No sane person could nourish malice for so long. If you've got a pack of cards, I'll play you any game you like, the stake being Congreve. Science has done more toward the detection of crime than any thing else, so they say, but oh, do give me the human mind:"

"I'm damned if I'll gamble Congreve away," Mahew protested, outraged.

"Yes, you will. We'll start an endless rummy game, like Camilla."

At eleven o'clock they were still playing. Congreve had changed hands eight times. Mahew was practically asleep, wheezing. By the fire, the dogs slept, four warm, brindle bodies. The cards dropped out of Mahew's hands, and he grunted. Parry got up and went to the telephone.

"London call," he said to the sleepy operator.

Through a haze of sleep, Mahew caught disjointed, jagged bits of Parry's talk, meaningless.

"...In the blitz...Presumably the 1940 installment...might be later of course...I know it's a long time ago, and that it's too late tonight... You're telling me...Yes, that's the name...Age? Don't know... Thanks...Take these phone numbers. If I can't be got at one, then I'll be at another...If not....No, no messages to anyone...If you've anything to say, give a message for me to ring through to you..."

"What the hell?" Mahew woke up. "I feel like death—I'm going to bed." He stumbled to his feet; the dogs woke up and staggered after him.

Parry heard them going up the stairs. Mahew went into his dressing room, got into his pajamas and betook himself to Mrs. Mahew's bedroom. Her bedside light was on, and out of one eye she regarded him amiably.

"I've got your cold, so we may as well share the agony," he said.

"By all means." She moved over, and he crawled thankfully in beside the comfort of her. "Poor old Mahews," she mumbled. "They're getting old."

All four dogs jumped on the bed and settled themselves on top of Mahew, who groaned. Mrs. Mahew put out the light, and delicately wiped her nose on her husband's pajamaed shoulder. For a time he slept, then woke up, half suffocated.

"Get off, you fat bastards," he said to the dogs, trying to dislodge them. After a sharp struggle, he gave it up, and somehow wormed his way out of bed. In the darkness, he groped his way to the door and opened it.

"Come on," he invited. "Chup-chup-chup."

There were four thumps as the dogs jumped off the bed and followed him. A light shone under Parry's door. Mahew turned the handle with caution. Parry was asleep, with the light on, the bedclothes pulled over his head. Mahew patted the end of the bed. "Up—come on, hup."

Weighed down by dogs, Parry slept peacefully on. Mahew stopped to turn the light off, and paused, wondering what he'd been up to. On the bedside table, his notebook, a large one, was open; he appeared to have been amusing himself by some strange, solitary game. Roughly drawn was a picture of what looked like a sausage, only it had two pygmy arms, two eyes, a nose and mouth, and was swathed in what looked like a sort of sheet. Out of its mouth spouted a balloon, inscribed, "Out, out damned spot." Then came a row of question marks, "????????????" and the entry, "Didn't expect that, so of course was surprised." Then more question marks, "????????"

Mahew stared, fascinated, and unashamedly turned the page over. On the next page Parry had written, "He does that part of it so he doesn't do the other part of it. The murderer does. So what? The butcher, the baker, the candlestick maker."

Mahew put the light out, and groping his way in the complete darkness, stubbed his toe on a chair and swore. Somehow, he got back to his place beside Mrs. Mahew. He was filled with a nasty foreboding that tomorrow would bring with it more, and quite horrid unpleasantness. He shivered. It was rather cold without the dogs.

CHAPTER 19

MAHEW and Parry set off so early on their day's work that it was still nearly dark. But at least the fog had cleared, and a soft, transparent mist proclaimed that it might possibly be a fine day.

When they got down to the Central Police Station, Congreve had just arrived on his bicycle. No word had come in from Norton, nor from Arnoldson. Nor was there any message from the constable to whom Parry had delegated the depressing job of keeping watch over Harry's cottage during the night.

Congreve gave them some disgusting tea at the station, roped his bicycle on the back of the police car, and as a pale sun broke through the mist, they started off, for what seemed like the hundredth time, to Shotshall. Mahew's cold was so bad that he was past taking an interest in anything. Even the peculiar entries in Parry's notebook had ceased to intrigue him. All he could think of, for the moment, were the aches and pains in his bones, his perpetually running nose and the wheezes in his chest.

On their way out of the town, they stopped at the hospital. But Abbot had gone home to get some sleep.

"Stop at Dr. Abbot's for a moment," Parry said to the driver.

"Yes, sir."

"Have a heart," Mahew croaked. "Can't the poor blighter have half an hour's peace?"

"No," Parry said, without heart. "Is this the house? Sound your horn."

The driver sounded his horn in loud, strident blasts. At the same time a large mail plane roared overhead. The mixture of noises was enough to rouse the dead. They roused Abbot. His head, disheveled, appeared from his bedroom window.

"Go to hell!" he shouted. "What d'you want?"

Parry stuck his head out of the car. "Any news? If so I'll come in. If not, ring me at the Shotshall pub, or come up there."

"I'll ring you." The window slammed down, and the utterly worn out Abbot went back to bed.

"He's a damn nice chap," Parry said, as the car got under way again.

They dropped off Congreve and his bicycle at the Shots Arms. Arnoldson was breakfasting, waited on by a flushed and overexcited Winnie. He said he had nothing to report. If so, thought Parry, why did he have that gloating look on his face? He was beginning to mistrust Arnoldson, from his motives to his morals.

"Congreve?" Parry pulled at his lower lip, and beckoned Congreve outside the pub with a jerk of his head. "Listen, go and pay a nice social call on Captain Belairs. You might bring the conversation round to the subject of health."

"I bet I get a mouthful," Congreve said. "All about malaria in the 'Imalayas, ticks in the jungle and snake bites in Burma. Still, seeing as 'ow I'm so ignorant, it may improve my education. I never can get the 'ang of it whether Poona's a real place, or just a music 'all joke."

Mahew and Parry left him thoughtfully pumping up his back tire, and took the car on to Molly's cottage. Norton greeted them rather like a dog that'd been chained up for days never expecting to be let loose again. He was a quite deplorable sight, unshaved, hungry, his uniform plastered with half-dried mud. He held the door open with an air of agitation, and was evidently bursting with something.

"Well, Norton?" Parry greeted him. "What sort of a night did you have? You can crack off home when you've told me."

"Oh, Lord," Norton groaned. "I don't know what you'll say, Inspector, when I do tell you. Sorry your cough's so bad, Major Mahew."

"So'm I," Mahew said, gingerly sitting down in Molly's armchair. "What's happened?"

"It was this way," Norton started to explain. "Like you said, Inspector, round about 2 A.M. this morning, I took my boots off, and sneaked off in my socks to have a look round for that broom."

"And did you find it?" Parry asked, hoping to cut a long story short.

"Well, in a manner of speaking, no. It found me, right on the head."

"What the devil d'you mean?" Parry stared, no longer anxious to curtail Norton's story.

"I got as far as the middle of the road, just outside the gate here, and then I skidded in the mud and fell down. I hadn't my light on, so I couldn't see what I was doing. It was that awful, it really was. I tried not to make no noise, but I kept falling down every time I got up, and then I found one of my socks was half off, and I was keeping treading on it with my other foot, if you see what I mean, sir?"

Parry saw, and shook with inward laughter. "Yes—I see. And then?"

"So I simply had to turn my light on," Norton apologized, "and then it happened."

"What did?"

"The broom."

"The broom?" Even Mahew's cold-muffled interest was roused. "It happened?"

"It simply came from nowhere, and landed, wham, on my head."

"But who was at the other end of it?" Parry asked.

Norton shuffled his feet. He'd been afraid no one would believe him, and behold! they didn't. "There wasn't anyone at the end of the broom. It just landed," he repeated rather hopelessly, "wham, on my head. Zonk. Out of the blue, if you could call that black fog the blue."

Parry swallowed a laugh. "Then someone must have thrown it at you, mustn't they?"

"But who?" the bewildered Norton said. "There wasn't no one there at all, and not a sound. Directly I put my torch on, the broom just fell out of the sky on my head. Tell you the truth, it near knocked me out, and by the time I got my sock on, and got hold of the broom, if there was anyone around, they'd gone. I went over to Miss Merridew's, and all I could hear was her snoring upstairs. Then I went along to Shots Hall, and not a sight or sound of anyone. So then I went up the road, and down the road, and as far as I could see in the fog, there wasn't no one there either."

"Preposterous," Mahew remarked, starting in on yet another handkerchief. "Brooms can't fall out of the sky, Norton."

"This one did," Norton said stubbornly. "Wham."

This time Parry laughed outright. "Listen, Norton, between the time the broom descended, like the sword of Damocles, on your defenseless head, and the time you went in search of prowlers, how long elapsed? Seconds? Minutes?"

Norton scratched his unshaven jaw. "Well, I fell down again when the broom hit me, then I sat down and pulled my sock on and did up my sock suspender. Then I got up, felt my head, looked round for whatever it was that hit me, found the broom lying in the road, decided it was the broom what had fallen on me, picked it up, looked at it, and then I started to hunt round."

"In fact," Parry suggested, "from the time the broom hit you, to the time you started off to look for the broom thrower, a matter of minutes might've gone by, mightn't they?"

"I couldn't rightly say. I was that surprised."

"Never mind. Let's have a look at it."

With great care, Norton produced a small, stiff-bristled broom, rather muddy, out of a corner. There was a chunk of bristles missing from the middle of it. "I handled it with gloves on when I found it," he said, with no little pride.

"Good—" Parry took a small wooden box out of his pocket, and in a moment had dusted the broom handle with white powder. There were no finger marks, only smears. Well, anyhow, he thought, if there'd ever been any finger marks, Norton, even with his gloves on, would have effectually cleaned them off. Not that it mattered. The murderer was always so careful to touch nothing.

"Cut off home, Norton," he said. "Anything else, before you go?"

"No, sir, nothing."

"Half a minute," Parry called after him. "If you wait down at the pub, I'll send the chap who's at Harry's cottage along, and the car can take you both home. Have a drink on me, in the meantime, you look as if you could do with it —that is, if the gentleman from the brewery'll trust me to pay up eventually."

Norton, very thankfully, went, and Parry and Mahew got into the car and drove to the bottom of Harry's lane. The morning mist had cleared, and from a washed, pale blue sky the sun shown, so that the water in the ruts and potholes were pools of silver. The fields were green, sparkling, and in the distance rooks cawed. Mahew swore as they plodded through the mud; Parry's mind went back to the evening before, when Flik had run beside him along the same track in the dark and fog, and Abbot, silent and long-legged, Gwen and Miss Merridew clinging on behind, with their cries of horror, muffled and strange.

The constable who had spent a miserable night at Harry's had nothing to report at all. He had whiled away his time by testing for fingerprints, and found none but Harry's. Everything was just as Parry had left it the night before. There seemed no sense in searching the small old cottage all over again. He'd been over it almost inch by inch already.

The three men went back to the car, Parry and Mahew dropping off outside Molly's cottage, while the driver went on down to the pub to pick up Norton and his bicycle.

"Now what?" Mahew said. "God, I wish I was home in bed."

"With the dear dogs? Blast you, I'm still paralyzed from the waist down—of all the filthiest tricks. Now we'll search round and see if anyone's lost a broom lately." Parry still held it under his arm, as if it were a gun. "We'll take the first. And that's Miss Merridew of the curtains."

They went up the short path, and Parry knocked on the door. A face bobbed from behind the living-room window, and in a moment the door opened. Miss Merridew greeted them with her usual confusion.

"Major Parry? Oh, and Inspector Mahew—how nice. Oh, no, Major Mahew and Inspector Parry—how very nice. Do come in—isn't it a lovely morning? Too bad the weather's been so nasty for you, it always is, isn't it? Sometimes, that is, but not now."

Mahew rolled his eyes to the ceiling, as though he prayed for deliverance, which, indeed, he did. Not looking where he was going, he fell over an electric flex, and found himself clawing for support to the sewing machine, now coyly hidden under a frilly cover.

"Hell," he swore with feeling.

"Oh!" Miss Merridew cried. "I'm so sorry. Oh, dear, this room's so small, isn't it—or rather, it isn't the room, but having to have everything in it."

"Cozy," Parry soothed. "Have you lost a broom lately?"

Miss Merridew perceived the broom, and uttered little whinnies of delight, like a child finding its lost toy. "My broom! I was wondering—I couldn't remember. Fancy, I never remembered lending it to you, how stupid of me. And I was wondering—"

"You didn't lend it to me," Parry pointed out. "It was found out in the road."

"In the road? Gracious me, how careless of me. And I can't even remember leaving it in the road, either."

How long, oh Lord, how long? Mahew champed inwardly. Was she forever going to babble these inanities?

"Very likely you didn't leave it in the road," Parry said, "it's only just turned up. Try and think when you missed it, Miss Merridew."

Miss Merridew tried to think, and at last succeeded in doing so. "Let me see, now. Yes, I remember now—yes, I did miss it, and thought I must've put it away in the wrong place, not in the garden shed. Let me see—it must've been, I think, last Friday, when I thought to myself, now where can the garden broom have got to? Yes, last Friday, I remember, now. And I didn't lend it to anyone, I'm sure."

"D'you keep your garden shed locked?" Parry asked patiently.

"No! Oh, dear, no. We haven't any criminals in Shotshall " Miss Merridew suddenly turned white, and put a small, shaking hand over her mouth. "At least, we hadn't then—last week," she quavered. "And all the time we had, and they took my broom."

Barmy, Mahew thought, fidgeting. The subject of the broom was getting like a nightmare. Hoping to change the conversation before he went mad, he pointed rather wildly at an excellently done pencil sketch of a man's head. "Very well drawn," he exclaimed. "Really good."

There was a sudden silence. Then Miss Merridew nodded, her nod more like a bow of reverence. "My cousin, Mervyn Crawford."

So that was Mervyn Crawford? thought Parry. In a way, he wasn't bad looking. Fortyish. Maybe more, maybe less. Only there was something wrong about the drawing. It gave the impression that it wasn't a true likeness.

"Dear Flikka drew it for me—after—after—" Miss Merridew's voice faltered, and her mouth sagged.

"After his death?" Parry said brutally.

"He died of the blitz," Miss Merridew said.

Strange new disease, Mahew thought. "And she was brought to bed with a fine blitz." Only it was a he. "He caught the blitz, complications set in, and he died." He was, he decided, a little delirious. His head, anyway, was blazing hot. Out of the corner of his eye, he saw a long black M.G. turn up into the drive of Shots Hall. Parry saw it too.

"Well," he said, "we mustn't keep you any longer. I'm glad we've been able to return you your broom."

"So kind of you," Miss Merridew was all smiles again. "Such an old friend, if you understand what I mean?"

"Perfectly," Parry assured her, and pushed Mahew out of the door in front of him.

"She's barmy," Mahew said when they got out in the road. "Oh, Lord, where do we go from here?"

"A little gravelry is indicated, I think. Clive's car and others've most conveniently scattered some nice gravel out into the road from Shots Hall drive. It matches up very prettily with the gravel Congreve picked up in Mrs. Vale's front cat run."

"Your high spirits," Mahew said, "not only make me sick, but they're out of place. You're a ghoul, Lane."

"That's rather what I feel like." Very quickly, as if he was twitching one of his shoestrings tighter, he stooped and picked up a handful of gravel from the road outside the entrance to Shots Hall. Somehow, the action made Mahew feel quite literally sick. It was so cold-blooded.

"We'll now stroll a little way down the road," Parry said. "That is if you don't mind helping me with a short experiment."

Mahew made an inarticulate noise in his clogged throat and followed. Where the road took a slow bend to the left, Parry stopped. They were just in sight of the pub.

"Got a watch?" he asked.

"Yes."

"Then turn your back, wait five minutes, then walk straight down the road, go in the back door of the pub, stand outside the sitting-room door for a couple of minutes, not more, walk out of the back door again, and start up the hill the way you came."

Grumbling under his breath, refusing to admit his interest, Mahew turned his back. The minute hand of his watch crawled with the awful slowness of a horse-drawn hearse in a traffic jam. He stamped his feet, trying to warm them, thankful for the warmth of the vagrant sunshine. After what seemed like a lifetime, the five minutes was up, and he turned and walked down the hill, feeling absurdly self-conscious. He found that it took him four minutes to reach the back door of the pub. This surprised him, as he thought it was much closer. When he got to the back door he paused, then lifted the latch and walked in. The sitting-room door was half open. He could see Arnoldson at the table, writing industriously, while Winnie halfheartedly flipped a duster over the hideous furniture. One minute passed; Winnie said, "I wouldn't go into domestic service if you paid me £500 a year."

"No one's going to pay you £500 a year," Arnoldson said without looking round. He hadn't seen Mahew.

The two minutes were up. Mahew let himself out and began to walk up the hill. When he had got halfway to the place he'd stood and waited with his back turned, he heard Parry whistle, and stopped.

"Well?" Parry caught up with him. "Did you hear anything?"

"Only Winnie and Arnoldson. Winnie said she wouldn't go into domestic service if she was paid £500 a year, and Arnoldson said no one'd pay her £500 a year. That's all except for the man from the brewery breathing heavily in the four ale."

"That's that, then." Parry looked satisfied. "If anyone was hiding in the abattoir when Flik went in to get the bottle of gin, then she didn't hear them chucking gravel at Mrs. Vale's window. It was too easy. I watched you coming down the hill through that slit of a window, waited till the back door of the pub shut, then hopped out of my hiding place, heaved the gravel across the road, and hopped back again. I think Mrs. Vale's now having hysterics, thinking my gravel's the herald of another murder."

"Let's hope it's not. Where do we go from here, Lane?"

"You look as if you ought to go home. Why don't you? I don't want to be the direct cause of your getting pneumonia, even to pay you out for smothering me with dogs."

"I'm not going home." Mahew was stubborn. "Look, here comes Congreve." In a manner unbecoming to his rank, he pulled off one of his gloves, put his fingers between his teeth and whistled. Congreve looked up, and pedaled a little, but not much quicker.

"This is rather a public place." Parry steered for the narrow track off the road where Abbot had turned his car, and leaned his back against the gate into the field. "Have a nice time with Captain Belairs, Congreve?"

"No. Oh, Lord, 'e's a bore. You just ought to 'ear 'is theories about the murders. Then I got 'im started on 'is 'ealth—that was worse. I'm surprised 'e's not dead. Anyway, I found out what was wrong with 'im when 'e sent for old Bannard on November 10th, 1942."

"How d'you get him on to the subject safely?" Parry asked.

"Oh, just said 'ad 'e got flu in the awful, dreadful, shocking epidemic in November 1942, and 'e said, no 'e 'adn't. So I said, gor, wasn't 'e lucky to've been the only person what wasn't ill then, and 'e got quite snotty and said 'e was ill."

"What with?" Mahew asked. He was getting rather sick of these long repetitions of other people's conversations.

Congreve grinned. "'E just said with 'is old trouble and then told me to go to 'ell. So I went."

"I see." Parry pulled at his lower lip. "There seems so much to do that I'm damned if I know where to start."

Mahew burst into a fit of coughing, then groaned.

"I'd like to get rid of Arnoldson this afternoon," Parry pondered. "He gets under my feet and into my hair so that I can't think straight."

"Why not send him over to see Camilla?" Mahew suggested.

"We will." Parry led the way down the hill to the pub and a much needed quick one, thinking hard.

Congreve broke in on his thoughts with a discreet cough. "Sir? I don't think Captain Belairs likes Mrs. Ashley. I think 'e'd like to see 'er get in wrong."

"His wish," Parry said, "may be realized," and thought, oh, for the motive, for the motive.

As they went down the road, he looked back over his shoulder to where the tower of Shots Hall stood up gray in the wintry blue of the sky. Even on a fine day it seemed forbidding, watchful; remote and secret as Flik herself.

CHAPTER 20

CLIVE stayed for lunch with Bee and Flik. For all his scrounging, he hadn't been able to find them a lady to oblige. None of the ladies who obliged when they felt so inclined were going up to Shots Hall to be poisoned, so they'd told him when he'd interviewed them. He felt sick at heart, and terrified for Flik's sake. People were saying appalling things about her. Like snowballs their suspicions and their dirty stories were accumulating to fantastic proportions.

There seemed nothing, so far, he could do for her. The one thing that might help, she wouldn't hear of. She wouldn't marry him, and that was that. To add to his gloom, he had a feeling that she'd taken a fancy to Parry, and Parry was very attractive. He was also the man who, at any moment, might come and take her away to the police station. From liking Parry, he began to hate him.

After lunch, he took himself off. He didn't want to go, but Flik, though she was as always kind to him, seemed to want him to. So he went, while she stood in the door and watched him pull his leg into the car after him, then watched him drive out into the road.

Miss Merridew looked up from her letter writing and watched his departure down the road as well. Poor dear Clive, she thought. He was so nice, with his soft fair hair and his charming ways. Such a pity—poor dear Clive. If only she could do something about him, but it was so difficult. She tore another page from her writing block. Her handwriting was exquisitely neat and as precise as her conversation was not. Behind her, the fire crackled in the grate, beside it, steaming in a saucepan, her afternoon drink of hot milk, which she had at exactly the same time every day. On the table an empty glass with a spoon in it stood ready, and a silver bowl filled with sifted sugar. She sucked her pen, searching for the words that always muddled themselves in her head, still staring out of the window. Coming along the road, walking slowly, was Flik. The pale sun was caught in her hair, and under it her face was more like marble than ever, lovely and composed.

Miss Merridew, inspired, wrote a little more, then folded the finished letter with a feeling of something accomplished, something done. She got up and carefully poured the steaming milk into the glass, added a great deal of sugar and began to stir the concoction round and round. Flik opened the gate, came up the path, tapped on the front door and opened it.

"Flik, dear?" Miss Merridew called, just as she always called even when she knew it was Flik.

"No curtains today?" Flik sat down by the table, leaning her arms on it.

"Not today, dear. I thought. I'd have a little rest. They look pretty, don't they?" Miss Merridew took a tentative sip of her milk, dipping her tongue into it like a little cat. "Frills may be old-fashioned but I do like them."

"Yes. Yes, Susan. Clive's still on the hunt looking for a lady to oblige."

"Dear Clive. So kind—I do hope she will. Or hasn't he found her?"

Flik looked down at her hands, gloved in dark blue buckskin. "I don't think anyone wants to oblige us and risk being poisoned. You remember what Parry said last night? Someone knows the clue to the murderer and they're in danger."

"I really don't understand —" Miss Merridew shook her head tearfully. "All too dreadful—" She began to sniff, then blew her nose in a valiant effort not to cry. "Too, too dreadful."

"Dreadful," Flik agreed, her voice strained, almost harsh. "I must go and do some work of some sort. Have you finished the book I lent you, Susan, dear?"

"Your book? Oh, yes, your book. Let me see—oh yes." She trotted out of the room, and Flik, listening, heard her go upstairs. She came down again, still at the trot, a little breathless. "There, dear. I'm sure it's a very nice story, but don't you think a little hard to understand? I mean, so little punctuation, and no—what is it you call them? Commas upside down."

"Inverted commas? Some people think they're unnecessary. Goodby, Susan." Flik kissed her on the forehead and turned away abruptly.

"Oh, but I'll see you this evening," Miss Merridew pointed out. "So just *au revoir*. I'll pop over, dear."

When Flik had gone she thought, there, she'd quite forgotten to tell Flik about the broom and how queer it was the broom was found in the road. She sat down at the table again, and drank the rest of her milk now nearly lukewarm. It tasted queer. Yes, it tasted very queer. What a very queer taste, she decided. Bitter. It tasted bitter all right. Something was happening to her eyes. They suddenly felt all swimmy. Then her head felt swimmy. For a few moments she was filled with a vast energy and exhilaration. But that faded, leaving her heavy, almost helpless. She dragged herself out of her chair and swayed to the telephone in her narrow hallway. A doctor—who was her doctor? She hadn't had a doctor since old Bannard died—but there was that man—what was his name? Abbey? No, Abbot. She clawed up the receiver.

"I want Dr. Abbot's house. Dr. Abbot's house—yes, Dr. Abbot's house—Dr. Abbot—Abbot—"

She was so tired. She was going to fall down and sleep. Through the singing in her head she heard a voice, then her own voice from a long way off. "It's Miss Merridew—my milk—it was bitter—I feel ill—queer—ill."

Her fumbling hands dropped the receiver. Her heavy feet took her back to the chair she'd been sitting in. Only now there were two chairs. She pulled at the front of her blouse, sat down, and knew mistily that she had sat on nothing. She was lying on the floor, and the world was slipping away. Only she'd forgotten something. She struggled to her knees, groping. There it was. Now she was lying on the floor again—strange, strange, strange...

In his uncomfortable bedroom down in the town, Abbot tugged at a clean collar. He'd only just got back from the hospital. He supposed that this sort of thing was now going to happen every minute. Each of the inhabitants of Shotshall in turn would imagine they'd been poisoned, and every doctor in St. Arthurs would be hauled up to the benighted village. Nearly tearing his collar in half, he showered a thousand maledictions on Miss Merridew's head. Why did she have to pick on him, anyway?

As he got into his car, he remembered he'd forgotten to shave. The fact that he minded what he looked like only served to make him more angry; for who but Abbot cared what Abbot looked like? And Abbot had never cared before. Shooting off the main road and turning up to the hill that led to Shotshall, he thought that if he stopped at the pub Parry might be there, and he could give him the report on. Harry's postmortem. He drove wildly, his brakes screaming at every corner, as if he was pursued by devils of his own manufacture. Outside the pub he skidded to a standstill, and with quite unnecessary violence sounded his horn. From the window of the now closed four ale bar, Congreve's head appeared, a pencil sticking out of the only mildly inquiring mouth.

"'Ullo, doctor," Congreve said placidly, spitting the pencil into his hand.

"Where's Parry? Drinking?"

"Shall I ask 'im to come out, sir, or're you coming in?"

"I'm not coming in," Abbot said.

"You aren't missing anything, then. The whisky supply's run out. I'll tell the Inspector you're 'ere."

Abbot smiled wryly. He liked Congreve, who had the rare distinction of never having irritated him.

Parry came round from the back door of the pub. He looked thoughtful, and rather worried. He was actually thinking about Arnoldson, whom he had just sent off to see Camilla.

"Hullo, Abbot," he said, sticking his head in at the car window. "Done the postmortem already?"

"I hope I never see the inside of a pair of lungs, the outside of a pancreas, the workings of a dead heart or any of the other organs contained in the human body again. Here's the report on the postmortem. I trust you can understand it."

Parry took the obtusely worded document Abbot thrust at him and groaned. "I'm but an ignorant policeman, dragged up under the arches and then pitchforked into a reform home. Will you translate all this into simple words of two syllables?"

"All right, all right." Impatiently Abbot snatched his report out of Parry's hand. "Harry died as the result of cerebral hemorrhage induced by excessive and prolonged retching. He had a growth, probably malignant—I'll know that tomorrow—in his stomach, which had weakened his constitution, and judging by everything else I found he'd have died pretty soon anyhow. He must have first of all taken a fatal dose of morphine, and then very strong salt and water to induce vomiting, and I can't really tell you how many grains of morphine he did take—the dregs of his tea-cup showed morphine in them, and he must've died, as far as I can safely say, between, say, 5:45 and 6:30 yesterday evening. There was no sugar in the tea."

"No sugar?" Parry repeated, staggered.

"No sugar."

"And apparently he always took a lot of sugar. Jees—and the blood?"

"Burst a blood vessel in his throat from the strain of the retching. There looked to be more blood than there actually was. Here, take the report. I've got to go along and see old Merridew."

"Susan Merridew? Why?"

"She phoned me," Abbot fumed. "Talked some balderdash about her milk tasting bitter and she felt ill."

"God!" Parry tore open the door of the car and sprawled inside next Abbot. "Step on it no, wait a minute—Congreve?"

"Sir?" Congreve answered from the window of the four ale.

"Come on."

Congreve climbed nimbly over the sill and got in the back of the car.

"Hell," Parry swore. "The trap's sprung. I hope we shan't be too late. How long ago was it she phoned you?"

"I didn't take the time. Getting on for three-quarters of an hour ago by now." Abbot roared the car up the hill and pulled up with a jerk outside the trim gate of Miss Merridew's small house. Parry was first inside, then Abbot, then Congreve.

"She's in here," Parry said over his shoulder. "Don't touch a damn thing but her, if you can help it."

"All right, all right," Abbot said fretfully. "We aren't fools. Get out of my light." He knelt down beside Miss Merridew's crumpled little form, felt her pulse, then, methodically, quickly, he opened his bag and took out a hypodermic syringe and an ampule of atropine. "I'd say it was morphine again," he said, lifting her eyelids. "Get a bowl of cold water, and a towel. Flap her face and neck." The needle went home. He frowned, rubbing his rough chin on the back of his hand. "I can't give her an emetic when she's unconscious like this, it'd simply choke her—go on, Parry, flap away—that's more like it."

Parry felt, somehow, repulsed. At no time was Miss Merridew beautiful, but in her present state she seemed to him quite hideously plain.

"We must get her down to the hospital at once," Abbot said. "Not that she's in much danger now, but I don't want to take any risks. I'd say she had the constitution of an ox."

"Shall I ring through for an ambulance?" Congreve asked.,

"Waste of time. After they've fiddled about, we could've got her there and back again three times in my car."

"If we stuck her in the back seat," Parry suggested, "then I could hang on to her. I want to go down with you. I'll have to get a statement from her directly she's capable of making one. Abbot, can you wrap that milk glass in a handkerchief, or something, and put it in your bag? Upright—"

Abbot snapped his teeth together, champing. "What d'you think I'd do? Rinse it first and put it in upside down to drain?"

"D'you know what?" Congreve said, bending down and staring at

Miss Merridew's face. "She ain't as old as she looks, to my way of think-ing. Funny."

Funny was scarcely the word Parry and Abbot would have used to describe the situation, and said so fluently.

"Queer, not tee-hee," Congreve explained.

Very carefully, Abbot wrapped Miss Merridew's dentures, which he'd taken out as they threatened to choke her, in a bit of paper and put them in his bag with the glass. Parry stopped flapping the wet towel and looked up.

"Why take her teeth?"

Abbot stared at him. "You've no imagination. People with false teeth, women especially, are often very sensitive. She'd hate to make a state-ment to you with no teeth in her head. You're a fool. Get some blankets off her bed and then help me out with her."

Congreve got blankets, and they rolled Miss Merridew in them, so that she looked like an elderly papoose. With some difficulty they bundled her out of the house and propped her in the back of the car. Abbot opened all the windows, muttered that the fresh air would help more than any-thing else.

Parry took Congreve on one side. "Stay here, will you?" he said. "And use all your ten pairs of eyes. You can ring me at the hospital. I'll wait there till she comes to and is as capable of being as coherent as she ever is, which isn't saying much. Don't let anyone in—you can lock the door, and if anyone calls they'll just think she's out."

"Wonder who done it?" Congreve pondered.

"The wholesale dealer in morphine," Parry answered rather impa-tiently. "Who else?"

"Come on, can't you?" Abbot shouted from the car. "Get in with her, Parry, and bounce her about. She's beginning to come to after the atro-pine, and I don't want her to go into a coma again."

Parry got in as he was bid. Then he put his head out of the window and called to Congreve. "Ring Major Mahew at the pub, and tell him what's happened and where I'm to be found. And Congreve? Will you ask him to pay a visit to Shots Hall and find out what Mrs. Ashley and Miss Chattock've been doing today?"

The fantastic drive to St. Arthurs started. To Parry there was a night-mare quality about it that he'd never encountered in his wide experience before. The air tore through the windows, so that he felt he must surely freeze to death. Obedient to Abbot's orders, he bounced Miss Merridew up and down and from side to side as if she were some horrid rag doll. Every now and then she half opened her eyes, and made queer noises, like an animal. The sun went behind a bank of gray clouds, and the country-side took on an air of gloom. A wind was getting up; Abbot's hair flew in wild disorder in the draft.

Parry marveled that this raging, caustic man was yet so sensitive to human feelings that he could think of Miss Merridew's dentures. Like Flik, in some odd way, there were the threads of that nylon-like fine strength in him.

"Keep her bouncing," Abbot said. "How's she doing?"

"All right. And I think you're right. She's tough as you make them."

"She's the tough type."

"No, no, no!" Miss Merridew suddenly wailed. "She—she—"

The car lurched round a corner, and she fell against Parry. With distaste, he pushed her back in her corner and shook her.

"Wake up!" he shouted in her ear. "Come on—Miss Merridew, wake up—time to get up—"

The still rising wind whistled in the windows. Vagrant drops of rain hit the windscreen. The fields and woods were splotched with black shadows, like some skin disease that had overtaken an otherwise pleasant face.

"Oh," Miss Merridew bubbled. "Oh, oh— She—"

Who? Parry wondered, mentally and outrageously cursing Mahew for dragging him into this unsavory mess. Flik? All the time Flik.

"Wake up, Miss Merridew," he shouted again, wishing he could sock her in the jaw.

CHAPTER 21

MISS MERRIDEW was put in a private ward, while Parry waited downstairs in the matron's office. There, left by himself to kick his heels, he did some hard thinking. His thoughts weren't pleasant, and when Abbot looked in at the door he found him smoking his tenth cigarette, an ashtray full of half-smoked ends next him.

"You can come up," Abbot said. "She's still very dopey, but I don't suppose any more half-witted than usual. The devil himself can't have a stronger constitution than she's got. Heart and lungs like a two-year-old, whatever the heart and lungs of a two-year-old're like. I'm having the dregs of milk in the glass tested for morphine."

"Did she ask for her teeth?" Parry said curiously.

"Yes."

"When d'you think she'll be fit enough to go home again?"

"She'll have to go tomorrow."

"Have to?" Parry whistled softly between his teeth. "Why the hell?"

"She'll damn well have to go out tomorrow," Abbot said. "The ward she's in is wanted tomorrow for a mastoid. The mastoid can't be kept hanging about, if you can realize that. None of the others in the private wards're fit enough to be turned out on her account, and as for the public wards, there's a waiting list."

"Surely you keep some beds free for emergencies?" Parry asked, getting impatient.

"As you say, for emergencies," Abbot agreed acidly. "She's not an emergency any longer, or won't be tomorrow with her powers of recuperation. If you're so concerned about her, then I can get the District Nurse near that appalling village to go in and keep an eye on her in her spare time, which is nil."

"Can't you really keep her in after tomorrow?"

"I told you."

"There's no other hospital?"

"No."

"Nursing homes?"

"Damn you," Abbot swore beside himself, "if I thought I could get a bed in a nursing home I'd have told you. They're all full. This isn't London, this is a one-horse seaside town."

"Tomorrow?" Parry frowned. "Hell, I'll have to get busy."

"That'll be a change," Abbot jeered. "Come along, if you want to see the old woman."

For all that Abbot said she had a constitution like an ox, Miss Merridew, propped up in bed in a hospital nightdress, was a pathetic figure. She seemed to have shrunk to the size of a small child, and was having great difficulties with her dentures, which kept slipping forward out of her relaxed mouth. Abbot nodded his head at the nurse who stood by the bed, and Parry was left alone with his victim.

"Feeling better?" he asked gently.

Miss Merridew tried to nod and smile.

"Are you the doctor?" she asked in a clogged voice.

Parry groaned within him. Now the usual muddled conversation was going to take place, he supposed.

"No, I'm not the doctor. I'm Parry, Inspector Parry. You remember who I am, don't you?"

"Oh, yes, of course," Miss Merridew muttered vaguely. "Only I thought you were a major. Such a queer thing to happen—it was sour—no, not sour, bitter. It must be the cows. They turn sour in thundery weather, don't they?"

"Very likely," Parry agreed, curbing his impatience with admirable fortitude. "I'm sorry you were alone when you were taken ill. If Mrs. Ashley'd been with you she could have helped you, couldn't she?"

"Oh, dear—yes she could, couldn't she?" Miss Merridew plucked at the sheet puzzling. "Only she'd gone. I mean—she hadn't been there. Of course she hadn't been in at all," she added with a quick, nervous twitching of her fingers, like a guilty child. "Not at all. No one had been in. Flikka hadn't—"

"I see." Parry strolled round the room. Of course Flik had been in, and when she'd gone, Miss Merridew had drunk her milk. He ran his eyes over Miss Merridew's unromantic clothing, neatly folded and laid on a chair. On the dressing table other oddments were laid in a row with tidy hospital precision: a handkerchief, a door key, a crumpled letter. He glanced at Miss Merridew. She seemed to have forgotten he was there. He picked up the letter and read it quickly, then opened the door. The nurse hovered outside, waiting to throw him out when his time was up.

"Nurse?"

"Yes? Is she all right? Please don't overtire her or worry her."

"She's all right. Where was this letter? I mean, where did you find it?"

"Funny," the nurse said, "we found it tucked down the inside of her blouse in the top of her—erm—just as if she'd tried to hide it."

"People do such quaint things, don't they?" Parry smiled at the girl and put the letter in his pocket. "I'll go now, I won't bother your patient any more just yet."

On the staircase, he reread Miss Merridew's beautifully penned but chaotically phrased missive. There were a lot of underlinings, and a muddled account of the murders, the weather, hopes for an early spring when it would be so lovely to see the spring flowers showing, would it not? dearest Emily—whoever dearest Emily was. The letter ended:

> Well, dearest, I must stop, as I see dear Flikka Ashley, of whom I have often written you I think if I remember rightly, coming in at my gate to visit me which she so often does at this time.
> With dear thoughts,
>
> Your affectionate
> SUSAN MERRIDEW

Screwing up his eyes, Parry reconstructed the scene in his mind: Miss Merridew laying down her pen, blotting the fine writing, folding the letter, then greeting Flik with inanities as she came in. As plainly as though she was there before him, he saw Flik sit down very quietly, in her unfidgety manner, saw her immobile face, heard her calm voice answering Miss Merridew. As surely as if he had been there himself, he knew that Miss Merridew had got up and pottered out of the room on some futile errand. He could see Flik, when she came back, saying good-by, going, her back straight, out of the gate again—then Miss Merridew relishing her milk, tasting the bitterness, running her tongue round her mouth and tasting again, somehow getting to her phone. Then she must have gone straight back into her living room, groping her way while the morphine worked on her. Then the letter—what would an old friend, a loving friend of Flik's do? Leave the letter on the table where it'd be found? No, hide it—hide it somewhere—obviously someone who'd had an overdose of morphine wouldn't have the strength to tear it up and throw it in the fire. So hide it down inside her clothes.

Parry's methodical brain clicked over and over till it came to a standstill at the ever present barrier of the motive: the motive of the motive. Only Flik could provide that. Damn her eyes, he thought angrily, oh damn her eyes.

A nurse came up the stairs toward him, hurrying, a small white mask over her nose and mouth.

"Nurse?" he said. "I'd very much like to see Dr. Abbot, if I may."

"Dr. Abbot? Oh, dear. I'm afraid—"

"I'm Inspector Parry, if that means anything in your young and charming life."

Apparently it did.

"He's just going to give an anesthetic," she said. "An emergency case that's just been brought in. I think he's gone up to the theater already, but the patient hasn't been taken up yet, so perhaps he could give you a minute if you'll come up."

"Thanks a lot." Parry followed the girl back up the stairs, along a corridor and into a lift which sailed to the top floor. The hospital smells of antiseptic were everywhere. He liked them; they were so clean.

"If you'll just wait here." The nurse opened a wide, white door, and a blast of hot air rushed out and hit Parry in the face. He'd forgotten that operating theaters were heated to hothouse temperature, and wondered how in God's name anyone could work in such an atmosphere. He had a confused view of chromium plating, white enamel, of another masked nurse, and Abbot.

He looked almost terrifying but imposing in his white overall, his white skullcap and his mask. He stepped into the corridor, his hands thrust away from him. Behind him a nurse held out his glasses.

"Your glasses, doctor," she said.

"Never mind now. Shut the door." He looked down at Parry, and for the first time Parry, tall himself, realized how tall the doctor was, and that the unspectacled eyes that stared at him were extraordinary in their life and fire. "Don't come and plaster yourself all over me," he said. "Just as I'm cleaned up. What the hell is it now? I can only give you a few seconds. An emergency appendectomy's just been brought in, so they got their hooks on me. Well?"

"Is there no possibility of your being able to keep Miss Merridew in here after tomorrow?"

"My God, have I got to explain, to you all over again?" Abbot exploded. "If I stuck her in one of the emergency beds, then she might have to be hoofed out five minutes after she'd got into it. With this case that's just come in, that'll only leave two emergencies anyhow. To the devil with you."

Parry stuck to his guns. "This District Nurse you were talking about, would she be able to stay with Miss Merridew all the time when she goes home?"

"No!" Abbot almost shouted, seething. "How could she? With a huge district and patients all over the place? Maternity cases, influenza cases, God knows what to visit. Don't be half-witted."

"Then could some other female be found to stay with her?"

"Find her, then. Go on, find her. Now get out, will you? Here comes the appendectomy."

Parry shrugged his shoulders, and as the trolley was wheeled past him, bearing its burden, he got out. Without looking back, Abbot followed the trolley, and the door shut. Ignoring the lift, Parry went down the three flights of stairs. When he reached the hall, he realized he was stuck for a car. He knocked on the door of the matron's office. There was no answer. He supposed she was up in the theater. He went in, and shut the door behind him. Now what? If the expert scrounger, Clive, couldn't find a lady to oblige at Shots Hall, then it was unlikely he'd be able to find a lady to oblige Miss Merridew, who'd just had an overdose of morphine. A hotel? No, she might take it into her head to hire a taxi and drive back to Shotshall. Could she stay with the Ambroses? No, they were too scatty. They'd go off to the pub and spend half the night there, leaving Miss Merridew alone. Congreve and Norton could, of course, take it in turns to stand guard over her, but that wouldn't do at all. Nothing would do. Home she would have to go, tomorrow, and that was that.

Parry, who suffered from no false modesty, had a nasty feeling that he'd fallen down over this repulsive case, and that everything was coming unstuck on him.

He took up the matron's phone, and rang London

The answer to his last night's inquiries was entirely negative.

"No," said the voice the other end. "No trace to be found of anyone of that name. They seem to've neither been born nor died, and no identity card was ever issued to anyone of that name either. They didn't commit homicide, suicide, matricide or any other cide, or arson, larceny, bigamy or anything else."

"Hell," Parry swore, and rang off.

There seemed only one thing for it. He'd have to go to London himself. There was a train at five o'clock that evening. He couldn't get back that night, but that didn't matter. He'd take an early train in the morning or the afternoon. In the meantime, Mahew could take charge. Debating his many problems, he phoned through to Congreve. Congreve had used his ten pairs of eyes but had spotted nothing, so he said. Parry lit yet another cigarette, and got on to the Shots Arms. Mahew had just arrived back from an abortive visit to Bee and Flik. He'd got nothing out of them at all.

"Damn," Parry said, and told Mahew about Miss Merridew's letter to dearest Emily. Mahew was coughing so much that it sounded as though a pack of hounds was in full cry at the pub end of the phone. He seemed, in between his fits of coughing, to take singularly little interest in anything. Parry supposed the gentleman from the brewery was listening. He rang off, then got on to the Central Police Station and told them to send a car up to the hospital for him.

There was no time for him to go back to the Mahews' and collect what he wanted in the way of razors and toothbrushes for the night, but that worried him not at all. Everything he'd need was in his flat in town. He let himself out of the hospital, and waited on the edge of the pavement for the car. The afternoon was drawing in. Gusts of wind and rain came from the sea, and he could hear the roar of the waves in the distance. It was blowing up for a southwesterly gale, he thought. A feeling of dreariness and defeat suddenly came over him. Right under his nose three murders had taken place, and then Miss Merridew had taken morphine in her milk. And still he lacked the vital link in his chain of evidence. Damn Flik, he thought, and his mind dwelt with longing on thumbscrews, racks, rubber truncheons and other tortures designed to make people talk. Under that copper hair, inside that strange mind with its secret corners, dwelt something that was beyond all reason and logic. And there, until he found the key to unlock that mind, it would still dwell. He hoped Mahew had digested well and truly all his directions.

The police car came round the corner, stopped and turned.

"Station," he said briefly, and got in.

"Which one, sir?" the driver asked. "Police, or railway?"

"Sorry," Parry laughed. "Railway. I want to catch the five o'clock to Victoria."

Five minutes later, the immensely worried driver of Mahew's car swept up to the front entrance of the hospital, and getting out, opened the rear door.

"I tell you," Mahew wheezed, "I won't see any bloody doctor. Take me back to Shotshall—I've a million things to do. How'd I get in this car, anyhow?"

"I'm afraid, sir, I pushed you in from behind," the driver said. "You wouldn't by no means let me ring up your doctor, so it seemed the only thing to do." He stared anxiously at his chief's flushed face and glassy eyes, congested by much coughing. The wheezing of his chest was like the pumping of concertina bellows, and as unlovely. It was obvious to the driver that here was someone who was very ill indeed, and, murders or no murders, orders or no orders, needed expert attention. Somehow he got Mahew into the hospital, where a nurse pounced on him with professional enthusiasm and sat him down on a chair by the hall fire.

"Just wait with him, constable," she said, "and I'll fetch the house surgeon. He and Dr. Abbot're just through with an operation. Take it easy," she said to Mahew, who was not quite capable of doing anything else but swear.

He was still swearing when the house surgeon and Abbot came out of the lift, stinking of antiseptic and well scrubbed.

"What the hell?" Abbot said, staring at Mahew. "Here, help me along with him."

Mahew's temperature was 104 degrees. By the time his examination was over, he was quite delirious.

"We simply can't keep him here," Abbot frowned.

"We can put him in one of the emergency beds," the house surgeon, a man by the name of Larson, said. "But I don't like doing that, as there're only the two vacant ones now, and if we had a couple of bad accident or operation cases, we'd be stung."

"Couldn't agree with you more. Listen to me, ring up his house and see if Mrs. Mahew's capable of looking after him, and get her to ring his own doctor. I expect there's a District Nurse or someone available to give a hand over his way." Abbot ran his hands through his hair. More trouble, and he liked Mahew, who, fortunately, appeared to have an excellent constitution apart from his present ailment.

The soul of competence, despite her cold, Mrs. Mahew said she'd ring their own doctor, and could certainly manage to look after her own husband. Within ten minutes, wrapped in blankets and hot-water-bottled, a St. John Ambulance team had him under way, and Abbot breathed a sigh of relief. He had enough on his hands already without the added burden of a Deputy Chief Constable with pneumonia. Unaware of Parry's sudden departure, he was blissfully ignorant of the fact that the triple murder case was now left unattended, and that the man he loathed above all others would automatically take charge till Parry came back. He shrugged himself into his overcoat, and weaving a pattern of violent imprecations in his mind which included all the crimes of the Decalogue, wrathfully took himself off on his rounds. He wondered when, if ever, he was going to see Flik again. Like a wraith she haunted him, a wraith which, when he put his hand to touch it, vanished out of his grasp.

CHAPTER 22

THE object of Abbot's loathing, also unaware that he was temporarily in charge, looked at his watch and decided that hell, he couldn't stay much longer with Camilla, unless he could think up some good excuse to give Parry on his return to Shotshall. Anyway, he'd done his stuff. Questioned and cross-questioned her, happily unknowing that she'd amused herself by feeding him a pack of quite delightful lies about her past life, which, lurid though it had been, was nothing compared with her sprightly inventions.

"You certainly went it, didn't you?" he grinned.

Camilla looked at him under her eyelashes. "Do have another drink, honey," she tempted.

"Why aren't you drinking?"

Camilla, who never drank anything till evening out of regard both for her complexion and her lucid brain, smiled provocatively. "I had mine at lunch," she said. "Gin."

Well, Arnoldson thought, he'd done his duty. The duty that had to come before pleasure. He got up and transferred himself to the sofa next Camilla, breathing whisky on her beautifully dressed little silver curls, which she wore piled up on top of her head like some seductive sort of bird's nest.

"I like the way you do your curls," he said, poking a fat forefinger at them.

Camilla smiled, and did not flinch.

Outside, the wind gathered force, and the raindrops ran down the windows. But by her fire it was warm and scented. Arnoldson moved closer, and pushed his knee against hers.

"You must see my little garden house," she said in a throaty voice. Camilla's garden house was a toolshed, where, in the spring, her broody hens sat in coops on their clutches of eggs. "We can go out the front door."

"In the rain? It's cozier here—Camilla."

She got up, her hips swaying. "But it's even cozier in my little garden house. Central heating, and lovely divans.

Chewing his lips, Arnoldson followed her. At the front door she paused. "You go first, honey," she said, opening the door.

Arnoldson stepped out into the rain, wondering why the house wasn't good enough. He'd had so much of Camilla's drink, however, that he didn't much care if it was the house or the garden house, so long as she would play. Camilla steadied herself by holding on to the doorjamb. Then she lifted one shapely foot, and, placing it in the small of Arnoldson's back, expertly heaved. He shot forward onto his face into the mud of the path. He looked, Camilla thought, very funny like that.

"Good-by, you howling cad," she said pleasantly, and shutting the door, locked it. Even at her age, she was extremely choosy about her boyfriends.

Rage indescribable seethed through the ladies' man as he roared away on his motor bike. He was smothered with mud, and his *amour-propre* was lacerated. He'd make her pay for that, the bitch. Now he'd have to go back to St. Arthurs and change. Buffeted by the wind, he did an unsteady sixty to the edge of the town, then slowed down to a wobble and took the turning to his lodgings. The letter that had arrived by the afternoon's post completely soothed him, however. It was, indeed, almost too good to be true. He read and reread it as he changed, putting on his best suit and a tie that was nobody's business.

A quarter of an hour afterward he dropped in at the police station, thinking he'd phone Parry from there, making out he'd been back from

Camilla's for some time. More good news greeted him.

Brewin, now doing a spell of day duty, looked up when he came in, and said, "Been trying to get you for the last hour. Inspector Parry's gone to London for the night, and the Major's just been taken to his home in an ambulance with pneumonia." He shook his head. "Lord, I'm sorry, I hope he hasn't got it too bad."

Arnoldson digested this delightful information.

"Queen Anne's dead. I knew all that before you did. Parry put me in charge of the case before he left. What else d'you think?"

Brewin and two fellow constables eyed him in silence. If they'd ever thought him quite a good sport, they thought so no longer. Old, forgotten resentments piled up in their honest though not very brilliant minds, and blossomed there in sturdy blooms. And he was bloody drunk. They liked their drink, but they didn't get bloody drunk when they were supposed to be on duty.

"Must get cracking," Arnoldson said. "Now, perhaps—not even perhaps, but certainly, something'll be done about this mess. Scotland Yard—"He very nearly spat. "Mahew and his pet from London—" He strolled to the door, his hands in his pockets, one hand feeling the letter he'd just had. "I'll take one of the cars. Bransome can drive me."

"Kiss-me-boot," Brewin remarked to the ceiling in a loud, resounding voice, which hit Arnoldson in both ears as he went out, but did not make them burn.

The reluctant Bransome, a young and rather overawed member of the St. Arthurs' flying squad, obediently stopped at the Shots Arms, where Arnoldson told him to wait outside. Arnoldson went in the back door. Winnie was poking at a dirty saucepan with an even dirtier mop. When she saw him, she dropped both.

"Hullo, darling," she said rather doubtfully.

"Don't call me darling. Kept that bottle aside for me? Give me a drink then, and stop being a fool."

The infatuated Winnie, thus addressed by the man she looked on as her boyfriend, began to snuffle, and unearthed a half-full bottle of whisky from the bottom of the kitchen cupboard.

"If this is the way you start, then how're you going on?" she gulped.

Arnoldson took no more notice of her than if she'd been a small spider. He drank his drink in a satisfied silence, and left, as he'd come, without greetings. Winnie burst into tears.

"Gawd, what a turnout," said the brewery's man who was taking it easy in old Marsh's armchair, preparatory to opening up, which he was already late in doing. Mr. Fewsey, the butcher, had been hammering on the door of the saloon bar for what seemed to him like hours. As he hammered he shook his head from side to side, like a dog with canker in one ear. All disorganized. All the old habits and customs and routine gone by the board. The rain ran down the back of his neck, and the wind howled.

And in Miss Merridew's living room, Congreve wondered what was going to happen now. They'd rung him up from the town to tell him about Parry and Mahew, and a second call had just come through from Brewin. If Congreve had had any idea that Parry had gone off thinking that Mahew was safely in charge of the proceedings, he would have rung up Scotland Yard. He'd never rung up Scotland Yard in his life. But he'd have rung Buckingham Palace if he'd known how urgently Parry was needed.

For, confident that the news he'd had that day would break down the iron wall of Flik's reserve and that she'd crack, and the honor and glory of solving Parry's case would be all his, Arnoldson took her down to the police station and shut her up in one of the cells.

Norton, struggling through the storm, gave Congreve the news when he came to relieve him; and Congreve, scenting mischief, went straight to Miss Merridew's telephone.

"You mark my words," he said over his shoulder to Norton as he picked up the receiver, "'is ruddy 'oliness, Arnoldson, ain't up to no good. This all smells to me like old fish."

"Stinks," Norton agreed.

"'Ullo?" Congreve bawled into the receiver. An earsplitting crackle nearly deafened him. After a long time, a dim, harassed voice answered him. "London call—can you 'ear me? What?" he said.

"Sorry, main cable—can't get trunk—toll—not even—loca—tomorrow perhaps—"

Congreve put the receiver back. "And sweet Fanny Adams to you," he said. "Norton, the line's gone again, bad luck to it. Know what? I don't believe the inspector knew before 'e went that the Major'd been taken ill. 'E'd never 'av gone off and left Arnoldson in charge if 'e 'ad."

"What're we going to do about it, anyhow?" Norton asked rather helplessly. "I don't see we can do nothing. After all, the inspector must be back tomorrow, and then he'll put things right."

"'Oo knows," Congreve debated with relish, "what may 'appen before 'e does get back? Maybe two more murders."

"Perhaps Mrs. Ashley did do them." Norton was reluctant to admit such an idea, but it seemed to him, now, more than likely. "After all, someone did."

"No?" Congreve opened his eyes wide. "Go on? I'm off now. Don't know what you'd better do—'ang on 'ere, I suppose. Gawd, what a mix-up."

The force of the wind, when he got out in the road and pushed his bicycle against it, nearly knocked him down, and the salt in the rain stung his eyes. It was quite dark. He left his bicycle by the entrance to Shots Hall, and by the light of his torch, which showed nothing but the spewing silver of the rain, groped his way to the front door of the house. After knocking twice and getting no answer, he boldly walked in. Bee was at the telephone, furiously banging the instrument up and down, as if by so doing she could wrest from it some response.

"It ain't no good," Congreve said. "The main cable's gone."

The door crashed behind him, nearly catching his raincoat in it. All the hall lights were on, but even so the shadows still seemed to fill all the corners.

Bee turned, thumping the telephone down on its shelf.

"What the hell's gone wrong with the line?" she asked.

"I said, the main cable's gone. Miss Chattock, did Arnoldson 'ave a warrant for Mrs. Ashley's arrest, or what?"

Bee looked at him for a long time. Even this calamity had not appeared to have shaken her dignified exterior. "He hadn't a warrant. He said something to her I didn't hear, and she simply went. She simply went off with him just as if she was going shopping, the damn little fool. I tried to go too, but he shut me out of the car—"

"And off they went," Congreve finished for her.

With a calm fluency which roused Congreve's admiration on high, Bee proceeded to say what she thought of Arnoldson. "How Parry could have left him in charge, I don't know. Where's Mahew? What the devil's he up to?"

"'E's been taken 'ome with pneumonia, and as the superintendent's laid up with flu, Arnoldson's automatically in charge, as 'e's the senior of the rest of us."

"I wanted to get a taxi and go down to the police station and raise hell," Bee said.

"I 'aven't any doubt but what you do. But it wouldn't be much good. I'm on my way there myself, if I don't get blown away like the little bit of thistledown I am."

"Have a drink before you go," Bee invited him.

"Don't mind if I do, I'm sure," Congreve thanked her, and over a glass of the prewar whisky, cheered her up by telling her an imaginary story,about an imaginary funeral he'd once been to. Having thus fortified himself and his hostess, he went, leaving Bee alone with her horrified thoughts in the gray, empty, wind-beleaguered house.

It was downhill practically all the way to St. Arthurs, but even so, he had to pedal as though he were riding up a steep mountain. Several times he was blown off into the mud. Outside a pub near the sea front, he got off and thankfully went into the fug of tobacco smoke and beer. But even the noise of talk didn't drown the breaking of the waves over the esplanade, the hissing cry of blown spray, the boom of the gale. He shook himself, sending a fountain of mud and water on to the floor, and felt a hand on his arm.

It was Clive, his fair hair wet, clinging to his forehead.

"Hullo, Congreve? Have a drink?"

"Don't mind if I do," Congreve agreed for the second time that night. "Nasty evening, ain't it?"

"Bloody awful. Whisky?" Clive ordered two doubles. "I've just had to leave my car in dock. Came down again to the town to have a last try to get some sort of skivvy to oblige them at Shots Hall, and one of the big ends went. I'll have to put up at some pub, as I can't get a taxi driver in the place to turn out in this storm."

Congreve sucked his teeth slowly, meditating. "Pity," he said. "A car'd come in handy now. Arnoldson's just taken Mrs. Ashley away to the police station."

"What?" Clive stared, incredulous. "Arnoldson? That swine taken Flik? Where's Parry? And Mahew?"

Congreve told him.

Clive's face was white, and a little pulse beat in his forehead.

"I'm going to see Arnoldson," he said, and putting his glass down, limped out of the pub. He felt, suddenly, lonely and dispirited. He didn't feel young any more. His leg seemed a dead weight, a leaden limb he had to drag behind him. He was aware, yet not aware, that Congreve was wheeling his bicycle along in the gutter beside him.

His whole mind was concentrated on Flik, on the leering, pink-mouthed man who'd taken her away. He didn't think he was angry, but there was an awful coldness inside him that had never been there before. He didn't notice where he was going. He didn't notice the wave that drove him down the side street to the police station. He didn't notice Congreve open the door of the police station, an unbeautiful building that, with the adjoining wing where the cells were, huddled together in company with the mortuary, the corporation yard and the police court, as though all were bound together in the bonds of some unwilling and bigamous marriage. He only knew that suddenly he was in the warmth and light, a constable looking at him inquiringly while Congreve took off his raincoat.

"This gentleman wants to see Detective Sergeant Arnoldson," Congreve said. "Important."

"He's busy," the constable said. "But I'll send through to him. What name is it, sir?"

"Clive Harris. I've got a statement to make."

Somewhere a door crashed shut and another crashed open, blown by the drafts that whirled along the bleak stone corridors. Windows rattled and shook, and against the small, barred oblong of glass high up in the wall of Flik's cell, the spray whispered in wild, sibilant whispers. The four whitewashed walls sweated like the skin of an old, unwashed man. The one light set in the ceiling picked out the wooden bunk, the tin washstand with its tin basin, its jug and bucket, the hardwood chair, the stone floor, and Flik's white face and Arnoldson's flushed triumphant one. Outside the heavy door, a disapproving and angry policewoman, whom Arnoldson had summarily dismissed from the cell, stood tight-upped, swinging a bunch of keys. He hadn't any right to be in there alone with that lady, not in the state he was in, whatever she'd done, she kept telling herself. No right at all.

She looked round as Congreve came along the corridor.

"Been thrown out on my ear," she complained. "And he's the worse for whatever he's been drinking."

"Oh, 'e is, is 'e?" Congreve was interested. "Well, you can just go in and tell 'im Mr. Clive 'Arris wants to see 'im particular, as 'e's got a statement to make."

Without ceremony, the policewoman opened the cell door wide so that Congreve had a glimpse of Flik sitting taut on the edge of the bunk. He tried to wink at her, not in familiarity, but in reassurance.

"There's a Mr. Clive Harris outside wants to see you," Flik's unwilling jailer said sharply to Arnoldson. "He's got a statement to make to you, and it's important."

Arnoldson's face was still flushed when he came out to Clive, and round his eyes there were beads of sweat.

"Well?" he said aggressively.

Clive looked at him, hating him, and leaned heavily on his burdensome leg. "I came here to tell you that I murdered those three people." His voice sounded unreal in his ears, as if it was someone else speaking from miles away.

Arnoldson burst into a guffaw of laughter. "Trying to take the blame for your lady love?"

"My—what—?"

All Clive could see now was the pink face, the wet mouth, and he hit out at it, and hit again and again. His violence, however, was short-lived. There would be no need for him now to find a pub to put up in overnight. He had free board and lodging in a cell exactly similar to Flik's.

"Oh, why did you do that?" Congreve reproved him before he locked the door. "Now you'll be charged with assaulting a police officer. The Bench doesn't sit tomorrow, so you won't come up till the day after— still, lots of things can 'appen before then."

"That's what I'm afraid of," Clive said grimly, nursing his torn knuckles. "What a bloody fool I am. Now I'm no help to her at all."

Congreve sucked his teeth. "Never mind, Inspector Parry'll be back tomorrow, and I dare say 'e can fix things some'ow. One thing, Arnoldson won't go in and see Mrs. Ashley again, not with 'is face like it is. I'll see you get some tea and a sandwich. Anything else you want?"

Clive thought quickly. "Yes. Look here, Congreve. Will you get hold of Dr. Abbot and ask him to keep an eye on her? He's the police doctor, after all, isn't he? And she's his patient anyway. Will you do that?"

Congreve nodded. "I'll do me best," he agreed.

But when the weary Congreve was decanted off his bicycle by the gale on to Abbot's doorstep, he could get no answer to his persistent ringing. Abbot was out on a maternity case, hastily fetched by an alarmed husband who had run all the way; and his housekeeper had basely deserted her post and taken herself off to the nearest local for a Guinness. Usually the most conscientious of women, she had occasional bouts of thirst, when her motto was "Let 'em all ring." This was one of the bouts.

By the light of his torch, the paper nearly torn out of his hand by the attacking storm, Congreve scribbled a message and pushed it through the slit of the letter box. The draft that whirled under the door carried the scrap of paper far across the floor of the hall, lodging it in a dark corner. So Abbot passed an uneasy night in his hard bed, unaware that Flik sat sleepless on the edge of her wooden bunk at the police station, that Clive raged impotent in another cell, that Arnoldson was cooking up trouble while he thought unprintable thoughts. And at Shots Hall Bee sat upright in her bed, listening to the noises of the storm the creakings and rustlings of the lonely house, waiting for the morning.

Of them all, of all the people whose lives had been so suddenly disrupted, only Miss Merridew slept peacefully and soundly, watched over by a night nurse with freckles and an upturned nose.

CHAPTER 23

ABBOT'S housekeeper found Congreve's note when she was sweeping the hall floor. She took it up to him with his morning mail and the papers. For once he hadn't been dragged out of bed at some unearthly hour by someone who imagined they were dying, and he lay on his back for a time, staring at the ceiling, before he bothered to look at his letters. When he did, the shock galvanized him to feverish action, and he tore at his face with his razor as though he would masochistically flay the skin off it.

Why had that muddleheaded fool Parry gone off and left Flik to the mercies of Arnoldson? And what had Arnoldson found out that justified his taking this step while Parry's back was turned and Mahew out of the running? He dragged his clothes on, his fingers unfumbling but furious, and without waiting for his breakfast ran his car out of the garage. The gale had died down to intermittent gusts, and from the sea the aftermurk of the storm rolled in, a channel fog of low-blowing cloud and dark gray, fuggy rain that blanketed the town and the country round, blotting everything out except the immediate foreground.

Abbot cursed the fog, which would force him to drive at a crawl, and still cursing, backed his car on to the road, trying to ignore the panting man who gesticulated wildly at him. But he wouldn't be ignored. He almost flung himself on the bonnet of the car in his endeavors to attract attention, and the irritated doctor saw it was the panicky husband and father of the evening before.

"Well?" he said. "What is it? Must you try and commit suicide by getting run over?"

The man let go the bonnet and came round to the open window next Abbot.

"For God's sake, doctor," he jabbered, "can you come at once? It's the baby, he's dying. My God, he's dying."

Abbot ground his teeth. "Get in, go on, get in the back and stop dancing about."

The incoherent father stumbled in the rear door, and Abbot started on his unwelcome errand. The short drive seemed to last forever as he nosed the car through the fog. He had no thought for the baby he'd just brought into the hazardous world, but only for Flik and her plight. But Flik wasn't ill, and the baby was, so he'd have to attend to the baby first. He found the unfortunate brat being bounced about in the arms of its mother's sister, while the mother lay in bed crying loudly. The baby was also crying, in hard, gasping jerks, and its face was purple.

"Stop throwing it about," Abbot said. "Can't you hold it properly? What've you done to it, in the name of heaven?"

Breathless, the fond father began to explain. "He seemed to look so pale this morning, so we—I gave him a little drop of whisky."

"Whisky?" Abbot repeated in exasperation. "How much?"

"Only a tablespoon," blubbered the mother. "He looked so pale."

"God almighty. A whole tablespoon of whisky? Neat? A large tablespoon, I suppose?"

Abbot supposed rightly. Down its tender, unwilling throat, into its tender and unwilling stomach, a scalding dose of neat spirit of the worst kind had been forced in one fell swoop.

"Miserable little thing." Abbot glared at its parents, and set to work to undo the mischief they'd done, which took him some considerable time and trouble. By the time he was through, the morning was getting on, and his already jagged temper was in shreds. The fog, too, was thicker, so when he drove on his way it was at walking pace. As he passed the hospital, he thought of Miss Merridew, and his conscience pricked him. He turned the car and drove up to the entrance. Then he thought of Miss Merridew's milk glass, and hurried to the laboratory.

"About that glass I left here," he said to the white-coated analyst, "have you done anything about it yet?"

"Morphine."

"I see—I wonder how much the total dose was?"

"Not quite the mixture as before," the young man said. "There's not such a large morphine content in the dregs of this glass as there was in those three teacups."

"I see." Abbot rubbed his chin thoughtfully. Then that was why she'd made such a quick recovery. She hadn't had such a strong dose as the others. But quite strong enough.

"What a damned awful business these poisonings are," the young man pondered. "I hear Mrs. Ashley's been arrested."

Abbot's eyes narrowed behind his spectacles. So Flik's arrest was public property, was it? He hurried out of the laboratory and fell straight into the clutches of a nurse from the public wards.

"Oh, Dr. Abbot?"

"Yes, now what is it?" he fumed.

"That gallstone case of yours doesn't seem too well today. Can you have a look at her?"

Oh, God, now gallstones. Champing at the bit of his urgent desire to get to Flik, he followed the nurse to the bedside of his gallstone case. She was a fat woman, and had worked herself into a panic that she was rapidly developing more gallstones in place of the ones which had been removed. Valuable time was spent in convincing her that she couldn't be growing new gallstones as she now had no gall bladder for them to lurk in. Much more of this, Abbot thought, and I'll yell.

At last, however, he freed himself from the clutches of the nurse and his agitated patient, and ran up the staircase to the private wards, shuddering at the thoughts of having to listen to Miss Merridew's meandering and meaningless attempts at conversation. In the corridor off which the private wards opened, there appeared to be more trouble, and he mentally tore his hair. Outside the door of Miss Merridew's room, the day sister in charge of the private wards was hauling over the coals a young nurse who seemed almost on the point of tears. Abbot hesitated, wondering if he could escape, and was lost.

"Dr. Abbot?" The sister approached him, rustling. "I'm sure I don't know what you'll say."

"I'm sure I don't know either," he answered, "as I don't know what it is you're sure you don't know what I'm to say about." He was rather dismally aware that his remark surpassed, in its complicated structure, one of Miss Merridew's least lucid efforts. "What's happened?" he added.

"Nurse Halliday was silly enough to tell Miss Merridew about Mrs. Ashley's arrest. Apparently Mrs. Ashley and her aunt, a Miss Something, are very great friends of Miss Merridew's, and Miss Merridew was not unnaturally terribly upset by the news."

"I suppose she would be. I'll go in and smooth down the ruffled feathers."

"That's the trouble," the sister said with a wintry smile. "You won't find any ruffled feathers to smooth. I'd just made arrangements to have a second bed put in my number four private ward, as the patient didn't seem to mind, and then Nurse Halliday went and gave Miss Merridew the news." She shrugged her shoulders, glaring at the unfortunate culprit, who still hovered in the background. "Miss Merridew insisted, *insisted* on being sent back immediately, so that she could be of some help to this Mrs. Ashley's aunt, who apparently must be all alone. I don't see what possible help Miss Merridew thought she could be in her present woolly, weak state, but she *insisted*."

"You mean she's gone?" Abbot stared. "My God, she's a tough old boot, isn't she?"

"Quite remarkably so. I did everything to dissuade her, but I can't lock the patients in their rooms, you know, this isn't a lunatic asylum. She was up and out of bed, dressing, before you could say knife. Poor thing, and in such a state, crying her eyes out like a child. I tried to get her back to bed, but you'd be surprised how strong she is. In the end I had to give it up, so I got Brassey's taxi from down the road, and rolled her up in plenty of blankets. Miss Merridew assured me that she'd stay with Mrs. Ashley's aunt, where she'd be quite all right. I'm sure, doctor, I can't say how sorry I am."

"Not your fault," Abbot said, not caring a damn whether Miss Merridew had gone or not. "You couldn't help it, and anyhow it's her own lookout. I don't suppose for an instant it'll do her any harm. After all, she wasn't recovering from an operation. It's simply a case of her blood being upon her own head. She's quite irresponsible, as you've probably noticed."

Then he fled before anyone else could trip him up with further woes or worries. Now, at last, he could go to Flik. He weaved the car in and out of the befogged streets and roads, and drew up with a jerk outside the police station. He had no idea what he could do for Flik; no idea what had happened. Clive could look after himself. According to Congreve's brief note, the young man had hit Arnoldson and been incarcerated too. That wouldn't kill him. His heart, however, warmed toward Clive, who had done what he had so often wanted to do himself.

He nodded a greeting to the duty officer, who lifted the flap of the desk so that he could go in behind it.

"I want to see Mrs. Ashley." He found that there was an odd unsteadiness in his voice, and this roused him to anger with himself. "I'm her medical practitioner as well as yours, and her health's very groggy. Those cells'd kill off an all-in wrestler in this weather. Her chest's weak. I take it you don't want a case of congestion of the lungs on your hands?"

"No, sir." The duty officer, like the rest of the St. Arthurs police with the exception of Arnoldson, liked Abbot. They appreciated his honesty, and his flowery language was to them a constant source of entertainment. "Only you'd better have a word with Sergeant Arnoldson first, I suppose."

"May I inquire if that slab of mutton fat is in charge of this case? Where's Parry? Isn't he back?"

"He isn't, doctor. We expected him first thing. It's a b—it's a nuisance, the line's still being out of order. We can't get in touch with no one, and no one can't get in touch with us. Maybe the Inspector'll come on the 1:45 from Victoria, I mean, the train that arrives here 1:45. He can't've come by the 12:02, otherwise he'd be here by now."

"Where's Arnoldson?"

With a dislike he took no pains to conceal, the duty officer jerked his head at a closed door with "Private" painted on it. "In there. Writing. By the pages he's written he must be doing a book."

Without knocking, Abbot opened the door and went in, shutting it with an aggressive bang. Arnoldson's back was to him. His hair shone with oil as he bent over his literary occupation. He didn't turn round or speak; his shoulders proclaimed that he was too busy on important business to deign to notice anyone. Abbot's mouth tightened, and he looked over Arnoldson's head at what he was doing. It was evident that he was writing a lengthy report. On the page on the blotter in front of him, Abbot read words here and there. "On the 2nd December, Mrs. Ashley denied... but on searching the grate I found ..." Abbot felt sickened. Then he turned cold down his spine. For carefully laid beside the blotter and the accumulating pages of close writing was a copy of a marriage certificate. Flikka Ashley, James Gene Waldron (Private, US. Army), March 10th, 1943, Sefton-in-the-Marsh, Yorkshire. And Arnoldson was writing, "It is obvious that Mrs. Ashley, or rather, Waldron, wished to conceal at all costs the fact of her marriage, and that having discovered that the three deceased and Miss Merridew knew of it..." It seemed to Abbot that a rat was gnawing at his stomach. Two opened letters protruded from under a piece of blotting paper. Abbot could only see the halves of them, but saw they were addressed to Flik, and he guessed that Arnoldson had been to the post office that morning and impounded her incoming mail.

He reached forward his long, sensitive fingers, till they nearly touched Arnoldson's neck. But that wouldn't do. It wouldn't help Flik if he strangled the man who was trying to hang her for murder.

"Arnoldson?"

"Well? Well, who the devil's that? Get out. Can't you see I'm busy?"

"You amaze me." God give me strength not to kill him, Abbot thought. May the devil look after his own and protect him from me. "I'm going in to see Mrs. Ashley."

"Oh, you are, are you?" Arnoldson turned round, his battered face red. "Who said so?"

"I say so. I might remind you that I'm the police surgeon, and that one of my manifold duties is to see none of your guests die on you. Mrs. Ashley suffers from emphysema," he improvised wildly, "therefore the cold of the cells may bring on acute congestion at any moment."

Arnoldson had no idea what emphysema was, and taken off his guard was temporarily at a loss for what to say. Abbot took the opportunity to walk out of the room and shut the door. He nodded at the duty officer, and let himself through the door that led, by way of more doors and many corridors, to the cells. The policewoman was just coming out of one of the cells with an empty teacup in her hand. She smiled at Abbot, and looked relieved.

"Have you come to see Mrs. Ashley?" she asked.

"Yes," Abbot said. "I have."

"Well I'm glad you have, because she doesn't look at all well, and she's got a cough—come on. Doctor, they ought to do something about this place, it isn't fit for pigs, what with the damp and the smells."

She put the teacup down on the floor and pushed the cell door open wider. It was her duty to go in with Abbot, so she went, shutting the door behind them both. Despite her hard-seeming, plain face and her efficient feet, she was a kindly enough woman, and she felt for Flik a deep pity, which was mixed with admiration for her prisoner's quiet control and courteous manners.

"Here's the doctor, Mrs. Ashley," she said in a loud, cheerful voice.

The sight of Flik had the effect of paralyzing Abbot, so that for the moment he couldn't speak or move, but only look. She stood at the opposite end of the wretched cell, her back to the wall, her hands against it. As surely as if someone had told him, Abbot knew that she had washed herself with meticulous care that morning in the little tin basin. But Arnoldson must have taken her away without giving her the chance to bring any necessaries with her. For the first time he saw her without lipstick, without powder, just as she was; it was a shock to find she was so really beautiful, so flawless. Her eyes, which had been turned inward on her own thoughts, slowly came to life and looked at him squarely.

"Good morning," she said. "Or is it good afternoon yet?"

He must get rid of the policewoman, Abbot decided; somehow he must get rid of her.

"Good morning," he answered, and the effort of speaking was painful.

Flik coughed, a small, dry cough which seemed to shake her.

Abbot turned to the policewoman. "Would you mind going out to my car and fetching my bag?" he asked her. "I forgot it. I can give Mrs. Ashley a linctus that'll temporarily relieve her chest. Oh, and then could you send round to Brights the chemist and ask them for a small bottle of

Friars Balsam? If you felt in the mood, I could do with a cup of tea, I've been hard at it all morning."

"Of course, Dr. Abbot." The obliging woman went about his errands, unhurriedly. If Arnoldson could shut himself up in there, then why shouldn't the doctor, who was respectable? It'd be a smack in the eye for Arnoldson.

"Isn't Parry back yet?" Flik spoke with sudden urgency.

"No, he isn't." Parry, always Parry. Curse Parry.

Flik moved away from the wall. "Funny," she said. "I'd never thought of you. I kept trying to think all night of someone who could give me a hand, and I never thought of you."

"I'm used to that," Abbot said dryly. "I don't loom very large on your horizon, do I? Has Miss Chattock been to see you?"

Flik nodded. "The blessed Congreve sent a taxi up for her early this morning. Only there wasn't anything she could do. Arnoldson hasn't been in today. Why? What's he doing?"

Abbot nearly said he was getting together the evidence to hang her, but stopped himself just in time. "He's too vain. His face looks like a rotten bit of meat. Didn't you know your friend Clive Harris beat him up last night?"

"My God. Did he? Did he? What's happened to Clive, then?"

"He's keeping you company in another cell," Abbot said with a certain amount of satisfaction. "But no doubt when the omnipotent Parry decides to come back he'll arrange matters."

"Arnoldson was drunk."

Flik's calm scorn somehow filled Abbot with alarm. If she went on practicing this terrible self-restraint, she'd crack up. He fumbled in his mind for words. There was so much he wanted to say, and so little time, he thought, to say it. Only he must say it.

"Listen to me. D'you know your cat's escaped from its bag? D'you know Arnoldson's got a copy of your marriage certificate?"

"Yes. Yes, I know. That's why I came with him yesterday evening, without kicking. I thought if I didn't make a fuss, he mightn't poke about any more."

"Once and for all," Abbot said, his temper rising, "will you tell me what it is you're concealing? It's more than your marriage to that American, isn't it? Isn't it?"

"Isn't that enough? Isn't wanting to conceal that marriage a big enough motive for having committed murder?"

"Be quiet, damn you, you little fool," Abbot swore. "D'you want to put a rope deliberately round your own neck?"

She stared at him, a strange look on her face. "No." She moved her hands, a movement so suddenly helpless that Abbot softened, his fierce resentment of her and her loveliness dying in him. "Abbot? D'you know a fool when you see one? If not, then take a good look at me." She was talking, now, more to herself, as if she had forgotten he was there. "I've been nursing in the thing that goes for my mind what I thought was a sort of high ideal— No, that's not the right word. Never mind. But after a night in this charming residence I see I've been a fool. A wicked fool— After all, one often hears about people killing themselves and others by unselfishness. It isn't unselfishness, it's insanity. I've done incalculable harm. I'm responsible for Molly's, and Marsh's and Harry's deaths."

Abbot snatched her by the shoulders and shook her as if she had been an empty sack. "I don't know what you're talking about—a lot of bloody parables and bunk. Shut up, you lunatic. Shut up before I make you shut up. I don't want to know your damn secrets—my God, letting everyone think you'd been sleeping with a casual pickup, when all the time he was your husband." I don't know what I'm saying, he told himself, and let go her shoulders.

Flik sat down on the bunk, out of breath after her shaking, and Abbot felt incredibly foolish. Idly, she began to turn over the selection of dreary books that had been provided for her entertainment, while Abbot watched the white curve of her neck as she bent her head. Suddenly she seemed transfixed, her eyes wide, staring at a faded reproduction of a photograph in a book on horticulture. What had struck her, Abbot couldn't imagine; she had the look of someone who, groping in the darkness, had found a light.

"How's Susan?" she asked unexpectedly.

"The old fool took herself off from the hospital this morning when she heard what had happened to you. She's gone to stay with your aunt."

"With Aunt Bee? Abbot? Abbot, don't they really know when Parry's coming back?"

"No," he almost shouted. "Perhaps he won't come back at all. Perhaps they've handed the case over to someone else. How should I know? Anyway, he hasn't phoned. He can't, the lines've broken down."

"Once you said you'd help me." Flik's voice dropped to a wildly urgent whisper. "Will you help me? Will you help me to get out of here? Today, soon?"

"Get out," he muttered. "How? How the hell can I? For God's sake, what a wildcat idea."

"Please? You can think of some way. Please?"

The policewoman reappeared with the bottle of cough linctus and an enormous teaspoon. Something in Flik's manner affected Abbot with a rather terrible excitement, and he found his hand was shaking when he poured out the dose and offered the spoon to her. Her hand was perfectly steady.

"I'll come back again later," he said, knowing he was going to help Flik do the impossible and make a getaway. "Then I'll see about the steaming of your chest when the Friars Balsam comes. Good morning."

The policewoman followed him out of the cell and locked the door. "I think it's dreadful," she complained, "the way all the ratepayers' money goes on building amusement places on the sea front, when there's holes like this in the town. These cells are enough to give anyone pneumonia." She lowered her voice, looking over her shoulder. "I know I oughtn't to say things, but it's all wrong. Mrs. Ashley hasn't been charged, or anything. It's most irregular. We'll all get into trouble."

"Especially if Mrs. Ashley gets pneumonia," Abbot said maliciously, inspiration coming to him. "Which she looks like doing. I'll be in again as soon as I can."

I'm going to make a fool of myself, he thought angrily. And not only a fool. That bugaboo, the Medical Council, would strike him off the Register. He might even be put in jail; unless they decided he was mad, then he'd be shut up in a lunatic asylum instead.

CHAPTER 24

THE fog was so thick when Abbot drove back to the police station at half past two that it might have almost been the middle of the night. Instead of parking his car in front of the station, he drove round to the yard onto which the door to the cells opened. In the yard, with some difficulty, he turned the car so that its nose pointed toward a narrow alley that led past the mortuary to a side street. There was not a soul in sight. The windows of the passage that ran past the cells were too high for anyone but a nine-foot giant to see out of. So far, so good, he thought, cursing himself for his folly. The bonnets of two police cars showed dimly in the open garage at the far side of the yard. Abbot eyed them, wishing he didn't feel as if his teeth were going to start chattering. He walked round to the front of the station and went in the main entrance.

"Parry back?" he asked the duty officer.

"No, doctor, he's not. And if you want to see Arnoldson, he isn't back from his lunch yet."

"I don't in the least want to see Arnoldson," Abbot said with perfect truth. "I want to see Mrs. Ashley again. Her chest's in a bad way."

"Oh, Lord," said the duty officer. "Hope she won't die on us."

Without waiting for more, Abbot took himself off to the cells. In a room at the far end of the corridor he could see the back views of the policewoman and a constable as they crouched over a smoking fire. He hadn't reckoned on the constable as well, and inwardly cursed him. The policewoman turned round, got up, and came toward him.

"Mrs. Ashley's coughing very bad," she said. "The Friars Balsam's come."

"I want to sound her chest before you steam it," Abbot said, hoping he didn't sound as agonized as he felt.

The policewoman unlocked the door of Flik's cell, and stood aside for him to go in before her.

"Well, how are we now?" he asked in his best professional manner.

"We aren't too good," Flik said.

Nor did she look too good. Her face was unnaturally flushed, and there were deep marks under her eyes, which were very bright. He'd never get her out of here, Abbot thought desperately. She began to cough, and he took out his stethoscope.

"If you'll just pull your jersey up or down," he said, and burst into a sweat. He'd seen and listened to hundreds of women's chests, he'd prodded hundred's of bare female stomachs. But the idea of having to investigate Flik's chest filled him not only with embarrassment but a sick fury. She pulled her jersey up round her shoulders, and keeping his eyes fixed on the wall behind her head, Abbot went to work, his nerves jibbering, his hands shaking.

"Yes, thank you—" He nodded at the policewoman, beckoning her out into the corridor. "Mrs. Ashley's very much worse than I thought. There appears to be considerable congestion of both lungs. Looks to me like the onset of pneumonia, and that'd be a pretty pickle."

"My gawd," the policewoman said, showing considerable signs of panic. "Is she really as bad as all that?"

"There's only one way of finding out," Abbot said. "She must have an X-ray immediately. At once."

"But we—"

"You needn't tell me she can't be X-rayed here," Abbot snapped. "Of course she can't. I'll have to drive her to the hospital."

"But—"

"Of course, if you want her to die on you, then go ahead."

The last thing in the world the policewoman wanted was for Flik to die on her, and she said so, vehemently.

"Very well then—" Abbot's heart was beating so fast he thought it would burst through his ribs. "Apparently Arnoldson isn't back from his lunch, and we can't wait for him. He may take all the afternoon about it. He mayn't even come back here after his lunch, for that matter. The only thing for you to do is to cut along to the duty officer, explain matters, see what he has to say, tell him the matter is of the utmost urgency, and in the absence of Arnoldson, get his permission to come to the hospital with your prisoner." All that palaver should take quite ten minutes, he decided.

"Hadn't you better explain yourself, sir?" the woman asked.

"No time, no time," Abbot fumed. "I want to take Mrs. Ashley's temperature at once, and give her a dose of M. and B. I've got some out in my car at the back. Unlock the door into the yard, will you? Wait a minute, never mind, give me your keys and I'll look after myself."

The rattled policewoman, with docile obedience, handed him her bunch of keys, and went. Now for the constable, Abbot thought, and called to him.

"Yes, doctor?"

"Be a good chap, will you, and go along to the office and look up the times of arrival of every train Inspector Parry might come back by? Not only the trains to St. Arthurs, but to Pelsey, and Eastbourne and Hastings, in case he comes by another route and gets a car on here."

The good chap, all unsuspecting, went along. Abbot unlocked the door of Flik's cell and jerked his head at her. She got up off the bunk and silently followed him. He relocked the door, and unlocked and unbolted the door into the yard. Still in silence, Flik went out to the car, got in the back, and vanished under the motor rug. Abbot locked the yard door, and dropped the bunch of keys down a grating. There was one more thing to do. When he let the air out of the tires of the two police cars, the noise seemed to his fevered imagination like the wailing of banshees. As he started the engine of his car, he thought every policeman for miles round would come running.

"Where to?" Abbot asked over his shoulder.

"Home," Flik's muffled voice answered. "And thanks:" Past the mortuary, down the side street to the main road, Abbot drove with a reckless disregard for the fog and all it might contain. By now their flight would be discovered. But it would take some time to pump up the tires of one of the cars. Abbot raged under his breath. This was madness; at any moment the hunt would be on. The car bounced from right to left. A telegraph sprouted out of the fog nearly on top of the bonnet. A lorry driver leaned from his cab and bawled profanities about lunatics in charge of cars. The fog clung to Abbot's hair so that it dripped down his forehead, and his spectacles were misted up. This wasn't reality; he was dead and in hell, only there were no warming fires to soothe his cold, tired limbs. At first he didn't realize it was the Shots Arms he was passing. It was almost a shock to find he'd got there. Unconsciously he noticed there was a taxi drawn up outside the place. He missed his gears driving in the entrance of Shots Hall, swore, jammed on the brakes, somehow got into bottom, and shot up to the front door.

Flik appeared from under the rug.

"Sound your horn as if in rejoicing," she said.

Abbot blasted his horn in rage.

"What d'you want me to do now?" he asked. "Shoot someone? Dance a fandango?"

"Just come in and be yourself," Flik said, her voice tight. "I've been released. It was all an awful mistake."

She got out of the car, waiting for him, then opened the door. The hall lights were on, fighting against the gloom. Bee sat in her usual chair, her hair adamantly dressed over its old-fashioned pad. Opposite her, crouched on a sofa, Miss Merridew, wrapped in a shawl, wailed into a crumpled ball of a handkerchief.

"Flik?" Bee said. "Well, Abbot?"

"Flik?" Miss Merridew echoed, incredulous. "Flik! Oh, my poor darling child!"

Abbot wiped his spectacles and put them on again, waiting for Flik to give him some sort of cue. Waiting, too, for the sounds of pursuit.

"I'm back," Flik said, with what seemed to him quite unnecessary emphasis of the obvious. "Parry managed to get a call through from London. Arnoldson just made a hideous mistake, that's all."

Abbot felt, rather than saw, the flash of understanding that went between her and Bee Chattock. Bee knew damn well no hideous mistake had been made.

But she said, "I trust this'll give Arnoldson a lesson. He's been disgraceful. You'd better have a drink at once, Flik, you look all in. Susan, must you continue to howl?"

"I'm so relieved," Miss Merridew sobbed. "When they told me Flik had been taken away, I could scarcely believe it. How dared they suspect her?" She became almost belligerent, almost, indeed, coherent. "It was wicked! But now everything's all right; it is, isn't it, Flik dear?"

"Perfectly all right," she answered. She unbuttoned her coat, half took it off, shivered and pulled it on again. "I'm going to light the drawing-room fire. It's cold in here."

As Abbot watched her go into the drawing room and shut the door, he had an illusion of impending disaster and horror. When he spoke, his voice sounded so loud in the echoing hall that he thought he must have shouted.

"Parry shouldn't have rushed off to London, damn him. When the cat's away—" He left the inadequate proverb unfinished. What in the name of the devil was Flik doing? From behind the closed door of the drawing room there came an odd scrabbling noise. Bee heard it too. Not so Miss Merridew, who was trying to stifle her tears by blowing her nose. One minute passed, two, three, four—a dreadful eternity.

Then Bee stiffened in her chair, and Abbot turned colder than ever. A car was grinding up the drive; doors banged. The front door burst open and crashed shut.

"We took a taxi down to the police station to see if we could see Flik, and they told us she'd just—"

Abbot swung round and pounced on the babbling Phil Ambrose, who was clinging on to Tim's arm. "Be quiet," he glared at her.

"They said someone'd let the air out of the police car ti—"

"Be quiet, I tell you."

"They tried to take ours, but we bunged off before they could—"

"Phil, honey, perhaps—"

The drawing-room door opened slowly. There was mud on Flik's shoes, on her dark blue slacks. Behind her the drawing-room lights shone, outlining her head. But in the cavern of the hall it seemed the fog had gathered, seeping through the walls, creeping down from the ceiling.

"Flik!" Phil gulped, leaning forward till her hair fell over her face.

"We've got a taxi outside," Tim said. "It's all yours if you want it, and we'll come with you to wherever—" He stared at her, and didn't finish what he was saying.

Her lips moved, but she said nothing. The look on her face appalled Abbot. She might have walked straight out of some torture chamber.

"Dear Flik!" Miss Merridew was like some old, faithful dog as she got off the sofa and tottered toward her. "You ought to go to bed, dear." Her small hands fumbled for Flik's arm.

"For God's sake," Tim bawled, "come on, Flik, while the going's good."

Hell, thought Abbot. Hell, hell. Why couldn't he think straight? Why couldn't he do something sensible? Why couldn't he wipe that look off Flik's face and then strangle all these bloody people? This slyly watchful house—the fog—why didn't old Chattock say something? But Bee still sat in her winged chair, her eyes fixed on Flik; Miss Merridew still fumbled for Flik's arm; the Ambroses still clung to each other as though they themselves were in some mortal danger.

And then the front door swung open and remained open, as Congreve held it for Parry to come in before he let it crash shut again.

To Parry, ever sensitive to atmosphere, the scene seemed as if it might have been deliberately set for the last act before the curtain came down. He pulled his hand out of his pocket and held out to Flik a small, sodden bundle of what Abbot first thought were labels, but then saw were empty seed packets.

"You weren't far ahead of me and Congreve, were you?" Parry said.

"About five minutes," Flik answered in a dead voice. She slipped her hand inside her coat, and took out several little bits of crumpled paper, closely written on with an indelible pencil. "So you guessed too? Old Harry's farewell letter—I should have thought sooner. He trusted me too much. He thought I'd remember at once."

In front of his eyes, in a flash back as clear as the rising sun, Abbot saw the crouching figure of the old gardener on that dripping evening, a dim figure in the mist, sticking little labels in amongst the rotting fireflowers of the monstrous rock garden; and heard his old, tired voice— "Miss Flik, I've labeled everything what's underground in the rockery— if I died tomorrow you'd still be able to find out just by looking at the labels—and don't you forget it." And Harry'd died that night.

Parry held his hand out, and Flik put the bits of paper in it.

"The significance of what Harry said to you that evening before he went home dawned on me just before I left town. I got out at Pelsey to save time, and took a taxi to Shotshall."

He didn't ask how Flik had got out of the cell. Congreve must have told him Arnoldson had taken her away the day before. He smoothed the sheets of paper, spreading them out fanwise. "Page one, page two, page three— Dear Miss Flikka—" His quick eyes ran along the lines of writing. "In his way, Harry was the cleverest of us all, wasn't he?"

For one moment, Abbot thought Flik was going to crack, to cry. But she only put the back of her hand against her mouth and dug her teeth into

it, leaving two regular, reddened semicircles. With a sudden, savage desire to protect her, he moved next to her, but without the courage to touch
her. Phil's mouth opened, and a small sob came out of it. Abbot found
himself staring hypnotized at Parry.

"It's my unpleasant duty," Parry began very slowly, and Abbot's heart
contracted, for it wasn't Flik he was looking at, "to—" He jerked his head
round. "Stop her!" he exclaimed.

But with amazing agility, Miss Merridew had scuttled to the far end
of the hall; the door leading to the kitchen quarters slammed in his face,
there was a rattle of a key being turned, of bolts being shot home. He
and Congreve threw their shoulders against the thick panels, heaving
and grunting.

"The side door—outside—" Flik shook herself as if she were freeing
her body of some invisible shackles; and Abbot ran beside her, out of the
front door, down the drive, Parry and Congreve, Phil and Tim with them.

"Hell," Parry swore. "She's locked herself in."

"Wait. Listen." Flik lifted her head, stiffening.

From down the road came the bang of a door shutting, muffled by the
fog, but distinct.

"She locked the door from the outside and took the key," Parry said.

"She's taken another key." Flik began to run again. "The key of my
shed—it's always on the hook in the kitchen."

As they stumbled down the muddy track that led to the stone shanty,
Abbot heard another car drive up to Shots Hall, and voices.

"We'll never open this door," Flik panted. "It opens outward. Oh, my
God, what's she doing? Oh, God, what's she doing?"

For from the other side of the door came a dull, feverish hacking of
metal on stone, and giggles, little bubbling giggles. Parry heaved impotent at the door; it didn't even creak.

"Just a moment, sir." With loving care, Congreve produced, with the
satisfied air of a successful conjurer, a small roll of tools he had once
bought off a burglar before he went down for two years. "'Ope there
aren't bolts inside too, Mrs. Ashley?"

"No," Flik said wearily. "No, there aren't—Oh, God, listen to her."

Unconcerned by the noises within, Congreve, unfumbling and admirably nimble-fingered, set about picking the lock, which he did with remarkable ease.

"You'd better stay outside," Parry said to Flik gently. "You and the
Ambroses. It won't be nice."

"I'm coming in."

The door swung open. The unscreened lights blazed, hard and cruel, on the small bedraggled figure that giggled, salivating at the mouth, and hacked and hacked with the strength born of insanity, with an iron-headed hammer at the face and breast of the sleeping sea-green mermaid. Then all at once, before Parry could take it away from her, Miss Merridew dropped the hammer, and pawed and scratched at the face she'd marred beyond all repair, at the breast, chipped and scarred, babbling obscenities that shocked and appalled even Abbot.

"Come away, Flik." He took her arm, and white-faced, she went with him, the Ambroses, Phil in tears, trailing behind.

Round the corner Arnoldson came pounding, his bruised face oozing sweat, his breath a white cloud in the fog, as though he was breathing smoke engendered by a fire inside him.

"What the bloody hell's going on here?" he demanded, lunging at Flik. "You bitch—"

With one accord, as though by some carefully prearranged signal, Tim and Abbot delivered two right hooks with simultaneous satisfaction, and Arnoldson went down for the count.

"That's the first time," Flik said in grim amusement, "I haven't seen him bounce." She shivered, her teeth making small chattering noises; and with inexpert fingers, Abbot tried to turn up the collar of her coat over her ears, so that she wouldn't hear Miss Merridew.

CHAPTER 25

THE drawing room Abbot had approved of when he'd first seen it was bright with firelight, and the quiet light of shaded lamps. The crystal glasses on the low, round table sparkled with rainbow daggers; the bottle of prewar whisky was clear amber beside the deeper amber of the 1904 Amontillado sherry. And the lights caught in Flik's hair, so that it shone like a chestnut burnished from long use in games of conkers. The five men—Clive, newly released from his incarceration with his ear still full of well-directed fleas delivered by Parry; Parry himself, his dark, pointed face tired; Abbot, disheveled in body and mind; Congreve, as ever placid; Norton, perched stiffly on the edge of his chair—each seeing her from their own different and private angles, marveled that she showed so little trace of the last few nightmare days and nights. She'd even taken the trouble to change into the plain, tight black suit and crisp white shirt of

Sunday's awful cocktail party.

"Sherry," Bee said without looking up. "And give these people and yourself some more whisky, Clive." Straight-backed, indomitable, she spread the crumpled sheets of Harry's last letter on her silk lap, reading them for the first time. And as she read the painfully scrawled words, she had the feeling the old man she'd known for such countless years was standing beside her as he'd so often stood, cap in hand, waiting for her orders, only to argue about them when he got them. Outwardly unbending, her heart was deeply moved.

"Page one," she read. "Dear Miss Flikka, I am taking the liberty of writing you in case things go wrong with me. I am writing on December 3rd in the tool shed at the hall, and when I go this evening I'm going to tell you that if I die you have only to look at the labels in the rockery. Then you'll see the seed packets I used as labels is all addressed to you, and has each one a sheet of this letter inside it. Down in the village they say you poisoned Molly and Marsh, and I won't have that. I think Miss Merridew done it, but I want to make sure. Continued in packet marked Easter Roses."

Bee picked out the page headed, "Page two," and went on reading. The clock on the mantel shelf struck eleven—only six and a half hours since the wretched, raving creature'd been taken away from Flik's shed.

"I thinly Miss M. is wrong in her head, and no one what wasn't wrong in their head would kill people like that. I know she is queer. One evening last summer I knocked at her door to ask if she wanted any wood chopped, and as she didn't answer I went in. She was in her sitting room, bobbing and bowing in front of that picture you drawn of Mr. Crawford after he died of the blitz. She was saying, you'll hang by the neck like he did, I'll see to it. I didn't know what she meant, but I could see she was wrong in her head. Her face was all twisted up, and there was spit on her mouth. I went home. Continued in packet marked Sweet Peas."

Bee wasn't easily horrified, but Harry's ungrammatical scrawl drew for her a picture of utmost horror. "Page three," she read on. "I didn't think no more for a bit, till Molly and Marsh was poisoned, and then I thought a lot. Plenty of the villagers may be soft, but they aren't mad like I reckon Miss M. is. Only I couldn't think why she done it, except she wanted to put the blame on you. But I am sure she done it. Just now you and that London policeman and Miss M. were talking in the road when I came along, and when you said I looked right ill I saw Miss M.'s face. She looked that queer, as if she was scared I'd die suddenly before she done something to me she wanted to do. So I thought it's me next she's after. She looked crazy only you and the policeman didn't notice. Continued in packet marked Nasturtiums."

Bee was aware that Flik and Parry were talking quietly about nothing, but took no notice of them. She searched for page four with her hands, while her mind searched back into the past, remembering, amongst Harry's queer, muddled philosophy of life, the equally queer sparks of wisdom and insight.

"Page four. Miss Flikka, I never told you or Miss Bee that there is a lump in my inside what will finish me sooner or later, so if it's sooner or later it don't matter. I'm going to make sure if Miss M. poisoned Molly and Marsh or if she didn't. When I go this evening I'm going in to Miss M. like I want to ask if she wants any woodcutting tomorrow. And I'm going to tell her I heard the policeman say he hasn't no idea who done the murders. So I'm going to put the idea into her head another murder is needed to prove who done the others. Then I'm going to tell her you promised you were coming to see me half past six this evening with some medicine, which is some drops to put in my tea. You ain't of course, but I'll make her think so. Then I'm going home and I'll have a cup of tea all ready on the table. Continued in packet marked Aubretia."

Oh, God, thought Abbot drearily, are we never going to get through with this night? Under his tired eyelids he watched Flik's and Parry's clear-cut profiles against the fire, and knew that Clive was watching them too.

"Page five." Bee picked up the last page. "I'm not going to put any sugar in my tea, so if she puts something in it I'll taste it when she's gone. If she does put something in it I'm going to drink a lot of salt and water so that I sick it up, and then I can tell, and no one won't say you done it any more. If Miss M. doesn't come, or doesn't put anything in my tea, then I'll burn these bits of paper and the packets when I come next morning. I wouldn't get anyone in trouble if they hadn't done it as mud sticks. Dear Miss Flikka I am your obedient servant Harry."

Bee folded up the five sheets of paper and handed them back to Parry. "Poor, queer old man," she said. "As you remarked today, he was the cleverest of us all."

"It's a pity he wasn't just a bit cleverer," Parry said. "It never occurred to him not to drink the tea at all, but to simply hand the full cup over to the police for analysis."

Bee tst-tsted impatiently. "Don't confuse wisdom with learning. Harry had glimpses of wisdom, but his learning was nil. I don't suppose he even knew what the word analysis meant, or that things could be analyzed. He did the best he could, and he died doing it."

"He'd have died anyway," Abbot said, rousing himself. "That growth of his was malignant."

Flik threw her cigarette into the fire with a quick gesture of sudden, dreadful tension. Abbot thought, if she doesn't burst into tears or something human like that, she'll have a nervous breakdown.

"He died trying to save me, anyway," she said. "All alone, so horribly. He was damned brave—" She lit another cigarette, snapping her lighter on and off with taut fingers.

"Now then—" Parry became businesslike, covering Flik's moment of emotion by talking. He didn't want her to crack yet, if anything would ever make her crack. There was a lot he wanted her to tell him. He felt immensely sorry for her, but she had to go through with it. He smiled at her, trying to look comforting. "It's hard to know where to begin, isn't it, Flik?" he said.

"What about," Congreve suggested, "beginning at the beginning?"

Bee gave him a withering stare. "My whisky appears to have dimmed your originality of ideas. Give me some more sherry, Clive, and don't wave the bottle about like that."

"Sorry," he said. He'd forgotten there was anyone else in the room but himself and Flik. She seemed to fill it so that everything else faded into a jumbled background, out of which she emerged as the one reality. "Sorry," he repeated, handling the sherry with more care.

Flik pushed her hair back behind her ears. "Parry? Poor Susan—is she—"

"She was certified insane at eight o'clock this evening," Abbot said with frank brutality. "She's been taken to Massingham asylum. She'll never be able to come up for trial." He forbore to say, however, that Miss Merridew had made her exit from public life in a straitjacket, babbling that she was the high priestess of some heathen cult which existed in her disordered imagination. He thought it appalling that she should be kept alive. She'd be given treatment, probably lead quite a pleasant existence, and live till she was a hundred—after poisoning three harmless people for the purpose of getting Flik hanged. He caught Flik's searching look and added, "My good girl, she's perfectly happy."

Flik nodded slowly. "I'm glad. After all, I suppose I'm responsible for the whole horrible business, even for poor Susan going mad."

"Didn't you know," Parry asked, "that there was madness in her family? We found this evening that her grandfather died in Massingham asylum, aged," he added wryly, "eighty-seven. He was Masey Herbert's grandfather too."

"And who the hell," Bee demanded, "is Masey Herbert?"

Parry raised his eyebrows. This was a relief, anyway. "So you and Flik didn't know Mervyn Crawford's real name was Masey Herbert? I'm glad you didn't hold out on me there, Flik, at any rate."

"I never knew," she said dully. "I thought Mervyn Crawford was— Mervyn Crawford." She turned her head away from him to the fire. "It all started because of him. You'd like me to tell you, wouldn't you? I don't know if Susan said anything about him, and me?"

Miss Merridew had, in her hour of comparative sanity, when she'd made her statement before she'd started raving. But Parry wanted Flik's version.

"Go ahead," he said quietly, and, lighting another cigarette, prepared himself to listen, at last, to the unburdening of her strange, secret soul.

CHAPTER 26

FLIK stood up suddenly and faced the room, holding her back very straight. It was as if she were nerving herself to face some kind of tribunal.

She's an amazing person, Parry thought, and said, "Yes?" encouragingly.

"It was before Susan's father died, in the end of 1939, I met him first. He used to come down and stay with Susan. He seemed such a lost dog. I never asked him what his job was, if any. I don't see why one should question people. If they want to tell you, they tell you."

They do like hell, Abbot said to himself. More likely they were stricken dumb; Flik's beauty was the kind that led to incoherence. Bee glanced at Clive out of the corner of her all-seeing eyes. Tonight he'd ask Flik yet again to marry him. And yet again she'd turn him down.

"Maybe he hadn't a job," Flik went on, her sentences becoming more and more clipped. "He just said he wrote a lot, and Susan said he was a brilliant author, that he'd once had a book published. Only I somehow guessed his brilliance only existed in Susan's mind. I don't know why, but that made me terribly sorry for him. I didn't realize he was in love with me till the end of 1940, when he asked me to marry him. I didn't want to. I—that is, I didn't know what to do, as I didn't want to hurt him. But he must have guessed at once I wouldn't marry him, and he went crack, right off the deep end. We were out for a walk when it happened.

He had a sort of fit. Dreadful—horrible—"

She bit her lip, and Parry saw that she was shaking.

"I got him out of the fit somehow, but I knew, then, he wasn't sane. That evening he went back to town, to the air raids, and I never saw him again. Two days later I got a raving letter from him saying I'd encouraged him to think I loved him, that I'd broken his heart, and by the time I got the letter he'd have hanged himself. That same morning I found Susan'd dashed up to town, and I guessed he must have written to her too. Only I didn't know, I never found out, never, if she knew he'd written to me as well."

"She did know," Parry said.

"When she came back a few days later she looked awful, simply awful and twenty years older, so I knew he must've really done what he said he'd do. Only Susan told me, and Aunt Bee, and everyone, that'd he'd died in the blitz—of the blitz, were her exact words. And she stuck to it, putting him on a sort of pedestal. She asked me to draw a head of him, and I did. I expect you saw it, Parry?"

"Yes," he nodded. "And it struck me and Mahew as not being a true likeness. Why?"

"I made his eyes look normal, that's why. Anyhow, as Susan seemed to want everyone to think he'd died in a raid, we thought it better and kinder to pretend—Aunt Bee and I—that we believed her. It never occurred to me she really blamed me for his suicide. It never occurred to me she was hating me like hell all the time, planning her plans to revenge him. It wasn't till today I knew she wasn't sane herself."

Flik's voice trailed off, and her eyes took on their odd look of being turned inside her. Clive leaned forward in his chair, longing to go to her, to comfort her. Staring down at his sensitive fingers, Abbot stretched them on his knees, cracking the joints one by one. He wasn't enjoying himself. It was as if Flik was dragging her clothes off, to stand there naked for them all to see.

She jerked her shoulders back. "When Molly was poisoned, I never dreamed Susan had killed her. I realized things looked very bad for me, and all the time there was something puzzling me. It was Molly's savings club card being full. Norton told me. And the broom. Molly'd broken her garden broom, and yet some broom had swept her bit of path that night. It was when Marsh was poisoned too I saw a glimmer. I forget who told me, but someone said his card was full too. And neither of them should've been. There was one more week to go before everyone was due for their last stamp. That made me think of Susan, because it was she who called once a week on the villagers to collect their sixpences and give them their stamps. And I knew from something Molly said the day she died that she certainly had her last stamp to come. When I said she had no visitors, I didn't count Susan. She—poor Susan, she just didn't count. She was taken for granted, like the butcher's boy, or the baker's man. Then the broom— Norton?"

Norton shuffled his feet. "Yes, Mrs. Ashley?"

"You remember about midnight Sunday when I called out to you when you were patrolling? I was really on my way to Susan's—Miss Merridew's—to look for the broom. I had an awful idea that hers had a chunk of bristles out of the middle of it."

"You ought to be in the police," Congreve said, with unwonted lack of tact.

Flik laughed, a tight, bitter laugh. "My only excuse for practically handing her poor Marsh as a present was that I didn't realize, then, that she had anything to do with Molly's murder. On Sunday morning I told her I was going down to the pub at half past four to collect the damned gin, and she knew as well as everyone else in the village did, that he had a cuppa at half past four every afternoon, and that he liked a lot of sugar. Oh, God—then Harry. Parry? You saw me look in his table drawer after he was dead? I was looking for his savings club card. And it was full. Susan had called on him too. I suppose she took my cigarette ends out of an ashtray and stuck them under Marsh's grate—"

"That's precisely what she did do," Parry said.

"After Marsh," Flik went on, the defiance in her voice dulling down to a bleak monotone, "I guessed Susan wanted me to hang for murder. To hang at the end of a rope, because Mervyn had hung at the end of a rope. A sort of just retribution."

"And still," Parry interrupted, "knowing all this, you kept it to yourself? Three people'd been poisoned, you guessed who the poisoner was, and knew the one thing I didn't know to make a brass-bound case against her—the motive for the motive. I knew her primary motive was to throw the guilt on you, but I didn't know why. But you knew."

Clive blew up, his face scarlet. "Leave her alone, can't you? Hasn't she been through enough hell already without you rubbing it all in, you damned policeman?"

"Clive?" Bee was authoritative, commanding. "Be quiet. However right you are, I won't have this shouting and bawling in my house. Give everyone another drink, and in the name of the devil let's get this disgusting business over."

I couldn't, thought Parry approvingly, agree with you more, my dear

Miss Chattock. And Abbot, muttering inaudible bad language, thrust his empty glass at Clive; he'd had enough whisky already, but now he was in the unhappy mood to have too much. Flik let Clive refill her glass, and for a moment stared into its golden depths. Then she raised her head and looked straight at Parry.

"Well?" she said quietly.

"Well?" he repeated, half mocking.

There was a short, uncomfortable silence, till Abbot's temper became suddenly more audible, rising in a crescendo of irritation.

"Hell and damnation," he swore. "Are we to sit here all night holding a bloody inquest on everyone's motives for what they did, or didn't do?"

Flik held her glass very tightly. "Parry," she said, "my evidence against Susan was only circumstantial. I was responsible for Mervyn's—Masey Herbert's—suicide. So I was responsible for Susan poisoning Molly, Marsh and Harry. Can't you see that? It was my fault. I felt I ought to take the rap. And suppose I'd accused her, and was wrong? Mud does stick. At least, that's what I felt about it till I'd spent a night in that cell and'd had time to think straight. Then I realized I was wrong. I realized poor Susan must be off her head, that she was a menace, that she might go on and on killing people. When Abbot told me she'd left the hospital and gone to stay with Aunt Bee, I was scared stiff she might do something to Aunt Bee too. Then I saw a picture in one of those dreary books they gave me to read when I was at the police station. It was a rock garden in winter, with a lot of labels stuck in it, and I remembered the queer thing Harry'd said before he died, and I guessed the labels were some sort of message for me, and that he knew something about the murders."

"So you suborned Abbot to help you break out?" Parry smiled.

"I had to know for sure. I'd no idea when you'd get back, and I knew Arnoldson wouldn't let me out, or take any notice of anything I said."

Parry raised his glass to Abbot. "A most masterful stroke, Abbot. I've had to square the entire St. Arthurs police force, all eight of them, to keep their mouths shut about this afternoon's performance. Luckily they're only too anxious to oblige. No one likes being made a fool of. Abbot, you've no respect for the law."

"For once," he admitted, "I'm in complete agreement with you."

Parry looked up at Flik, finding her as ever admirable, even though she'd caused him so much extra work and annoyance. "You're a quixotic young woman, aren't you? I guessed you were trying to shield Merridew. Before I left for town I phoned Mahew and asked him to see you and tax you with it straight out. But instead, the poor old chap was carted off home with pneumonia. I've had cases before when people've thrown spanners in the police works trying to protect someone and even take the blame. So very helpful."

"Shut up," Clive muttered. "You weren't so damn bright yourself."

Flik turned on him. "Clive, you're unfair. It was all my fault."

Oh, God, Parry wondered, am I ever going to get to bed this side of the grave? "Let's skip the recriminations," he said as patiently as he could. "You all know the bones of the case now. Revenge. In her statement, it appears Merridew was madly in love with her cousin, imagined he was in love with her, and that Flik had stolen him from her with malice afore-thought. She brooded for years, planning first this revenge, then that. Finally she decided Flik must hang; only she couldn't think how to manage it. Now then, Congreve told me that in 1942 old Dr. Bannard reported the loss of a package of Barbitone which he said was taken from his car. Only it wasn't Barbitone. It was morphine. Bannard went to visit Belairs one night, and Merridew, on her way home from seeing some sick farmer's wife, spotted his car, and out of curiosity started poking about in it. She found the morphine thought it might come in handy, and took it home with her. She hid it, all nicely packed in its airtight glass tubes, in that wooden candlelamp affair in her sitting room. The lamp was hollow— what d'you say, Flik?"

"I said," she repeated, "so that's why it never worked."

"To cut a long story short," Parry went on, wishing he could cut it altogether, "she had the morphine, but couldn't think how it would come in useful to hang Flik, till she hit on the idea, this winter, of poisoning the old Chattock retainers and arranging things to look as if Flik had done it. We'll take Molly first. She melted six grains of morphine in an aspirin bottle, dodged across the road in the dark and fog just before she knew you, Flik, would be going in to see the old woman, made an excuse to sell her the savings stamp before it was due, and while Molly was looking for her sixpence, put the morphine in the tea. When she heard this door bang like the crack of doom, she simply said good night and went home. As for Marsh, you'd told her you were going down to the pub at half past four Sunday to get the gin, so a few minutes earlier she armed herself with some of the gravel from this drive, went down to the pub, knowing the people in the only three cottages she'd have to pass would probably be napping, dealt with Marsh in exactly the same way she'd dealt with Molly, then went and hid in the gents' lavatory."

Bee snorted in disgust, but said nothing.

"When she saw you come down the road and go in the back door of the pub, Flik, she hopped out of the gents, woke up the ever curious Mrs. Vale by chucking the gravel at her window, then hid in the gents' again till the coast was clear. As for Harry, it worked out exactly as he prophesied in his letter. You know the rest, except she took a shortcut across the fields at the back of her house to his cottage. Flik? I had a bad moment that evening when I found you in your shed with mud on your gum boots, obviously having been out instead of working."

"I simply went for a walk along the road. I wanted to think."

Parry swallowed a yawn. He was almighty tired, and, all at once, sick to death of humanity, the involved and so often unlovely working of human minds, both sane and insane.

"I got a line on Merridew," he said wearily, "when Congreve told me the Ambroses had mentioned there was one more week of savings club stamps to come. Merridew let out to me what no one else bothered to tell me, and that was that she did the stamp selling and sixpence collecting. And her three victims' cards were fully stamped. Then there was her alibi of her curtain machining. The machine was going all that time during the period when Harry must've been given poison. But it was an electric machine. I spotted it when Mahew and I went to see her and he fell over the flex. Easy just switch it on, and let it grind away. Then there was the business of the Hunter girl yelling out about blood and sick after she'd found Harry dead. Merridew echoed, 'Blood? Blood? Blood?' as if she couldn't believe it. Of course she didn't expect blood when she'd fed him morphine."

"Why in heaven's name," Bee demanded, "did she give herself morphine?"

"Oh, that?" Parry gulped down another huge yawn, "that was the trap I laid for her. Don't you remember when we were in here the evening before I announced there was one person in the village who unknowingly held the clue to the murderer's identity, and that they were in danger? She swallowed the bait."

Flik nodded, thinking of Miss Merridew's letter to dearest Emily that Parry had showed her. And still all she felt for the mad creature was profound pity. "How did you know about Mervyn Crawford coming into it? How did you find out that wasn't his real name?"

"From the way you didn't seem to want to talk about him, from the queer way Merridew spoke of him, and her queerer phrase, he died *of* the blitz, I was sure he fitted into the pattern somewhere. Oh, the red herrings that have bestrewn my path—the Ambroses with their black magic— Belairs with his hints—the Hunter girl with her poisonous herbs—Camilla who was once a drug addict—as for you—" Parry looked at Flik, and thought that if she wasn't so lovely, he could gladly strangle her. "However, Masey Herbert—I put through inquiries to London about Mervyn Crawford, and all that came of them was that he appeared never to have been born, existed or died. That struck me as so really odd that I made a line for town myself, to see what I could find out. I won't bore you with the routine work I did, but at any rate I discovered that Mervyn Crawford was the name he published his one very poor book under, years ago, and that he'd used that name for most purposes ever since. But his identity card was issued under his real name, and under his real name he committed suicide."

Norton edged himself further forward on his chair. "And the broom, sir?"

"The broom? It was hers. The might I told you to have a snoop round for it, she heard me speaking to you. She waited up in her bedroom window with the damn thing, and when you fell down and put your torch on, she simply heaved it at you, then got back into bed and pretended to snore."

Flik's mouth twisted as if she was in pain, and her fingers clung to the mantelpiece. Weren't her other grisly skeletons going to be dragged into the light after all?

"Merridew took the most appalling risks." Parry yawned outright, unable to control himself any longer. "But she thought that, like God, she was omnipotent. Lunatics are like that, you know."

Congreve glanced longingly at the almost empty whisky bottle. "She was a one, and no mistake," he remarked chattily.

CHAPTER 27

FORTIFIED by the knowledge that Parry would not only foot the bill but pick the bodies up on his way back, Congreve and Norton poured beer after beer down on top of Bee's whisky, while they warmed themselves in front of old Marsh's sitting-room fire, and Winnie and the brewery's man squabbled in the kitchen.

As Clive drove past the back of the pub he saw the light in the window but didn't stop. The car he'd hired in St. Arthurs while his M.G. was being put to rights had an ordinary accelerator pedal, and he fumbled clumsily for it with his unfeeling foot. At the turning that went down to the Ambroses, to Belairs, to Gwen, he stopped the car. He'd phoned Phil and Tim he'd go in and give them all the news; but now he felt in no mood for Phil's exclamations and Tim's inquietude. He felt in no mood for anything or anyone. Let them wait till tomorrow. He started the car again and drove off into the misty darkness, taking no notice of where he was going, not caring whether he ran into a ditch or not.

Like a will-o'-the-wisp, Flik's face seemed to dance before him, always evading him, just as she'd always evaded him, always would. Before he'd left, when she'd gone to make the tea Parry'd suddenly craved, he'd followed her to the kitchen, sure, somehow, that now all the horrible mess of the past few days was cleared up she'd change her mind and marry him. But she hadn't. She'd been sweet, kind, she'd even kissed him gently, very lightly, as a mother might kiss her child. But she hadn't changed her mind. Staring ahead of him into the beams of the headlights, he knew she never would. He hadn't waited for the tea.

The road twisted and turned, now narrowing to a high-hedged lane, now broadening out. He had no idea where he was till, turning another corner, the headlights picked out a white gate, tall clipped hedges, and the bare branches of an oak tree, curiously gnarled and deformed. He jerked the brakes on, the engine stalled, and a painful longing for company came over him. Tired and stiff he climbed out, switched off the headlights and opened the gate. He felt very lame, almost unable to pull his leg along with him. He knocked on the door; in the darkness he couldn't find the bell.

"Hullo?"

The door opened, and a warm streak of light shone out. Camilla had on some sort of housecoat; thick, deep red silk, which made her curls look very shining, like platinum.

"Clive, honey," she, said in a pleased voice. "Come in, my sweet, and have a drink."

"D'you mind? Don't you mind, Camilla? It's damn late."

"It's never too late for pleasant surprises." She put her arm through his, and shut and locked the door behind him. "I heard some wild rumor about Susan Merridew being hauled off to Massingham looney bin. Have you been to Shotshall?" Without waiting for him to answer, she deposited him on the low sofa next the fire, went to her drink cupboard and poured him out a whisky and soda from her meager supply. "Sweetie, do tell me all about it. Is it true? I'm all ears, like a jackass."

She sat down next him. Dully, Clive thought she smelled warm, and nice. Infinitely tired, he made himself tell her of that afternoon he hadn't witnessed, of the night he had. Of Parry's story, of Miss Merridew, stumbling over Flik's own story, leaving most of it out, so obviously glossing it over that Camilla guessed most of it. She looked at him covertly. The mist was still wet on his pale fair hair. He was staring into the fire so that she couldn't see his eyes. But she knew, as plainly as if he'd told her, that he'd had one last try for Flik and failed.

"Darling, what a time you've all had," she said. "You must be damn tired, aren't you? And flat. One always feels flat after the party's over."

"Yes, flat. Bloody flat."

Camilla took his empty glass away from him and refilled it. She was forty-eight, he was thirty, young enough to be her son, she thought placidly. She didn't go in for falling in love with young men. She was no more in love with Clive than she'd been with Tim. Tim had been fun to flirt with, till Parry'd warned her off. Then it hadn't seemed fun any more. She hadn't wanted to hurt poor rather silly Phil.

"I was just wondering," she said, "if you're feeling flat and bored now all the shouting's over, if you'd care to stop here for a day or two. I'd adore a bit of company. I'm getting so sick of playing rummy with those deadbeats. I could lock the door and put a natty little notice outside, 'Gone away to town: Or, *'Madam est partie pour Nouvelle Zealand,'* or just, *'Eingang verboten.'*"

She laughed, and her laugh was honey-thick, and Clive at last turned round and looked at her.

"You'd be so bored, Camilla," he said quickly. "I mean, you know I'm not in the least amusing."

Oh, poor Clive, she thought. Hungry for comfort, even hers. Pleading for his wounds to be healed. She ran her fingers over his hair, smiling at him.

"Do stay a while, Clive, sweet," she begged.

"Camilla? Can I? Can I really? Are you sure? I haven't anything with me."

"I've got a razor and a clean toothbrush," said the provident Camilla. "That's all you need." That, indeed, was all they ever needed. "I always keep a razor in case I start growing a beard, and clean toothbrushes in case one of my girlfriends drops in," she lied unblushingly, just in case Clive had any false illusions about her.

She twirled a strand of his fine hair round one of her fingers, and he suddenly put his face against her shoulder, hiding it like a small boy.

"You smell so lovely," he mumbled. "D'you really mean you—want me to stay?"

"Clive, darling, it'd be heaven. Did you know you had hair like silk?"

"Have I?" The deadness had gone out of his voice.

Camilla looked over the top of his head into the fire, pulling him absently closer to her. Men might lose their legs, their arms, their eyes, but the worse wound of all, the most agonizing, was a wound to their vanity. And yet, like all wounds, like all scars, there was a balm, a drug to ease the pain if not to cure it. Amused, and a little complacent, she wondered what the hell would happen to men if all the women in the world were virtuous, if there were no sisters of mercy like her to restore their often shattered pride in themselves.

And while Camilla in her usual efficient way set about reestablishing Clive in his own estimation, Arnoldson, his battered face congested with still simmering rage and bad whisky, wrote a letter of resignation to Mahew. Parry's remarks that afternoon had been brief, but they'd had a sting in them like a hornet's. As he folded the letter and put it in an envelope, the memory of them returned with vivid accuracy, word for word, with horrible persistence. He stuck the stamp on the envelope, banging it in place with his fist as though it were his bitterest enemy. Now that bastard Congreve would be promoted and take over his job, the grinning ape. He belabored the stamp with renewed energy.

A protesting thump sounded on the dividing wall between his bedroom and the next, and the voice of his fellow lodger, muffled but distinct shouted, "Stop that bloody row, you drunken, unfrocked policeman."

At Shots Hall the lights still shone. On the silver tray by the fire the empty teapot was cold. Sitting upright in her chair, Bee dozed, implacable even in repose.

Now, Abbot thought, I'm going. I'm going home to bed. I'm through. I'm not going to sit here for the rest of the night for the pleasure of watching that girl, or woman, or whatever she is, staring into Parry's eyes. With enormous difficulty he got up, stretching his aching body.

"I'm off," he said. "See you at the damn inquest tomorrow. I'll let myself out."

"Hey," Parry protested, "wait a minute."

But Abbot had gone, slamming the door behind him with a gesture of finality. The hall fire was still burning, the logs a red glow. Suddenly the idea of having to drive his car back in the clammy darkness seemed to him an unspeakable effort. He was cold all over. Outside he would feel colder still, not only his flesh, but his spirit. He crouched down in the big armchair by the fire, holding his hands to the blaze, trying to bring some life back into them. He didn't realize he'd fallen asleep till he heard Parry's voice in the hall, and Flik's. He tried to cough, to say something, so that they'd know he was there. But he found he couldn't cough, and his voice seemed to have become paralyzed, just as his body seemed incapable of movement.

Parry threw his cigarette into an ashtray and took Flik's arm. Under his hand he could feel her stiffen. He laughed, and shook her gently.

"Before I go," he said, "I've got something here for you. I thought you'd rather not have an audience, and anyway it's got no bearing on the case at all. You knew Arnoldson'd got hold of a copy of your marriage certificate, didn't you?"

"That's why I went with him to the police station with such lamblike docility. I thought if I didn't make a fuss, he mightn't dig about in my life any more."

"I guessed that. He'd hired some private nark to nose out your past. You might like to have it—the copy of the certificate, I mean."

Abbot heard the rustle of paper, and Flik's quickly indrawn breath. Then Parry said, "I take it the letter to Molly you purloined and burned was about James Waldron, the man you married?"

"Yes. Yes, it was." She looked up at Parry, her eyes wide with one of her flashes of almost brutal frankness. "I met him in town. He was only a private, but he seemed nice, and intelligent and cultivated. I thought I'd feel less disreputable if I was married. It wasn't funny having to take the blame for my divorce from Mac Ashley, and feeling responsible for Mervyn's—Masey Herbert's—suicide didn't make me feel any more respectable. And that's not all," she said quickly, as Parry opened his mouth to interrupt. "I'm illegitimate; my mother wasn't married. She was Aunt Bee's sister. She died when I was two, and she never said who my father was. The Chattocks were always so grand to me, but one way and another I didn't seem to've repaid them very well. I thought if I married again and went to America when the war was over it'd clear up some of the mess I'd made in their lives. Only it turned out to be a worse mess. Waldron was a bigamist."

"And that, of course, was Arnoldson's case against you," Parry said. "His nark seemed to've done the job properly in the way of routing out your past. Arnoldson's theory was that Molly, Marsh and Harry had discovered about Waldron, and you'd murdered them to stop their mouths. It's no disgrace, though, to've unwittingly married a bigamist."

"Oh, my God!" Flik exclaimed. "But so ignominious. And I was terrified that if I made a fuss when Arnoldson took me off that he might go a bit further and find out my mother wasn't married."

"When did you find Waldron out?" Parry asked curiously.

"The night of the fire here. He got in a panic he was going to be burned to death. I suppose he wanted to confess his sins before meeting his Maker." Her voice was icy with scorn. "So he told me. Then he rushed downstairs in his pajamas. I hid his kit under my bed, got back into bed myself, and hoped I'd be suffocated. Only Arnoldson hauled me out. He'd seen Waldron down in the hall, and then spotted his notecase on my table. I couldn't tell him the man was my husband, because he wasn't. I—he— Arnoldson—said he'd keep his mouth shut about my boyfriend if I'd— I'd—"

"You needn't explain," Parry said in disgust. "I can imagine what he suggested. Very pretty."

"A friend of mine in New York's been keeping an eye on Waldron for me. He broke his thigh a couple of weeks ago. If only it'd been his neck instead."

"He's done the next best thing," Parry said, feeling rather like Father Christmas about to deliver the presents. "He's just died of pneumonia."

"What? What?" Incredulous, Flik grabbed Parry's coat collar, her white face flushing. "What the hell d'you mean, Parry?"

"Arnoldson helped himself to your morning mail. One of the letters was from your friend in New York."

Abbot pressed his eyelids so tightly together that he saw red flashes inside them. He heard a second rustle of paper, Flik's exclamation, "I'm free—" and mimicked in his mind, cruelly, I'm free, Parry, and I love you, Parry, and now you can marry me—Damn you. Still he couldn't speak or move, or stop himself listening. Nor could he stop himself opening his eyes. She and Parry stood very close to each other. Parry was smiling, and the look on Flik's face was as if a light were shining behind it.

"Oh, my God, Parry, I'm free," she repeated, and her voice was expectant.

And Parry leaned down and kissed her on the forehead.

"No one could be gladder than I. And I won't tell on you. You're the loveliest person I've met, bar my wife."

Abbot had an insane desire to scream like some hysterical woman, and knew that he wanted Flik's happiness more than anything in the world. And Parry, might his guts rot, had a wife tucked up his sleeve. He somehow shut his eyes again so that he shouldn't see whatever look was on Flik's face now.

"I didn't know you were married." She spoke lightly, too lightly.

"I never talk about my private affairs when I'm doing a job of work. If I did, I'd start thinking about her to the exclusion of all else. You'll have to come up to town and meet her, and we'll have a party.'

"I'd love to."

"That's a date then. Now I must go, my dear. I'll save you all I can at the inquests and after. I think Masey Herbert can be pretty well glossed over, and Waldron doesn't come into it at all."

Parry buttoned up his overcoat, and Flik opened the front door for him. He looked down at her again, and smiled. "You smell so nice. It was the first thing I noticed about you, I think."

The door thundered shut, and the hall gave back its echoes.

Abbot made a dismal and hopelessly unsuccessful effort to behave like someone suddenly aroused from deepest slumber.

"I never noticed you there," Flik said.

"You never do, do you?" His voice seemed to him like a tin pot cracking; and seized with a kind of anguished fury, he laid hold of the poker that'd been put in the place of the one he'd broken, and attacked the fire with the savage intensity of a homicidal maniac. As the poker broke in two, he flung the handle in the fire and sent the other half after it, burning his hands. His spectacles, dislodged from his nose by the violence of his actions, fell in the grate. With loathing, he picked them up and hurled them into the heart of the red-hot ashes, where, for a few moments, they blinked at him foolishly.

"I hope you feel better now," Flik said, and began to laugh. "I do."

"What the hell're you laughing at?" Abbot staggered to his feet. "Stop it."

But she went on laughing, and he knew the moment had come when at last her self-restraint was going to crack.

"Flik—" He didn't know what to do. He was a doctor, but he didn't know what to do. He took her by the shoulders, felt them sag, and moving his hands, put them under her arms, holding her up. "Oh, my God, Flik," he muttered. "Oh, my God, Flik—" Her laughter changed to an awful shaking, and he held her tighter and tighter so that she wouldn't fall down. Then, suddenly, she wasn't shaking any longer. Through her thin suit he could feel the sweat breaking out, icy cold, like the sweat that breaks out sometimes on people when they are dying; and in helpless terror he wondered if she was going to die, now, in his arms, with her hair against the stubble of his chin.

"Flik—Flik—for God's sake."

She lifted her head, and the sweat on her face was wet on his hard jaw, not cold now, but warm. After all, he wasn't going to have yet another dead body on his hands, for which he was truly thankful. Only this particular live body caused him almost as much embarrassment. He ought to let go of it, but he couldn't. He ought to do something about it, lie it on the sofa, take its pulse, pour brandy down its throat.

"Abbot?"

She was staring up at him, right into his eyes, a straight embarrassing stare.

"Well?"

"Once I saw you when you were asleep. You had your glasses off. I didn't realize till then you had such long, dark eyelashes."

"It must have been an edifying sight," he said bitterly.

"I didn't realize, either, till now, that you had gray eyes."

"Oh, damn my bloody eyes," he fretted. Why couldn't he let her go?

Her hands moved over his shoulders; and, as she had done once before, she again, only more vividly, experienced the illusion that under his flesh his bones were long and thin and very fine. And without his glasses the structure of his face, hard and fine-drawn, was as firmly chiseled as one of her own carvings, his eyes now oddly unangry.

"I've done with chipping at blocks of wood, and hammering at rocks," she said. "It seems so stupid when nature makes such a much better job of carving human likenesses. I think that's why I thought I was in love with Parry. Nature made such a damned handsome job of him. I expect I could carve quite a good head of him, but I couldn't ever reproduce you from a block of wood."

She sounded, to Abbot, almost childishly puzzled. "What the devil're you talking about?" he asked.

"I'm not sure. But I think it's in the last extremes of adversity one runs headlong into the truth one never realized before just like running into a brick wall one hadn't noticed was there. "

"If you're going to start talking in parables again, then you can go to hell," Abbot said; and held on to her with furious tenacity in case she might go as far as the fireplace.

"I'm not talking in parables. I was just wondering if by any chance you might possibly like to marry me. Because if so, I'd better warn you I'm not in the least domestic."

"I'm forty-eight, twelve years older than you, and I hate domesticity as much as I hate suppurating appendixes. I—" Abbot broke off, stammering, wondering wildly whether he would have somehow to make a formal proposal, or whether she had the sense to know how much he desperately wanted her.

"Thank you," she nodded. Her eyes were too tired to keep open any longer. She shut them, contented and at last at peace, her ghosts laid. Then she felt Abbot's shoulders shaking, and aghast that she might have in some way hurt him, unable to endure the thought, she opened her eyes again.

But he was laughing.

"What're you laughing at?" she asked, curious.

"I was just thinking," Abbot said, his face against her hair, "that adversity makes strange bedfellows."

THE END

Inspector Parry's second and final case
Murder at Beechlands
0-915230-56-9
will be available Summer 2003 from
The Rue Morgue Press
Parry has to pick out a murderer from an eccentric list of suspects who are stranded by a snowstorm in a private country hotel in Sussex.

Rue Morgue Press Books

We specialize in reprinting mysteries from the 1930s through 1950s, releasing one new title a month. All books are quality trade paperbacks, usually with full-color covers. To find out more, to get a catalog, or to suggest titles, call 800-699-6214 or write to P.O. Box 4119, Boulder, CO 80306.

Titles as of June 2003

Cannan, Joanna. *They Rang Up the Police.* An English village mystery set in 1937 featuring Inspector Guy Northeast. **Cannan.** *Death at The Dog.* An English village mystery set in late 1939, the second and final book featuring Northeast. **Carr, Glyn.** *Death on Milestone Buttress.* Murder on a mountain in Wales. **Clason, Clyde. B.** *The Man from Tibet.* A 1938 locked room mystery set in Chicago with Prof. Westborough and a mysterious Tibetan manuscript. **Coggin, Joan.** *Who Killed the Curate?* The vicar's wife turns sleuth with hilarious results. **Coggin.** *The Mystery at Orchard House.* The vicar's wife continues her odd sleuthing among the guests of a small hotel. **Coles, Manning.** *The Far Traveller.* A 1950s comic ghost story in which a long-dead German nobleman returns from the grave to star in a movie being made about his tragic death. **Coles.** *Brief Candles.* The first of three comic ghost stories featuring the Latimers, two Victorian gentleman and their pet monkey, who, as tourists, were killed during the Franco-Prussian War and who rematerialize in a small French village. **Coles.** *Happy Returns.* 2nd Latimer. **Coles.** *Come and Go.* 3rd Latimer. **Davis, Norbert.** *The Mouse in the Mountain.* A comic private eye novel in which a P.I. and his Great Dane solve murders in Mexico during WWII. **Davis.** *Sally's in the Alley.* 2nd Doan and Carstairs. **Dean, Elizabeth.** *Murder is a Collector's Item.* A 1939 screwball mystery set in the Boston antiques world with Emma Marsh, currently out of print from us. **Dean.** *Murder is a Serious Business.* 2nd Emma Marsh (1940). **Dean.** *Murder a Mile High.* 3rd Marsh. **Little, Constance & Gwenyth.** *The Black Gloves.* From the queens of the wacky mystery, this one is set in East Orange, New Jersey. **Little.** *The Black Honeymoon.* **Little.** *The Black Stocking.* **Little.** *The Black Paw.* **Little.** *The Black Coat.* **Little.** *Black Corridors.* **Little.** *Black-Headed Pins.* **Little.** *Great Black Kanba.* **Little.** *Grey Mist Murders.* **Little.** *The Black Eye.* **Little.** *The Black Thumb.* **Little.** *The Black Shrouds.* **Millhiser, Marlys.** *The Mirror.* Our only non-vintage mystery, this is a wonderful time travel (sort of) novel set between 1900 and 1978. 6th printing. **Norman, James.** *Murder, Chop Chop.* Set in the 1930s during the Sino-Japanese War and involving the eccentric foreign community. **Pim, Sheila.** *Creeping Venom.* Irish village mystery. **Pim.** *A Brush with Death.* Irish art and gardening mystery. An earlier title, *Common or Garden Crime*, is currently out of print. **Rice, Craig.** *Home Sweet Homicide.* Three children help their mystery writer mother solve a murder in this 1944 Haycraft-Queen Cornerstone mystery. **Russell, Charlotte Murray.** *The Message of the Mute Dog.* Spinster sleuth solves murder at a defense plant on eve of WWII. **Sheridan, Juanita.** *The Chinese Chop.* Lily Wu and Janice Cameron solve a murder in a Washington Square boarding house. **Sheridan, Juanita.** *The Kahuna Killer.* Lily and Janice return home to Hawaii. **Sheridan, Juanita.** *The Mamo Murders.* Lily and Janice find murder on a Hawaiian ranch.